Bound by Fire

Rogues of Magic Book 3

Tiffany Shand

DEDICATION

For my mum, Karen.

CHAPTER 1

Urien Valeran appeared in a flash of light in Ranelle's chamber. "I have a new task for you." He wished he could be there in person, but he couldn't risk Ann sensing his presence, or his plans would fall apart.

Ranelle, one of his newest slaves, scowled at him. Her long red hair, pale skin and dazzling emerald eyes seemed to glow in the sunlight coming through the open windows. "What do you want me to do now?" She sighed.

If anyone else had dared to act defiantly, Urien would have killed them on the spot, but he admired this woman's strength. Most didn't have the nerve to stand up to him. He found her oddly refreshing. Besides, she'd proved too valuable to kill. Killing her would take away one of his greatest assets, and he wasn't about to squander that.

"I want you to tell me more about Edward Rohn. I've always known he was different—more powerful than he appears. But I've never been able to find out much about him."

He thought gaining control of Ranelle and her people had been pure luck but finding out her people were the sworn enemies of the lykaes was better than he could've ever hoped for.

Ranelle shook her head. "I've already told you everything I can about the lykaes. Why is Rohn so important to you?"

"Because you know more about him than you should—more than any enemy leader should know." Urien smirked. "My father always kept Edward close to my sister, and I suspect he knew who and what Edward really is. I want to know more."

"Why?"

Urien reminded himself not to lose his temper. The only thing he despised about Ranelle was that she questioned him. None of his other followers ever dared to do that, at least not if they wanted to keep their lives.

"A few weeks ago, one of my wyverns went to Trewa to deliver my sister a message. I saw Rhiannon and Edward using magic I've never seen them use before." Urien paced the length of the room as he spoke. "From everything you've told me, a lykae shouldn't possess any magic. I know an archdruid bound them centuries ago so they would never be a threat to the druids or the elders." Light flashed around the projected the image of his form. "I've seen Edward use magic myself as he grew up alongside my siblings. I want to know where that power comes from—what is he?"

Ranelle raised her chin. "What makes you think I can tell you that?"

Urien suppressed a sigh. "I know my father crossed over into Lulrien not long before Edward washed up on the shores of Trin. He didn't land there by accident, someone sent him. I want to know why. You are a representative of the council. You know far more than you have told me."

"I can't tell you anything else." Her gaze dropped to the floor.

"Come now, you don't want me to have to force the answers out of you, do you?" He reached across the table in his study next to the orb that was projecting his image to Ranelle and raised the Arcus stone, which glittered and hummed with power.

Ranelle flinched as the stone appeared on the projection. He knew it caused her pain every time he used it.

"Tell me," Urien said as his fingers wrapped around the ancient stone. "I will get answers from you one way or another."

She took a step back as if that would protect her from the stone's power. "He's an overseer. He was sent to protect your sister, to guide her."

Urien's eyes widened. He hadn't expected that. Overseers were guardians—warriors sent to watch over their charges by the council. He thought they'd been wiped out centuries ago. "Is that why he and my sister have such a strong connection?"

Maybe I can use that to my advantage.

Ranelle shook her head. "No, there is a bond between them. Their magic is bound to each other. Darius linked them together."

His eyes narrowed. "Why would my father do that?" He gripped the stone, feeling its power hum between his fingers.

"I can't answer that. Your sister is very powerful. Having an overseer to guide and protect her would ensure she never misused her power."

"Tell me more of this bond." Urien rubbed his chin, feeling a day's worth of stubble there.

"I don't —"

Urien tutted. "Now I know you're lying."

"I don't know how deep the bond goes between them, but I know they're stronger when they're together. Your sister and the other rogues are getting close to passing through the mist and will soon arrive in lykae lands."

Urien beamed. He knew Ann wouldn't be able to resist coming here if it meant helping her precious Edward. He never understood why the damn lykae meant so much to her. Ed might be strong and fast, but he had a weak character. *Too much of a do-gooder.*

"You shouldn't have forced me to contact Edward like that." Ranelle paced the length of the room. "Using my people is one thing, but if the council finds out I'm helping you…"

Urien could see the room itself had walls with creeping vines and tree rings etched into the wood. Urien found it fascinating how these people lived in a giant tree and wished he could see the place for himself. So far, he'd only had dealings with Ranelle herself and hadn't met any of her other people, not that it mattered as long as she obeyed him.

Urien gave a harsh laugh. "The council are nothing more than mere puppets to make the five lands think there's some sort of governmental order. The elders are the ones with the real power. You're mine now, and you'd do well to remember that."

Ranelle looked away, clutching the hem of her long green gown, which appeared to be so sheer it might as well have been see-through. "What good does bringing Rohn here do?"

"How do you know Rohn so well?" Dodging her question, Urien crossed his arms, making his form flicker.

"I knew him when he was a boy," Ranelle answered. She didn't elaborate any further.

"Odd, given that your people are the mortal enemies of the lykaes," Urien remarked. "If you play your part, we won't have any problems. How is the mining process coming along?"

"Fine. My people have been digging deep within the earth. I want to know what it is you're looking for." The fiery redhead put her hands on her hips. The gesture made her beautiful face look even more attractive.

Pity he couldn't reach out and touch her. He did enjoy his chats with her. He had known she would make a useful ally, and she had so far. It didn't matter how much she protested, Ranelle had no choice in helping him. Either she complied, or her people would suffer for it. Finding the Arcus stone when he had scoured Darius' secret chamber back at the palace in Larenth had been a stroke of luck. He might not have found Darius' secret vault, but he'd found some items of use. Including the Arcus stone—an ancient object of power that had been designed by an archdruid centuries ago to bind Ranelle's race to their human form. He kept Ranelle bound to human form because she proved more useful that way.

"What I'm searching for isn't your concern. I told you, you'll know it when you find it," Urien said. "Do as you're told, and I'll give you what you want."

"You'll give me freedom for my people? You'll release us from the curse?" Ranelle hugged herself. "How do I know you won't go back on your word?"

"You'll have to trust me. I'm a loyal man, I don't go back on my word."

"Your father did. You may not be archdruid, but you are—"

"Silence." Urien picked up the Arcus stone from the table next to him. It glistened like a large diamond as energy hummed through his fingers. Gods below, he loved the feel of its power.

Ranelle's mouth snapped shut.

He adored the feeling of having complete control over another living being. This must be what his druid ancestors had felt. They, and the elders created laws and spells to bind certain races of Magickind. This was what he'd been born to do. His demon mother had tried to gain control of Caselhelm, but the elders despised her. They wanted someone capable of being the archdruid again—of being their avatar here on Erthea. By using blood magic to pierce through the toxic mists into the lost realm of Lulrien, Urien had gained the elders' favour once more. If he could get them something else they wanted, they'd promised to help him destroy his sister and make him archdruid.

"Your job is to keep the workers in line and keep digging until you find what I'm looking for." He rubbed his chin. "Maybe you could send Edward a message and insist he leave my sister as well."

Ranelle hummed, but her lips remained frozen in place.

"I don't care how you do it." Urien waved his hand. "I know Edward loves her, play on his role as overseer. Or have the council order him to stay with his people." He loosened his grip on the Arcus stone.

"I can't. He was tasked to protect her. She's his charge," Ranelle protested, letting out a deep breath. "They are—"

"They are *what?*" Urien demanded. He still had no idea how Ranelle knew so much about Edward. At first, he'd thought it was her connection to the council. But he now suspected it went much deeper than that. Urien had ordered her to tell him, yet somehow, she had avoided giving him any real answers. It seemed the stone couldn't force her to do everything.

"Nothing." Ranelle shook her head. "I don't see why you need to part them."

Urien took a step toward her and reached out as if to touch her cheek. "Do you want to be free from your curse, or not?" he asked. "I could leave you as you are. Force you to remain in your human form. Such a waste. Your race used to be noble and powerful once. Now you're weak and pathetic."

Ranelle's jaw clenched. "I still have some power, and I won't let you use my people to start a war."

Urien laughed. "There's nothing you can do about it, is there?" The stone flashed between his fingers. "You don't have enough power to overcome this."

Ranelle's green eyes flashed. "I could tell your sister the truth. Convince her to help me," she hissed. "She's the archdruid. I'm sure she could break the binding spell. Even here, we've heard tales of how powerful she is—more powerful than you or your father."

Urien gripped the stone so hard he suspected it might break. "On your knees." The stone flared with light.

Ranelle's brow creased as she attempted to resist the force from the stone's power.

"Kneel," Urien commanded. "Shift."

Ranelle sank to her knees, her eyes taking on an emerald glow. She clawed at the floor as her body writhed, and her bones and muscles popped.

Urien loved to watch her change form. "Stop." The stone hummed again as he forced out his command.

Don't, Xander's voice whispered inside his mind. *You're hurting her.*

Ah, little brother has decided to make an appearance again. It had been almost four months since Orla had placed Urien's soul inside Xander's body. Xander's voice plagued and tormented him for weeks until Urien had used blood magic. Using the blood from numerous slaves, Urien had crafted a spell to block out Xander, which gave him some much-needed peace.

Urien grinned as Ranelle's body froze mid-shift. She opened her mouth to scream, but no sound came out.

How can you take pleasure from this? Xander hissed. *She's in agony.*

Oh, do be quiet, brother. Enjoy this while it lasts. Once I get Ann to break the spell that binds us together, you will both be gone, and I'll be back in my own body.

Urien hovered over Ranelle. "Remember, when you meet them, you will tell nothing of my plan to Ann or her friends. If you try, I'll end you and your people." He held up the Arcus stone, which glittered with power.

Ranelle moaned as she lay slumped on the tiled floor. Her body was half shifted, her arms a mass of bone and twisted cartilage. With a groan, her arms shifted back. Tears rolled down her cheeks.

"Besides, when you find what I'm looking for, we'll both get what we want," Urien continued. *And I'll have an entire army capable of conquering all five lands. The next realm war will begin.*

Urien drew back from the orb that projected him to Ranelle. His study looked more the way he wanted it now, full of his own things. The secret compartment containing a few of Darius' artefacts stood open on the wall behind him. This was the greatest gift his bastard father could have ever given him. While Ranelle and her people dug and searched for the hidden door, he'd work on removing the spell Darius had used to bind him and his siblings together.

Thanks to being back in the elders' favour, they'd given him a book on binding spells in the hope he could lift it. Elder magic fascinated him, it went far beyond what the druids or the Gliss were capable of, but for the spell to truly work, he needed to find his own body. The only person who could lead him to that was Edward Rohn.

Urien recited the summoning spell and waited for the elder to appear.

Constance, his lead Gliss, came in, her nose wrinkling at the sight of the dead Ursaie at his feet. Blood magic seemed to be the only effective way of summoning the elder messenger who'd been helping Urien.

"My lord, I bring good news," Connie said. "Gillie and Nordige are under our control. I've sent more Gliss to keep watch over the towns."

"Excellent. Any news on the re-emergence of Trin?" A few weeks earlier, Ann had taken the druid isle from Urien's grasp. As archdruid, she'd used the isle's power to submerge it beneath the sea. It had also restored the power of the ancient standing stones at Trewa to block any attempts of invasion, leaving both sacred sites inaccessible to him while undermining his claim to be the true archdruid.

"Not yet, my lord. We have most of Caselhelm under our control," Connie said." But..." she hesitated.

"But what?" Urien drummed his fingers on his desk impatiently. Why hadn't the damn elder turned up yet? He'd said the invocation.

"The people are talking. Word has spread about how your sister came here and destroyed the throne."

Urien gritted his teeth at that. Ann humiliated him in front of leaders from around the five lands. He reminded himself it didn't matter, because he had got rid of his mother and secured the way to Lulrien. He'd have a new throne built when the time was right.

"Let them talk. Rhiannon still has a price on her head, as do her other rogues." He waved his hand in dismissal. "Leave me." A guard came in, and he and Connie picked up the dead body and dragged it out of the room.

A blonde-haired elder appeared in a flash of golden light. His piercing blue eyes bored into Urien. Power rolled off him like waves of lightning.

Urien envied that power and wanted it for himself. "Arwan." He bowed his head and hid a grimace. He despised doing that. An archdruid bowed to no one, and Urien suspected he was meant to be much more than that.

Arwan's lip curled. "Why are you calling me again, boy?"

"To tell you the good news. I found an ancient text that once belonged to my father," Urien explained. "It speaks of the door used to shut the demons and other evils in the underworld away during one of the first realm wars." He held off on telling the elder about his plan of using Ranelle and her people to open it. He hadn't found the door yet, but he would soon enough. Urien failed to keep his excitement out of his voice.

"What of it?" Arwan flicked a speck of dirt from his blue velvet tunic. The elder always dressed sharp and perfect.

"My mother's people wreaked havoc on the five lands once—they can do so once again when I free them."

"The other elders like the state of the five lands just fine." Arwan grimaced at the pool of blood on the floor.

"Think about it, Arwan. Don't you want another realm war? A *true* realm war like those of the ancient texts?" Urien grinned. "Where thousands die, and entire races fall into memory?"

Arwan smirked at that. "We'd like that, but what we want most of all is your sister. You must kill or capture her. She's a thorn in our side."

"Oh, don't worry. I'll force my sister to lift the spell that protects us from death," Urien said. "One way or another."

CHAPTER 2

Ann Valeran crouched low, watching as a group of skeletal-looking beasts swarmed along the forest trail. *More banelings.*

She gripped the hilt of her knife with one hand as fire flared in the other. Her blonde hair blew in wisps under the hood of her long black cloak. The cloak kept Ann concealed, thanks to the magic woven in its fabric.

Ceara shifted beside her, her pale white skin and long black hair flecked with dust. Her leather bodice and trousers hadn't fared as well as Ann's own clothes. She arched an eyebrow, as if to say, *"Can we kill them?"*

The Gliss gripped her shock rod with one hand, keeping her free hand poised and ready to use her empathic power. Ann doubted Ceara's power would do much good against these creatures.

Ann shook her head, sending her senses out and scanning the area for any signs of the mists that separated Asral from the other four lands. They were close to Lulrien, a land that had been lost over the centuries.

Jax and Ed were concealed a few feet away behind another tree.

Ed—with his long brown hair, golden-brown eyes and black ranger clothing—blended in better than any of them. As a lykae, he would be able to see and hear the oncoming horde first. Jax, a crow shifter with stone magic, crouched beside him. Jax's dark skin and clothing made him blend in almost as well as Ed, apart from his bald head, which gleamed in the low sunlight.

Ceara prodded Ann, looking expectant. *What are we waiting for?* she asked in thought.

Ann rolled her eyes. *Learn some patience, woman. I thought all Gliss were patient, given how many months they spend trying to break people.*

I still don't understand why we are going this way. Ed having a strange dream isn't enough to put our lives at risk, Ceara remarked.

Ann repressed a sigh. Now wasn't the time to talk about Ed's dream, but they hadn't come here just because of it. Since her bastard half-brother, Urien, had broken through the toxic mist that separated the border between Lulrien and Caselhelm, different creatures had come through it. Not only had Urien torn a hole in the mists when he had killed his mother Orla using blood magic, but he'd gained control over a dragon-like species. Ann and the others had spent the last month tracking the movements of the wyverns across Caselhelm. The latest sighting had led them here.

Banelings were skeletal cat-like creatures with razor-sharp claws and fangs. Their bodies had no fur and held no blood or organs. They were one of the first things Urien had brought through.

One of the banelings turned, hissed, and bounded toward them.

Ann muttered a curse, leapt up, and threw a fireball, sending the creature staggering backward.

"About bloody time." Ceara grinned and pulled out her rods as she jumped up.

"Do you think about anything other than killing and torture?" Ann muttered.

"Of course I do. I think about staying alive."

Ann threw her knife at the next baneling. Ed shot up and blurred into the distance at the oncoming horde of creatures.

Jax drew his double-edged staff, swinging it as the creatures came at him. He sliced the first baneling in half.

Another baneling screeched as it bounded toward Ann. She blew it up with a well-aimed fireball, pulled out another knife, and threw another at it. Her heart pounded as she spotted more of the oncoming swarm. What did Urien hope to achieve by sending these nuisances after them? They couldn't kill her. He would know that.

Laughter rang in the air. "Can't defeat all of them, can you, little druid?"

Little? Seriously? Ann glanced at Ceara and Jax, but they seemed oblivious to the voice. A chill ran across her senses, warning of a presence, one she'd encountered before but had not yet been able to identify. She'd first come across the strange entity when it had started following her back in Trewa, the druid's settlement. She'd hoped it wouldn't make an appearance again. What did it even want? And why did it keep tormenting her like this? Ann had suspected Urien had sent it to spy on her, but now it didn't seem so. The strange shadow creature—whatever it was—seemed unaffiliated with her elder brother. Oh, Urien sent people to spy on her—she had no doubt of that. The strange shadow seemed different somehow.

Ann gritted her teeth. Light flashed and a blur moved past her, then laughter echoed around her. *Ignore it. It's trying to distract you,* she told herself.

"Why are you wasting your time with banelings when there's an even greater threat nearby?" the voice asked.

"What?" Ann dodged another baneling, ducking and rolling as it came at her. She shoved a fireball into its mouth, exploding it from the inside out. Too bad all the creatures bothering her wouldn't die that way.

Grabbing her fallen knife, Ann scrambled up. She sprinted after the presence that she felt fleeing. "What?" she called. "What do you mean?"

More laughter, a harsh cackling that set her teeth on edge.

Her black leather cloak billowed behind her as she ran after the presence. "Come on, where are you?" She'd fully crossed over into Lulrien. Trees blurred past as she ran. No sign of the toxic mist, or any dragons. One way or another she would find out what this entity was and what it wanted.

"Ann!"

She heard Jax call after her but ignored him. She had to find out why this strange entity kept toying with her. What did it even want? Using a spell, maybe she could reveal its true identity, then bind it, question it, and find out why it kept stalking her and her friends.

Ann ran faster, spotting the silhouette darting above the tree line.

What Magickind could move that fast? She thought only Ed could move with supernatural speed, but that didn't look like his kind of power. Plus, as far as she knew, lykaes couldn't turn into shadow creatures.

She felt the urge to hurl a fireball at it, but knew this thing went way beyond the capabilities of her druid magic.

She sensed the minds of other creatures nearby and watched as the creature approached five silhouettes in the distance. She had no idea what they were. Ann hadn't expected to encounter other beings so close to the border.

What are they?

Judging by their pointed ears, she guessed they might be elves.

More laughter. "I wonder how they'll react to your presence," the voice said. "Will you tell them who you really are? I doubt even the archdruid would be welcome here."

Ann stopped, breathing hard. *Why am I even following this thing?*

She winced at the mention of her title. Although she accepted being the archdruid, she had no territory or real authority within the five lands of Almara. Five years had passed since her parents had been murdered by Urien and she had been accused of committing the terrible crime. becoming a rogue along with her best friend—Edward Rohn—and his foster siblings.

Something blurred along the tree line. Ed? No, she didn't feel his presence nearby. The shadow thing? She caught a flash of the creature's burning amber eyes as it stalked through the line of trees. The shadow thing seemed to have disappeared as fast as it had come, this creature was a different entity altogether. Were her stalker and this newcomer somehow connected? If so, how?

She gasped as realisation hit. *Blessed spirits, it's a lykae!*

Her fingers warmed as a fireball formed in her palm. She hurled it at the lykae, who blurred away and snarled, his gaze now fixed on her—all five elves lay dead on the ground.

Crap! Ann had sparred with Ed over the past few months, trying to match his strength and speed. With the help of her senses, she'd been able to anticipate some of his moves, but he'd been holding back, so she doubted she'd be so lucky with this lykae. Where had it come from? Did that mean they were getting close to finding where Ed had come from?

She raised her hand, sending flames shooting across the grass, but the lykae blurred out of the way again before they had the chance to touch him. The feel of his power radiated through her mind, and rage rolled off him, stronger than anything she'd felt before.

Ann raised her hand, drawing her power to her. "Stop!" she commanded.

The lykae staggered to a halt mid-blur, then laughed. "Your magic is useless against me." He had a mop of long, messy black hair, skin so pale it was almost translucent, and grey eyes. His body looked muscular and his clothes were torn and filthy. He shook off her magic and had her by the throat faster than she could blink. "You smell divine," he hissed. "I've never met anyone with power leaking from them before."

Ann clenched her fist, drew magic, and punched him in the face, feeling the crack of bone. Though she was unsure if it was hers or his. He staggered back from the force of the blow. "What are you on about? My power isn't leaking."

His eyes burned red. "I'm going to enjoy killing you."

He made a grab for her, but she blocked him, then spun into a kick, sending him staggering. The lykae snorted, blurred, and grabbed her, sinking his fangs into her wrist.

Ann cried out as his fangs ripped through her soft flesh like tiny knives digging into her.

Ed shot toward them like a tornado, knocking her and her assailant to the ground. He tackled the other lykae away from her. The two lykaes were a blur as they wrestled each other.

Ann clutched her bleeding wrist and scrambled up. The other lykae tore into Ed with his claws and fangs. Ed yelped as the other lykae's hand plunged into his chest. Ed might have been strong, but his attacker seemed much stronger.

"No!" Ann cried. A burst of magic shot from her hand, blasting both men apart. Ignoring her throbbing wrist, she let her magic flow free. She clenched her fist as she forced her will into her power. *"Ceangail agus greim air."* The words to an ancient binding spell flowed from her lips easily, even though she'd never used it before.

The other lykae gasped, clutching his head. "You are no match for me." He laughed as he fought through her magic and lunged toward her again.

Ed leapt up and grabbed the lykae.

Hold him, Ann said.

He's stronger than me. I don't know if I can kill him. Ed struggled, holding the other lykae in a headlock.

We're stronger than him. She raised her hand again, drawing more magic to her. Her eyes burned with fire as power whirled up from deep inside her.

With a crack, the lykae's leg broke as she focused her power on him, swiftly followed by the other leg.

Ann, what are you doing? Ed's eyes widened in alarm.

The other beast struggled, and Ed moved to strike him down.

"Wait!" Ann moved forward, still keeping the beast locked in her power. "Where did you pass through the mist? Where did you come from?"

The other lykae laughed. "Why would you care?"

Ann, let's kill him and be done with it, Ed hissed. *I can't hold him for long.*

She raised her hand again. This time, the lykae's arm cracked as his right shoulder came out of its socket and his arm twisted at an odd angle.

The lykae hissed in pain. "I'll enjoy draining you dry, witch."

"Druid," she corrected. "Why do you even want blood?"

Ann, we need to kill him, Ed snapped. *He's not like me. He's different.*

Different how? She frowned.

He's consumed by rage—bloodlust. My beast warned me of it, and I'm inclined to agree with it. He's stronger than me.

"Because I need it to survive." The other beast laughed. "You're both too weak to kill me."

He grinned at Ed. "You're so close to losing control, I wonder how you don't bleed her dry. You can feel her pulse, can't you?"

Ed's eyes flashed. "I, unlike you, control my beast."

"She's pretty. Perhaps I'll play with her before I drain her. I'll—"

Ed snapped the beast's neck in one swift move.

Ann let out a breath and let her hand fall to her side. Her temples throbbed, and a wave of dizziness hit her. Where had that come from? Being a druid was all about nature and balance. She'd never used her power like that before—to deliberately inflict pain and suffering rather than in self-defence.

The binding spell was one her father, the former archdruid, had taught her. People within the five lands had always despised the archdruid for the power and control they wielded. Ann had always wanted to be different from the archdruids of the past. Instead of hurting and enslaving others as the archdruids of old had done, she wanted to fight for justice and a better world. Using a spell passed down by her ancestors might not have seemed like much, but part of her had enjoyed using the dark side of her power.

"What was that magic you used?" Ed asked her.

She shook her head. "Just a binding spell." She didn't want to talk about what she'd done, not here.

"You're bleeding," Ed said as if he had just noticed the bite on her wrist.

"And you have a hole in your chest." Ann made her bag appear and yanked a piece of cloth from it, using magic to wrap it around her injured wrist. She knelt and saw the gaping wound where the other lykae had punched his way through flesh and bone. "You're not healing." Her eyes widened. Ed always healed fast after getting injured—which had proved to be a common occurrence in their lives on the run as rogues.

"Yeah, I noticed." Ed gave a grim smile. "Guess I'm not so invincible after all."

Jax and Ceara came running over. Both looked out of breath.

"Everyone alright? Ann, why'd you run off earlier?" Jax asked. "All the banelings are finally gone. Nasty buggers." He leaned on his staff for support, breathing hard.

Ceara pushed her long black hair off her face and brushed dirt off her leather corset. "At least Urien hasn't sent another dragon after us yet." She cringed when she saw the hole in Ed's chest. "Ew, what did that?"

"It was another lykae. Bloody strong." Ed gasped as Ann touched him.

Ann placed her hand on his chest, calling up magic and muttering a healing spell. *"Leigheas agus arís eile a bheith ina iomláine."*

Ed yelped as if he'd been stung and gritted his teeth. "Please don't do that again."

"I don't know if I can heal this if your body keeps resisting my magic." Ann's stomach twisted. If she couldn't heal him, he might…

"I'll heal on my own. Maybe more severe wounds take longer," Ed said. "Just bandage me up and let's—"

The other lykae shot up before Ed or Ann had a chance to react, lunged straight for Ann.

Ceara grabbed Jax's staff and stabbed the beast in one swing. The bladed end pierced through his chest. "Lesson for today, children. The only sure way to kill a lykae is…" She yanked the staff out and swung it around to slice the beast's head off. "Like this."

This time, the lykae dodged the staff and knocked it away. He sank his fangs into Ceara's neck, bit down, then pulled back. "You're tainted by dark magic." He spat a mouthful of blood out in disgust.

Ceara smirked. "Time to put this rabid dog down."

The lykae blurred, going straight for Ann again. She transported out of the way in a flash of light before he had a chance to get to her, reappearing a moment later. Why wouldn't that thing die?

Ed jumped up, grabbed the other lykae, and pulled his head off in one swift move. He staggered as he dropped the head. "You could have told me that before now!" He glared at Ceara, and Ann wrapped an arm around him.

"You never asked," Ceara replied, clutching her neck. "Argh, that will leave a mark."

"Let's get out of here." Ann touched the pendant at her throat, and a glowing wooden door appeared that led to a hidden vault appeared. It was a place that existed between the worlds and outside time and space. Her father had used it to store all of his magical knowledge, objects of power, and secrets in. At least they would be safe there before they crossed through the mists that led the way further into the lost realm of Lulrien.

CHAPTER 3

Edward Rohn tried to ignore the aching in his chest and the pain radiating through his ribs as Ann led him into his room. The vault contained a large library, a couple of work rooms, and several bedrooms. The extra rooms had all appeared, as if by desire. His own room contained little more than a single four-poster bed draped with blue linens, a wooden table and chairs, and whitewashed walls. After five years of being on the run, Ed didn't own much in the way of clothes or possessions. Life as a rogue didn't afford any luxuries, and since they often moved around, they couldn't afford to waste time carrying possessions with them. Ed slumped onto his bed. The wound hadn't bled as much as he expected, which seemed odd, and he couldn't understand why it hadn't healed already. Any other injuries he'd had since his lykae nature had emerged had healed within hours, if not minutes, depending on their severity. But he'd never fought another lykae before. Where had it even come from?

His mind went back to the dream he'd had a few days earlier and the message he'd received that had sent them venturing to Lulrien to search for where he'd come from before he landed on the island of Trin at age ten.

"Rohn? Rohn, hear me," a voice said.

Ed glanced around to find himself surrounded by clouds. He frowned, he couldn't see anyone around him.

"Rohn of the lykae," the voice said. "Overseer."

Ed's frown deepened. Overseer. He knew that word but couldn't quite remember what it meant or what it entailed. "Who's there?" He sniffed, but caught no scent of anyone. Yet the presence felt almost familiar. Who was it?

"The way through the mists is fractured. You must return home. War is brewing. You must stop the lykaes from going into another war. Darkness now holds your homeland," the voice continued. "As an overseer, it's your duty to return and help to help your people."

Ed's mind had wandered back to when he was a boy.

"Rohn, as an overseer, you are tasked with protecting and helping. This is what you will learn and train for as you grow and become a man," the same voice said. "Your task is to watch over and protect Rhiannon Valeran—the archdruid's daughter. Rhiannon will one day take her father's place. Guide her. You may forget where you come from and who you are, but you'll never forget your

22

duty."

Ed blinked and found himself back among the clouds. "Wait, my duty is to protect Ann. She is my charge, I can't leave her."

"You've done your duty. You've guided and protected her. Now it's time for you to return home."

Ed shook his head. "No, I won't leave her." He couldn't imagine leaving Ann. They had rarely been apart during their fifteen-year long friendship.

"You must. Your duty demands you go where you're needed," the voice said. "There, you will find answers to what you seek."

"I can't leave her."

The beast clawed at the cage of his mind, breaking him out of the memory of the dream. It'd been on edge ever since it had sensed the waves of rage coming from the other lykae. Seeing it bite Ann had sent his own beast over the edge, and it had been hard to rein it in again. It felt restless, edgy, and like it wanted to kill again, despite Ann no longer being in danger. Ed glanced down. The wound still hadn't begun to heal, and blood seeped through his bandages.

Ann came back in with a healing kit. "Think, you must know something about how lykaes heal."

He slumped back against the bed. "I'm trying, but I was still young when I left them," he said. "You wanted to track that wyvern down and find out where Urien got them from, didn't you?"

"No, not when you're like this."

"Ann, if anything happens to me…" He took hold of her hand.

"Don't. You're not going to die. I won't let you." She smiled and sniffed. "I'll find a way to save you—I always do. We've been through worse than this."

Ed watched her pulse throb in her neck and heard the sound of her blood singing through her veins. He closed his eyes, trying to ignore what the other lykae had said. The words echoed through his mind.

"Just rest," Ann told him. "You'll make yourself worse if you keep moving."

Ed sighed. He hated feeling useless. They'd come to search for the mist and track down one of Urien's wyverns, and it felt like they had been doing anything but.

Over the next few hours, he drifted in and out of consciousness. Ann and the others came in and out, bringing books and talking among themselves. He didn't catch much of their conversation but gathered they hadn't found much about how to heal him.

Ed closed his eyes again, thinking of the dream. Who had contacted him? And why now, after all these years? Ann became archdruid five years ago.

Still, he didn't doubt his overseer status. The memory felt very real. He'd been sent to watch over Ann and protect her. They'd learnt magic together growing up, and he had often helped her with spells.

If one of the council members had contacted him, could he reach them again? Why had they been so secretive about their true identity? As an overseer, he should be connected to the council, but could he reach them in his weakened state?

Ed sent his senses out into the world, hoping to trace the connection to the council. He had no idea if he needed to say any words of power or cast a spell for it to work. His thoughts drifted away until he found himself back in the clouds he'd seen in his dream.

What is this place? Does it exist outside time and place on another plane, like the vault? Ed guessed it didn't matter.

"Hello?" he called, glancing around. "Are you here?" Ed had no idea what or who the voice who'd contacted him had been. What should he call them? He considered the possibility of it being Urien trying to trick him like he had tricked Ann before. But Urien would have no way of knowing Ed was an overseer.

"Ed? Ed, wake up." He heard Ann's voice and felt her touch his shoulder.

Argh, not now, Ann! Ed growled. He needed to concentrate if he was going to find the person who had sent him the message to come to Lulrien.

"Come on, whoever you are, please answer me."

Light flashed, and Ann appeared beside him.

Ed's eyes widened. "What are you doing here?"

"You wouldn't wake, and I was worried…plus I sensed you using magic." Ann frowned as she looked around. "What are you doing?"

He rubbed the back of his neck. "Figuring out a way to heal myself."

Her eyes narrowed. "You're hiding something from me. I can feel it."

He sighed. He never could keep a secret from her for long. "It's nothing. Please go."

"Ed, you're lying there with a hole in your chest. I'm not leaving you." Ann put her hands on her hips. "So, tell me what you're doing. You've been acting strange ever since you suggested we needed to go to Lulrien."

"Ann, please go. I'll explain more later."

"No."

Ah, there's the Valeran stubbornness!

"I heard that." Her eyes flashed.

Ed gritted his teeth and cursed their direct mind link.

"Fine, I'm an overseer. Someone sent me a message saying I needed to return to lykae lands to stop a war from breaking out there." He didn't know how she'd react to the news, but he had to tell someone. There was no point in trying to keep it a secret any longer.

Her mouth fell open. "What? That's not possible! Overseers are—"

"Think about it. It's not a coincidence I landed on Trin. I was sent there for a reason—to protect and guide you." Ed glanced at the clouds, disappointed no one had appeared. "I don't know who sent me the message, but I know they're telling the truth. That's why I have to go back and find the lykaes. I can't do that unless I figure out a way to heal myself first."

"How do you know Urien didn't send it?"

Ed shook his head. "He'd have no way of knowing what I am."

"Don't be so sure of that. I wouldn't put anything past my brother anymore." She crossed her arms. "What are you looking for here?"

"I thought I could track down the person who sent me the message, but so far I haven't found anything," he said.

"You helped me back in Trewa when I recharged the stones." She took hold of his hand. "Maybe I can help you contact whoever it was. If they're on the council, I should be able to reach them."

"You hate the council."

"True, but I'm the archdruid. I have a connection to them—even if my father did break all ties with them—whether I like it or not."

"Are you sure you want to do this?"

"Of course. I'm not about to watch you die."

Ed gripped her hand a little tighter. He felt his own magic combine with hers as it had back in Trewa when they'd restored the power of the standing stones. The connection and power between them felt incredible. He focused on the voice he'd heard in his dream.

The clouds shifted until they found themselves in front of a large standing stone. A woman appeared in front of it, and the air around her shimmered with power. Her long blonde hair fell past her shoulders, and her piercing blue eyes narrowed on them. Light sparkled over her flimsy white gown.

"Why are you here, Edward Rohn?" she demanded. Her gaze flickered to Ann. "Why are you *both* here?"

"You don't look like one of the council leaders I've met before," Ann observed.

"Times change. You were only a child when your father brought you before the council."

"Who are you?" Ed asked the woman.

"Never mind that. Ed is injured, tell us how to heal him."

The woman's eyes widened. "Injured? How?"

"Another lykae with red eyes attacked us. He punched a hole through my chest. Now I can't heal." Ed rubbed the back of his neck, his mind racing with unanswered questions. He wanted to know who this woman was. Why did she want him, of all people, to help stop a war in Lulrien?

"You will need blood," the woman replied.

"I was told never to do that."

"Feed from the archdruid if you must, but be warned, this will deepen the bond between you," the woman said.

"What bond?" Ann asked. "How—?"

The councilwoman cut her off. "Rohn, remember you must return home. Your people need you."

"But why? I'm not—"

"This is your mission, overseer. Obey your orders." The woman raised her hand, and Ed's eyes flew open.

Ann sat at his bedside. "Bloody useless council," she muttered. "How are you feeling?"

Sweat dripped down Ed's forehead. He gave a harsh laugh. "I've been better."

"But she did tell us a way to heal you. That other lykae fed on blood, he said he'd drain me dry."

Ed groaned. "Don't remind me."

"What if lykaes *need* blood?" Ann persisted. "I mean, you eat raw meat now your beast is out, maybe blood could heal you."

Ed heard the thrum of her pulse as she came over to him.

Blood, the beast hissed. *Feed.* It had whispered that to him earlier, but he had ignored it. Ed hadn't been happy when he discovered his lykae nature, he'd be damned if he'd feed on blood now too.

"It's worth a try." Ann held out her wrist.

"No, I won't feed from you." He turned his head away from her. The lure of her pulse made his fangs ache.

"If it'll save you—"

"I won't do that," he hissed.

Ann put her hands either side of his head turned Ed's face back to her. "I can't lose you. If it saves you, then just do it."

"We don't know what blood might do to me. I might be like that other lykae—a soulless killer."

"You won't be. Come on, Ed, I know you. You don't have it in you to be like that."

Ed shook his head. She was wrong. The beast in him was capable of that, he'd felt it more than once. Every time he lost control, he'd felt the rage, the need for blood. If he gave into that, he doubted he could come back from it.

"No," he said, a note of finality in his voice.

Ann grabbed his hand. "You're never going to accept what you are, are you? You're still my Edward. You always will be. That's why I can't believe you're giving up."

My Edward. The words made his heart twist.

"I'm not giving up," he insisted. All Ed remembered was someone telling him never to drink blood. He couldn't tell who it had been or what they'd meant, but it had been a warning.

"You're afraid. Why would someone tell you not to drink blood?"

He frowned. "How are you picking up my thoughts so easily? I don't know why someone said that, but they must have meant that something bad would happen."

She shrugged. "My magic seems stronger. Ed, isn't any risk worth it if you get to live?"

Feed, the beast hissed. *Blood. Need.*

"What if I change?" he demanded. "What if I lose control? Would you stop me?" He gripped her hand. "I mean it, everything in me says I shouldn't. Could you kill me?"

Ann looked away, and a tear dripped down her cheek.

His heart broke a little every time she cried.

"You need to promise you'll stop me," Ed insisted. "If the beast takes control, I won't be your friend anymore. It wants you."

"Why does it want me?"

"Probably because you're the person I care about most in this world. You're everything to me." He reached up and touched her cheek. "I could feed from Jax or Ceara." He didn't want to give in, but he couldn't leave her. Ed didn't want to die, not like this.

Maybe it's worth the risk, I won't take too much.

Ann shook her head. "Ceara is a Gliss. The other lykae seemed repelled by her blood because of it. Just feed from me. I heal faster than they do." She took a deep breath and held out her wrist again. "I'll stop you if I have to," she promised. "Now feed."

The warning rang through his mind again. *Never take blood…*

His eyes flashed emerald and his fangs came out as he bit down into her wrist.

Warmth flooded through him the minute her blood flowed into his mouth. It tasted sweet, and he could feel the power in it. No wonder the other lykae had craved it so much.

Ann gasped, but she didn't pull away.

More. Feed, the beast whispered.

Strength and power flowed back into him, and the hole in his chest closed over, but he wanted more, craved more. He didn't just want her blood. He wanted all of her.

Ed let go of her wrist, caught hold of the nape of her neck and pulled her closer until their lips almost met.

"I can't find anything," Ceara said from the doorway.

Ann opened her eyes and pulled back. "See, you're already healed." She wrapped her arms around him.

Ed held her close, enjoying the warmth of her embrace.

Ceara frowned. "How did you do that?"

"Ed drank my blood." Ann tucked a lock of hair behind her ear.

Ed sat up, pushing away any lingering feelings of desire. "If we're going into lykae territory soon, we're gonna need a good cover story."

Ann pulled back and frowned. "Why didn't you tell me you're a—"

31

"Ceara, can you leave us alone for a minute?" Ed interrupted.

Ceara's eyes narrowed. "Oh, pardon me for interrupting anything."

Ed's jaw clenched. "You are not interrupting anything."

The Gliss waggled her eyebrows. "Looks like I already did," she snorted, headed out of the room and shut the door behind her.

"Well?" Ann crossed her arms.

Ed sighed. "I couldn't. I think it's supposed to remain a secret, but I could never keep anything from you." He ran a hand over his abdomen, surprised to find smooth skin and no trace of the wounds the other lykae had inflicted. "In truth, I don't understand all of it myself."

"You should have told me."

"Do you think that woman lied to us?"

She shook her head. "No. We'll find the lykaes as planned, but why do we need a cover story?"

"Because I can't risk them finding out who you really are."

Ann frowned. "Why not?"

"I remember they hate magic…but I don't know why. I think it'd be safer that way." Ed grabbed his pack from the floor and pulled on a clean shirt.

"Maybe we should find out more before we go venturing through the mist. Let's go into your memories again."

"Taispeáin cuimhní i bhfolach dúinn." Ann said the words of invocation, and the spell dragged them both under. She didn't know

why the spell took *her* into his memories but didn't mind.

They stood surrounded by blue trees once again. Their leaves were shimmering purple. Even the sky seemed brighter and sharper here. Ed's memories always seemed to bring him back to this place.

"Here again." Ed sighed, and Ann felt waves of frustration coming from him.

"This place must've been important to you. Don't try to force it, let your mind show you whatever it wants you to see."

"I want to know what that damn entity that keeps tormenting us is."

"Maybe your beast could help you remember," she mused.

His eyes narrowed. "How?"

"Try using it to help you remember your childhood."

"You want me to let it out again?"

"It'll only force itself out more the more you try to control it. Perhaps that's why you don't remember about life before you landed on Trin," she said. "You locked that part of yourself away."

"That's not true."

Ann arched an eyebrow. "You're always locking your feelings away. Try it, let the beast out."

Ed scowled, and his eyes burned bright emerald.

The sound of laughter made them both turn. A little girl with bright red hair ran past.

"It's her," Ed gasped.

"Who?" Ann frowned.

"A woman I met during our last encounter with Urien. She felt familiar to me, and I think that's her. We were friends. She told me to find her…"

Ann's frown turned into a scowl. "Why didn't you mention her before now?" He rarely ever kept anything from her. What did this woman mean to him?

"You're jealous." He stared at her in surprise.

"I am not. I'm suspicious." She crossed her arms. "Is she a lykae too?"

"I think so. There's no need to be—"

"Don't you find it odd you met another lykae months ago? If she knows who you are, why didn't she say anything?" His memory of meeting Jessa flashed by.

"Let's move away from this memory."

Ed's eyes flashed emerald. This time, they saw his younger self running through the woods, the strange glowing entity chasing after him. They had seen this memory of him being chased before and believed it had happened the same day he'd landed on Trin.

"Do you remember why it's chasing you?" Ann prompted.

Ed's eyes glowed brighter.

Ed gasped. His eyes flew open as he found himself back in the circle. *What happened?* Ann hadn't ended the spell.

He shot up; his vision blurred. A blast of light from the circle sent him crashing to the floor.

"What's wrong?" Ann scrambled up. She hadn't ended the circle yet, so neither of them could step out.

Ed clutched his head. "Argh, you need to get away from me." He doubled over. His body shuddered and he changed into the beast's true form.

Ann waved her hand, causing the circle to flash as its power dispersed. "Focus." She moved over to him and put her hands on his shoulders. "You can control this."

"It's so strong." His fangs and claws came out. "I think it's worse because it's the full moon."

Ann didn't back away. "Why are you doing this?" she asked instead.

"Because I'm tired of being locked away," the beast hissed.

"I keep telling him—I mean, you—to accept it." She sighed. "This is who you are now. Locking it away will only make it worse." She paused. "Did you remember anything else?"

He nodded. "Pieces are coming back. Why is this so strong?"

"You're stronger. Just focus on me." She knelt with him as he sank to his knees.

After a while, his fangs and claws retracted. "I think it's passed," he breathed.

"That's good." She yawned and slumped onto the bed, which had just appeared.

CHAPTER 4

Ann waited until later that night before creeping into the work room. She checked on a sleeping Ed before leaving his room. Unbeknownst to him, she had found a poison in her father's collection that would keep her in limbo for longer before her body revived itself.

Thanks to a spell Darius had cast before he'd been murdered, Ann and her siblings couldn't die. No matter the method of death, the spell regenerated them. Xander had even been set on fire and his body revived itself.

She lit the candles and shut the door before settling down in the spell circle. The room looked just as she'd found it a few weeks earlier. Oak hardwood covered the floor, and the walls were of whitewashed stone. Ann still found herself reaching out and touching the walls to make sure they were real. It still fascinated her to think her father had managed to create this place that existed outside time and place. A small altar sat at the far end of the room—something Ann found strange. The druids didn't worship any gods or deities and didn't have a strict religion like other races. Theirs was a spiritual tradition based on seeking one's own path. Spirits existed all around their world—and were both good and bad.

She placed a big cushion on the floor and sat on it, then lay down, pulling her sleep shirt down to cover her thighs. It would be better this way, she wouldn't fall and hurt herself. Her body might heal itself from fatal wounds, but non-life-threatening ones took longer. Pulling the cork from the vial she retrieved from a workbench, she gulped down the poison. It burned her throat as she forced herself to swallow.

Ann had told Ceara what she was about to do, but the Gliss had been half asleep from too much wine. Ed would worry if she told him, and Jax would tell Ed if she had mentioned it to him, so she avoided telling either of them anything. She'd cross over, look for Xander, then come straight back.

Ann gasped, feeling her throat close as she struggled for breath. Her lungs burned and her heart rate slowed. She closed her eyes and let death drag her away.

The blackness of limbo surrounded her when she blinked again. Shadows danced around through the haze of mist, and a coldness crept over her even though she was in spirit form.

"Xander?" Ann called. "Xander, are you here?" She'd managed to contact Xander's spirit a few weeks earlier but knew Urien had a tighter grip on him now.

Despite the gloom, she didn't fear this place. Ann rarely ever saw anything else here. Besides, this wasn't the land souls truly moved on to after they died. Good spirits got to move on to Summerland—a beautiful place full of peace and tranquillity— and bad souls were sent on into the underworld for eternal torment.

She moved through the shadows. "Come on, Xander. I know you're here somewhere." She sighed. "Please come here. You're stronger than Urien." She waited, but nothing happened.

Ann raised her hands as they flared with light and muttered the words of power needed to summon a spirit. "Alexander Valeran, I summon you here. Come before me."

She waited, the shadows making her uneasy.

"Annie?"

She turned to see her little brother standing there. "Xander!" She threw her arms around him, then hesitated. "Wait, it is you, isn't it?"

Urien had tricked her before by posing as Xander's spirit in an attempt to get her to lift the spell that bound the three of them together.

Xander's mop of black curly hair looked ragged, and there were dark circles under his eyes. "It's me. I've spent days trying to call you. Urien—" Xander shuddered and shook his head. "He's been using blood magic to suppress me. I haven't had any control over my own body. Sometimes I see what he's doing, but other times I'm locked away in the shadows, unable to see or do anything."

Ann's heart twisted at the thought of his suffering. "We don't have much time. By the spirits, I miss you."

"I miss you too. Urien is searching for something. Perhaps a weapon? Whatever it is, it's important."

"To do what?" By coming here, she'd hoped she might learn more about Urien's plans. So far, her network in the resistance hadn't been able to tell her much about what had been going on back in Larenth.

"To bring down the mist. He wants to make the other lands more accessible so he can recruit more demons," Xander explained. "It's more than that. He wants something else—something in Lulrien. He found some old artefacts that belonged to Papa."

Lulrien again. Everything seemed to keep pointing her there. First Ed's message, and now Xander.

"What did he find?" Darius had possessed dozens of artefacts— weapons and objects of power that he had gathered during his long reign as the archdruid. Some had been handed down through their family over the centuries. There were too many items for her to remember, let alone guess what they might be. "Do you know how Urien got hold of a wyvern?"

Xander's form flickered. "I don't know. My body is calling me back."

Ann gripped his hands, using magic to hold him there. "You need to tell me everything you can."

"There's no time. Urien knows I'm gone, he'll drag me back. I'm going mad being trapped in my own body and not being able to get out or control anything."

"I'm close to finding a way to unlink you and Urien. I will save you."

"Ann, you have to undo Papa's spell. It's the only way to kill him."

"I told you, I won't do that. You'd die too." Ann thought hard. She had to do everything she could to remain one step ahead of Urien. Her hands flared with power once again.

"Ann." Xander gripped her hands tighter. "I don't want to go back. Ann…"

"Listen, I will save you. I promise."

"You need to promise me you'll do with whatever it takes to stop Urien. Promise."

She shook her head. "No, not at the cost of your life."

"Some things are more important than me."

"Stay strong, little brother." She hugged him tight. "I love you." Ann's shoulders slumped as Xander's spirit faded.

Something darted through the shadows, and a chill ran over her senses.

"You walk through death, little druid."

Ann winced, images flashing by. "You again," she said, feeling the presence of the strange entity. "What is it you want? Or do you enjoy getting on my nerves?"

The laughter Ann had grown accustomed to followed.

"I mean it! Why do you keep following me and Edward?"

The laughter grew louder, and power flared between her fingers. Odd, she'd never been able to use this much magic on the other side before.

"I enjoy watching lesser beings."

"Are you an elder?" Ann frowned. If the entity *was* an elder, she had next to no way of knowing. Her father had kept her away from them for most of her life, but she had met a couple during her years on the run.

"What I am is not important." The entity darted back and forth between the dancing shadows. "You like playing here in the Grey, don't you, little druid?"

"The Grey? Is that what this place is called?" Fire crackled between her fingers as her magic ached to get out. *Stupid, I shouldn't show my ignorance to this creature.*

"Tell me what you want then."

"I'm curious to see how your war with your brother plays out," the voice said. "You walk in death as easily as one breathes."

"This isn't true death." Ann's druid fire danced across her fingers along with something else, orbs of light she hadn't seen before.

"I sense your power. It's growing, isn't it? You feel a magic in you that doesn't come from nature."

"I don't know what you're talking about." Ann moved back and snuffed out her fire, willed her spirit to return to her body.

Nothing happened.

More laughter echoed around her.

Ann's eyes narrowed. "What have you done? Let me out of here."

She threw a fireball, but her magic vanished into the blackness of limbo.

"Go ahead, use your real power, the power that's stirring deep inside you. You feel it, don't you?"

She drew more magic, and lightning crackled between her fingers. Ann stared in disbelief. She didn't have this ability—where had it come from? Was this the strange power the entity was referring to?

"That's it. *Dark* power. Give into it. Come and join me…"

Ann's hand shot a static charge through the air. The entity screamed as Ann blasted it again.

"Whatever you are, stay away from me."

Ann gasped for breath. Lungs burning, she opened her eyes and clutched at her throat. Blood dripped from her nose.

"Ann, what happened?" Ed asked, kneeling beside her. "I couldn't wake you."

She wiped the blood away and clutched her pounding head.

Ed wrapped his arms around her. "It's okay," he whispered. "I have you."

Ann clung to him, pressing her face against his chest. His body felt warm and safe.

He held onto her, running his fingers through her hair, and pulled her closer, cocooning his body against hers. "Sleep. I have you now."

Her body felt weak, drained. It'd taken a lot of power to hold Xander, and she had no idea what that lightning had been. Druids didn't wield that kind of power.

She needed energy after all the strength she had spent being on the other side. She'd sensed Ed's energy when he'd fed on her earlier. It'd felt stronger than anything the earth lines of Erthea could offer her.

She stared at him. "I need your energy."

"Take it." Ed gripped her hand.

Ann felt the strength running through his veins but couldn't reach it. "It's not enough, I need to really touch you." She ran her hands down the hard planes of his chest. "We need to be close." She cupped his face and kissed him, gasping as energy flared between them.

Ed's eyes widened in shock. They stared at each other before she grabbed him and kissed him again.

His fingers curled in her hair as he thrust his tongue into her mouth, making her moan.

She pushed him back onto the cushion, wrapping her legs around his waist.

This kiss felt like nothing she'd ever felt before. Orbs of white light danced around them as energy rippled over their bodies. Ann didn't just want him, she needed him like she needed air to breathe. As light washed over them, some of his energy seeped into her.

"Spirits, I want you so badly," he groaned.

"I need your energy. I spent too much when I was on the other side." She brushed her lips over his again. "I need you."

The orbs around them became brighter, flowing in and out of their bodies.

Ed's eyes burned bright emerald, and she felt him touching her mind, his desire just as strong as hers.

Ed let go of her, breathing hard, and wrapped an arm around her, pulling her close.

She fell asleep with his body wrapped around hers.

Ann woke the next morning. Her head pounded, yet most of her exhaustion had faded. She looked down to see Ed's body pressed against hers.

What have I done? She'd been so damn weak from the power she'd used in limbo. She shivered, remembering the strange blue lightning she'd used. *Where did it come from? What does it mean?*

More thoughts raced around her mind. She needed to find out what that strange entity was and what it wanted.

She glanced down and saw the marks on Ed's chest had faded into faint pink scars. How had she done that? Lykaes were resistant to magic, that much she knew for certain.

I can't believe I kissed him and channelled his energy.

She didn't know what she'd been thinking, this was Edward. They were just friends.

What would he think now? That they were a couple?

Stupid, stupid. Why did I even kiss him? She blamed Ceara's incessant nagging over the past few months. Ann tried to wriggle free of his embrace, but he tightened his grip. *Damn it.*

She didn't want to wake him, didn't want to have face him yet. No doubt he'd want to talk about what had happened. She drew magic, light flashed over her body, and she reappeared outside the circle. She opened the door and crept out into the passageway.

Jax grinned as she moved into the space they'd turned into a living area with a table and four chairs. "Morning. Bet you've worked up an appetite this morning."

Ann froze. "That…it isn't what you think." Her cheeks flushed.

"You and Ed sleep next to each other sometimes, I know that. But you were sneaking around when you walked out, which means you finally got it on. It's about bloody time, woman!"

Her eyes narrowed. "We didn't do…Hey, remember I'm in charge!" She put her hands on her hips. "I know you and Ceara have a bet going about Ed and I getting together, so stop pretending this isn't about money."

"Yes, oh mighty archdruid." He gave a mock bow. "But first, tell Jax everything." He grinned. "Plus, it's not about money. The Gliss and I want you and Ed to be happy."

She grabbed a nearby cushion and threw it at him. "There's nothing to say. Be sure to tell Ceara your bet is off. Nothing is ever going to happen between Ed and I."

"Come on, I've waited years for this. Something must have happened." He motioned to her. "Your face is all red, so you're embarrassed about something."

"You are insufferable." She threw another cushion at him and hurried off to her room. Her cheeks burned hotter than ever.

By the spirits, what have I done? She pressed a hand her forehead.

Ann banged her head back against the door and looked down at her wrists. The scars left from where Ed and the other lykae had bitten her had vanished. She knew she'd have to deal with Ed sooner or later. Jax and Ceara would pester them both with annoying questions. She had no idea what to say to him. Damn that blasted entity for trapping her on the other side!

Ann washed and dressed in her usual leathers. She searched through her bag in hopes of finding some extra food. No such luck.

"Breakfast is ready," Jax yelled. "Come get it."

The door opened and Ed came in, now fully dressed. "We should talk."

She ran a hand through her hair. What was she supposed to say to him? 'Sorry I kissed you? Sorry I made such a huge mistake?'

"About what?" She avoided his gaze and made a move to get past him.

"About what happened last night."

"I was weak, I took energy from you. What else is there to talk about?"

He gripped her shoulders, forcing her to face him. "It was more than that that. We kissed…"

"Please don't." She shoved his hands away. "Last night can't and won't happen again. Nothing has changed."

"Everything has changed."

She'd been afraid he'd say that. "What do you want me to say, Edward?" She crossed her arms and glared at him. He knew her well enough to know nothing could come of that kiss. She didn't do romantic relationships.

"I want you to finally admit, after all these years, there is something between us," he said. "There always has been."

"I can't and—"

Cupping her face, he kissed her, hard. She melted into the kiss, remembering how good it'd felt last night.

"Breakfast is getting cold," Ceara said from the doorway.

Ann shoved him away from her. "This...this won't happen again." Heat rose in her cheeks again as she hurried out of the room before Ceara had a chance to question them.

CHAPTER 5

Ed forced himself to eat breakfast, but the beast clawed at his mind, thrashing to get out. Kissing Ann, touching her had felt better than he could ever have imagined. Now he'd had a taste, he wanted more. But she acted like their kiss had been wrong, and he couldn't understand why. She'd kissed *him* and instigated the whole thing. He wanted her now more than ever.

Mine, the beast hissed. *K'ia. Make her mine.*

Ed had no idea what that meant but knew Ann wouldn't even look at him.

"So, what happened last night?" Ceara asked as they sat in the dining area. "I thought I heard you cry out for help. I remember you mentioning something about crossing over to the other side. Did you?"

Ann played with her porridge, twirling the metal spoon around her bowl. "I did," Ann said. "I saw Xander there, and that strange entity appeared too."

"What?" Ed demanded. "Why didn't you tell me last night?" He couldn't believe she hadn't mentioned it earlier. She might have felt weak last night, but that seemed too important a detail not to tell him.

"I don't have to tell you everything," she snapped and glared at him.

Jax glanced between them. "What is wrong with you two?" He frowned. "Did you have an argument last night?"

Both Ed and Ann ignored the question. Ed leaned back in his chair, daring Ann to say something. She didn't, instead she avoided his gaze and pretended he wasn't there.

"What did Xander say?" Ceara asked.

Ann shook her head. "He told me Urien wants something in Lulrien, but I don't know what it is yet."

"What else happened?" Ed asked, trying not to sound as frustrated as he felt. Not only was she avoiding him, now she was shutting him out as well. His beast clawed at the cage of his mind, wanting to get out. He ignored it. No doubt his frustration set it on edge.

"The entity tried to stop me from coming back, but I made it go away. We need to get on the other side of the mist." She gave Ed a pointed look. "And you need find your people."

"Ann, your wrists are healed. When did that happen?" Jax motioned to where Ed and the other lykae had bitten her.

Ann pulled down the long sleeves of her tunic down to cover her unmarked wrists. "My father's spell healed me. We should get moving soon." She made no mention of how channelling Ed's energy had healed her.

Ed clenched the table to calm his beast as it clawed for control. The wood splintered and the edge of the table gave way under his grip.

"What's wrong with you?" Ceara asked.

"Nothing. It must be getting near the full moon," he growled. "We need to go over our cover story for when we reach lykae lands." The full moon had already passed, but it was the only excuse he could think of.

Jax raised an eyebrow. "What cover story? Why would we need one?"

Ceara stirred her rakka tea. Ed hated the strong stench of it, but she always insisted she needed it to wake up in the morning. "Probably in case they try to kill us like that other lykae did yesterday," she said.

"The lykaes don't like magic, they won't be very welcoming toward Ann. We'll need to be careful whilst we are there," he explained. "I've been remembering more things about them recently."

Ann sipped her own tea. "I wouldn't worry too much. We won't be staying there long." She rose. "Hurry up and finish eating. We need to reach lykae lands today if possible."

They reappeared outside, the mist shimmering in the morning sunlight. Around them, trees stood like silent sentinels, and the smell of fresh dew filled the air.

Ed stared at the mist, wondering what awaited him on the other side.

"How do we get through?" Jax asked. "I've seen the mist before, but everyone told me it was toxic."

"I should be able to cross over, I must've done it before when the sea carried me to Trin." Ed glanced at the others. "I'll go through first and come back for you."

"What if you can't come back through?" Ann asked.

"Do you even care?" he retorted.

"Of course I care." She glared at him.

"You took enough energy from me last night to open the mist." Ed walked straight through the mist, and energy rippled over him. He winced, covering his eyes. On the other side, the sky appeared a brighter blue. Everything smelled and looked different. He could almost taste magic in the air.

His beast jumped inside his mind, almost purring with pleasure. It wanted to be loose, to run through this new, alien land.

Ed glanced back to see the mist had vanished. "What? No!" He couldn't be separated from the others, not yet. He wouldn't let his last words to Ann be ones of anger.

He blurred and shot straight back through the now-invisible mist to see Ann and the others all looking bemused.

Relief washed over him. He made a move to wrap his arms around Ann, then stopped. He doubted she'd welcome his embrace. "It's safe," he said instead.

"I've cast a spell to protect them from the effects of the mist," Ann told him.

Ed grasped Jax and Ceara, pulling them both through before going back for Ann.

"Let's go." Ed held out his hand to her but didn't meet her gaze.

"Please don't be like this." She touched his shoulder, and he brushed her hand away.

"How do you expect me to be?" he demanded. "If you want to pretend nothing happened between us, fine, you do that."

"What do you think *could* happen between us?" She crossed her arms. "You're leaving, remember? We might never see each other again."

"I'd never leave you—not for long, at least. I don't intend to stay with the lykaes forever," he snapped. "Though I may reconsider that now." He grabbed her hand and tugged at her arm, but she didn't budge.

"You're leaving. Whatever might be between us won't change that." She reached up and touched his cheek. "That's why we can't give into this."

Ed sighed, stroking her hand with the back of his thumb. "Like I said, I won't—"

"You don't know that. Don't make promises you can't keep.

52

There's no guarantee I'll be able to stay with you for long. I can't give into this then say goodbye to you. Please don't ask me to." She gripped his hand. "Let's go. The others will wonder where we are."

His eyes widened. "That's why you're pushing me away? You think we won't see each other again? Ann, that would never happen." He stroked her cheek and brushed her hair off her face. "I'm not giving up. I know you wanted me last night as much I wanted you. One way or another I'll prove it to you." He squeezed her hand, and together they stepped through the mist. Energy hummed against his skin again as they passed through.

"It's bright here," Jax remarked.

"And full of fae, from what I can sense," Ceara sneered. "Never did like the buggers."

Ed kept hold of Ann's hand as they moved along the track. To his surprise, she didn't pull away.

"What kind of fae?" Jax asked.

"Hundreds. Dryads, fairies... Only you could be excited about crossing over," Ceara scoffed. "This place is full of danger, remember that."

"It will be interesting to see some of the fae. Most of them were forced out of the other lands during the realm wars," Jax remarked.

They moved through the clearing.

"Do you remember anything?" Ann asked Ed as they moved ahead of the others.

"Bits and pieces. It feels so familiar, yet so strange."

"If that entity hadn't chased you out, you would have grown up here," she said. "Don't you wonder what that would have been like?"

"Honestly, no. If I had, I never would have found you."

She tugged her hand away. "Ed, we've been through this."

"One way or another, I'll prove to you we can—"

"What? Have a relationship?" she asked. "You know I don't believe in that romantic nonsense. Us being a couple could only ruin our friendship." She sighed. "I shouldn't have kissed you last night, I'm sorry."

"I'm glad you did." Ed smiled. "I want—"

The sound of laughter cut him off.

"Argh, not that thing again." Fire flared in Ann's hand.

What did you do to it last night? he asked.

Long story. I'll tell you later, she replied.

Ed's eyes flashed emerald as his fangs came out. His beast clawed at the of the cage of his mind, demanding to get out. He would have gladly let it out if he thought it would do any good. But neither his beast nor magic could touch the strange creature that had been stalking them over the past few months.

Jax and Ceara came rushing over.

"What's with the creepy laughter?" Jax asked, gripping his staff.

"That would be our unwanted visitor," Ann replied. Ed made a move to run after it. "Wait." She grabbed his arm.

What?

Maybe by chasing after it, we're indulging it, she said. *Maybe we should ignore it.*

"Stand down," Ann hissed at the others as they drew their

weapons.

"What?" Jax stared at her in disbelief. "We can't do that. What if it attacks us?"

"If it does, I don't think there's much we can do about it."

Ed straightened, feeling the beast itching to get out. His beast senses were heightened, sharper and louder than they had been on the other side of the mist. He motioned for the others to follow.

"What are you doing?" the voice demanded.

"We're not going to be your amusement anymore," Ann snapped.

The laughter grew louder. It set Ed's teeth on edge. Damn it, he wanted to rip the entity's throat out.

"Move," he hissed at the others.

The others moved further down the trail—except for Ann, who remained by his side.

Go, he told her.

Not without you. You're not the only one it torments. Her eyes flashed with power.

"You're walking back into danger, lykae," the voice hissed. "Do you really want to lose the woman you love?" The laughter followed. "And you, druid, you're walking down a dangerous path. I can't wait to watch how you and your brother will fight over this."

"Keep on watching, but we're done with you." Ann snuffed out her fireball.

To Ed's surprise, the entity zipped away, disappearing among the tree line. "It's gone." He breathed a sigh of relief, taking her hand again.

Ann drew away. "Is that true? Do you love me?"

Ed hesitated. He'd wanted to admit his true feelings for her for a long time now, yet he could never get them into words. "Of course I do. You are my oldest friend." The word 'friend' didn't sound right anymore. What were they now? What would she let them become?

Her eyes narrowed at that.

"Oh, come on, you can do better than that," Ceara remarked.

Ed flashed her a glare. *Would you please stay out of this?*

"What do you want us to be?" Ed asked. "We can't carry on being just friends. Not after last night."

"Come on, sister. Let's get moving." Jax grabbed Ceara's arm and dragged her further down the path, giving Ann and Ed some privacy.

"Hey, I want to hear what they're saying!" Ceara protested as they walked away.

"Why not? Why can't we go back to what we were?" Ann asked him.

Ed shook his head. What would it take to finally break down the walls around her heart? He'd find a way. He had to. "Because you are everything to me."

Ann sighed and looked away. "We need to get moving."

They moved on in silence until he stopped dead. Ahead loomed blue trees stretching toward the sky. They smelt sweet, almost like honeysuckle

"I don't believe it," Ed gasped. "They are real."

"Nice trees," Jax remarked. "Never seen anything like them before."

"We must be getting closer to Corenth," he remarked.

"What's Corenth?"

"The plains—I think that's where I'll find the other lykaes." It surprised him how many of his memories had come back.

Ceara crossed her arms and frowned at him. "I'd still like to know more about this dream you had that brought us here in the first place. Who spoke to you and what did they say?"

It's just like Ceara to be nosy and demand answers, he thought.

Ed hesitated. He hadn't confessed being an overseer to the others. Deep down, he knew he was supposed to keep it a secret, but how long could he do that for? He and Ann never used to keep any secrets from each other. Ever since discovering his lykae nature and realising the true depth of his feelings, he'd kept more and more from her.

"That voice said you were walking into danger if you go there," Ann said. "Are you sure we should risk it?"

"I have to find them, you know that." He couldn't ignore that dream.

"What else have you remembered?" Ceara asked.

Jax and Ceara continued to pester him with questions as they moved.

Ann, meanwhile, remained silent. Damn it, he wanted to talk her about the entity, about their kiss, about everything.

"Let's focus more on what we're going to tell the lykaes," Ed suggested. "Ann, maybe we should pretend we're married." Her eyes flashed, but he ignored her. "We did when we first joined the resistance. Jax and Ceara can still be my siblings, and no one here would know I'm connected to the archdruid."

During their early days on the run, Ann and Ed had pretended to be a couple so no one would suspect who they were. It had proved effective and hadn't been hard for them to pull off. Most people assumed they were a couple anyway.

Ann shook her head. "No, you can't be sure of that. I agree that I should keep my identity a secret, but with my glamour in place no one will recognise me."

"It would give you and the others an excuse to stay," Ed argued.

"I think it's a good idea," Ceara agreed.

Jax nodded. "Yeah, we're family. I don't like the thought of you leaving us either, brother."

Ann gritted her teeth. *Fine, but don't think this changes anything between us.*

I—

"Who's the leader of the lykaes?" Ceara's voice interrupted his thoughts. "Hello, wolfy? Stop staring at Ann and answer me."

Ed shook his head. "The alpha." He couldn't believe how much of his past and knowledge of the lykaes had come back after all these years. He didn't know why he'd forgotten it. Maybe it had been trauma from almost drowning?

"What's his name?" Jax wanted to know. "Although I guess that might've changed since you left them fifteen years ago."

"I…don't know."

Ed had told the others he was going to Lulrien to find his family and learn control from the other lykaes. It was true enough. He'd struggled to control his inner beast ever since he'd discovered his lykae nature.

He thought back to the strange dream and the woman he and Ann had spoken to the night before. Ed wanted to know more about her. How did she know so much about the lykaes and whoever they were feuding with?

Ed didn't think either the dream or the woman were connected to the entity that kept following them around. That seemed separate somehow, more of a pest than a real threat. The voice in his dream had sounded familiar, yet he had no idea who the woman might be. Why did she think he could somehow help the lykaes? He wasn't sure what being an overseer even meant for him now. He knew he'd been tasked to protect and watch over Ann, to guide her until she became the next archdruid. But even if he hadn't been an overseer, he would've stayed with her anyway.

"I still think you're stupid leaving us if the lykaes don't let us stay," Jax muttered. "Ann could just transport you back and forth, or you could use the vault and travel that way. You wouldn't need to leave us then."

He glanced at Ann, but she wouldn't meet his gaze. He had no idea where he stood with her now. Could they be something more? Deep down, he knew an overseer wasn't meant to get involved with the person they were assigned to protect, but he couldn't help it, he'd been in love with her for as long as he could remember. Did she feel the same way?

"I'm not leaving anyone. I'll make sure—" Ed froze, catching the scent of something foul. "I smell something."

Jax frowned. "What? I don't smell anything."

"Maybe that's because your senses are inferior to his." Ceara smirked at their brother.

"Maybe we should split up," Ed suggested. At least that would give him the chance to talk to Ann again.

"Good idea," Ann agreed. "Jax, you and I can—"

"Whoa, I'm not going with wolfy," Ceara protested. "Not that bird boy's much better company, but at least he won't try to drink my blood."

"That other lykae almost choked on your blood, so I think you're safe," Jax remarked. "And stop calling me bird boy, it's bloody annoying. Crows are strong and majestic, they're not just birds." He crossed his arms and scowled at her.

"At least Ed turns into something interesting."

"Hey, he might be able to move faster and rip things apart, but I can fly and make my skin impervious to most injuries. There is nothing wrong with my powers. You should all be grateful for them, given how often you send me off to spy on people." Jax returned Ceara's glare, and the two of them stalked off in the opposite direction.

"Are you okay with me coming with you?" Ed asked.

Ann nodded. "Of course."

Giant trees loomed over them like silent sentinels, filling the air with their heady scent. Ed didn't remember ever seeing trees so big before, not even in Caselhelm's great forests.

"Listen, about last night—" Ed said.

Ann looked away. "I'd rather not talk about that kiss anymore."

"I meant when I bit you. I don't want…I mean I…I don't want things to be strange between us."

"Everything is fine."

He rubbed the back of his neck. "Still, I can't feed on blood again. It's too dangerous."

"Agreed." She still avoided his gaze. He heard her heart pound, then noticed the flush covering her cheeks. "I needed to heal you. It won't happen again."

"Good. I don't want things to be awkward."

"They're not. You're healed now, so everything is back to normal. I'll pretend to be your wife." She took hold of his left hand and recited words of power that Ed recognised as words of a handfasting spell.

His hand glowed with light and radiated with warmth as fasting lines entwined around his wrist and Ann's. The dark blue lines wrapped around their wrists in an intricate knot, giving the illusion of them being bound by druid magic.

She turned away from him. He felt her scanning the surrounding forest with her mind as she searched for the mist.

"There's something else I should tell you." Ed paused, wondering if he should admit his true feelings for her.

"What?"

"I'm…I smell decay." His brow creased. "Lots of it."

"Where?"

"It's some distance away, but it's strong. My guess is its bodies—a lot of them. I'll check it out." He made a move to blur away.

Ann grabbed hold of his arm. "No, we should stick together."

"I won't lose control again if that's what you're worried about."

"We should stay close anyway. Another lykae could be around, it took both of us to bring one down."

Ed shook his head. "There aren't any other lykaes, I'd sense them if there were. I had an uneasy feeling for days before we encountered one yesterday, I'd know if there were more."

"See, you *can* control it." She smiled. "We should check out the bodies just to be sure. You can carry me."

He arched an eyebrow. "Are you sure?" He knew how much she hated being carried around and was surprised she'd suggested it.

Ann nodded and slipped her arms around his neck.

Ed picked her up as if she weighed nothing at all. Trees rushed past them as they blurred so fast Ed barely had time to enjoy the feel of his arms around her.

"Argh, how do you not get ill from doing that?" she gasped as Ed set her down. Her legs wobbled, and she almost fell over.

"Sorry." Ed wrapped his arms around her again to steady her. "It doesn't bother me. Guess I'm used to it."

She took a few deep breaths and settled on a tree stump. "Where are the bodies?"

Ed motioned to a small wooden dwelling made out of branches.

Almost like a makeshift hut. "In there." Had the other lykae come from here?

Ann stood up, wobbled again. "Let's go."

"Are you sure you're alright?" He touched her cheek.

"I'm fine, don't fuss over me."

He grinned. "You never like anyone taking care of you."

"I'm fine. Really." She frowned. "Stop looking so guilty. You didn't take too much blood, and the lykae bites didn't affect me."

"You don't feel fine, you feel dizzy and sick." Odd, he seemed to be able to pick up her feelings more easily now than usual. Had him feeding on her blood created a deeper connection between them, or was it something else?

Her eyes narrowed. "How do you know that?"

"I feel it."

Ann's mouth fell open. "Do you think it's a side effect of you feeding on my blood?"

Ed shrugged. "Maybe, maybe not. I've always been able to sense when you needed me or were in danger."

She nodded. "As I have with you. Do you sense *everything* I feel now?"

"Just glimpses of it," he admitted.

"Well, don't. We might know each other better than anyone else, but I don't want anyone sensing my every thought and feeling."

Ed wondered if his new ability would give him the chance to find out how she really felt about him. He considered using their connection to find out, but decided against it. "Now you feel nervous."

"Edward!" Ann gave him a shove.

He smiled and picked her up, carrying her through the doorway.

Inside the hut lay body parts from animal carcasses and other remains, including what looked like bits of armour.

"This must be where the lykae lived," Ed remarked.

"Do you think it came from the same place you did?"

He shrugged. "I have no way of knowing. It would never have answered our questions, it was too consumed by rage."

"I hoped he might have been able to give you some answers."

"Me too." He sighed. "We should burn this place."

"Why?"

Ed shook his head, instinct had taken over. Would he ever understand his beast, or what he really was now? "It feels like the right thing to do."

As fire flared between Ann's fingers, Ed noticed something glistening among the debris.

"Wait." Ed gripped her arm, then knelt to retrieve a silver medallion with a wolf's head on it.

"What's that?"

"I have no idea, but this symbol seems familiar to me. Maybe we've found a clue to my past after all."

Ann set the den alight, watching the flames consume the entire dwelling. One good thing about druid fire was it burned quick and stayed in a concentrated area. Otherwise she might have set the whole forest ablaze. Ann rummaged in her bag, pulled out a scrying mirror and muttered a spell to show them the way to the lykaes.

"Tispeáin an bealach go dtí an likaes."

Nothing happened.

Ed stood still, running the medallion between his fingers.

"Did you remember something about it?" Ann asked.

He shook his head. "No, it's just a feeling." Ed took hold of her hand.

Ann looked down when he didn't let go of her hand. *Damn Ceara for putting ideas in my head.* Her skin felt warm against his.

"Why are you feeling nervous again?" Ed asked. "And why did Ceara put ideas in your head?"

"Stop that!" She tugged her hand away. "This is getting annoying. Hey, while we're on the subject of feelings, why don't you tell me yours?"

His frown deepened. "What do you mean?"

"Come on, I know when you're hiding something from me. Spit it out." Ann bit her lip. "Is it about last night?"

"No…Nothing is bothering me."

She rolled her eyes. "You've never been good at lying to me."

"We should work on our story. They'll ask us questions about our relationship."

She snorted. "That will be fun. Let's use the same story we used when we stayed with the resistance."

The beast growled at the edge of Ed's mind, warning him of danger. He pocketed the medallion. "We've got company."

CHAPTER 6

Ed stared at the five lykae men in surprise. How hadn't he sensed them coming? He'd sensed the other lykae who had attacked them the day before.

All five of them were dark-haired with pale skin. They all wore loose leather doublets and leather trousers. One of the lykaes—a man with a mop of long, dark, curly hair—stepped forward.

"You're trespassing here," he said, his pale blue eyes flashing with amber light. "You aren't welcome in these lands. How did you even get through the mist?"

"We're not trespassing, we're on our way to talk to your alpha." Ed's beast rose to the surface and he knew his own eyes burned with emerald light. He wasn't sure how much to tell them to start off with.

He'd only been ten years old when he left the lykaes and landed on Trin. Would these people even remember who he was?

The lead lykae gave a harsh laugh. "My alpha doesn't welcome outcasts. You'd all best be on your way. Lucky for you, I'm feeling generous today—if not, you would all be dead by now."

"Wow, so much for a warm welcome," Ceara remarked, her hand going to one of her shock rods. Light flared between her brows as her empathic power came to life.

The lead lykae's fangs came out as he made a move toward Ceara.

Ann raised her hands, and Ed caught hold of her wrist. *Don't, it would be safer if we didn't attack them. Stand down, don't use any magic or make any threatening moves toward them.*

He stared at the leader, noticing he seemed familiar. "Marcus, is that you?" Ed frowned. Images of a blue-eyed boy flashed through his mind. He remembered playing in the woods with him as a child.

The other lykae's eyes narrowed. "You know me?"

"Yes. It's me, Rohn." Ed blinked, surprised he'd referred to himself by his last name. He'd wondered if he'd had a different name before he ended up with the druids, but it had never mattered to him. He'd always felt his name was Edward, and he always would be, even if he found out otherwise. That was who he was now, and he wouldn't change his name, no matter what.

Marcus' eyes widened in shock. "Rohn? No, that's impossible." He shook his head. "Rohn was my cousin. He disappeared—who are you to bring him up? You are not one of us. Leave, before—"

"It's me. I know it's been a long time, but I am Rohn." The name had always seemed to fit, and Flora had told him he'd muttered it during his ramblings when he'd first arrived on Trin as a half-drowned orphan. So she had kept it as his last name.

"You lost your cousin fifteen years ago, right?" Ann asked. "Well, this is him. That's why we came here, to help him find his family."

Marcus stared at Ed. "The alpha will know. Come, we'll take you to him. But I warn you, if this is a trick, you will all pay with your lives."

The other lykaes followed close behind them as Marcus led the way back to the village.

Ed didn't like the hostility coming from them. It set his beast on edge. Yet he knew these men were his kin.

Are you sure this is a good idea? Ann asked. *These lykaes are strong. If we have to flee—*

Ann, I have to find my family—or at least try to. I have so many unanswered questions. Ed took hold of her hand again, feeling the waves of anxiety coming off her. *Plus, I have to see if I can help them somehow.*

What if they can't be trusted? she persisted.

If they turn against us, we'll leave, he said. *Don't mention you are the archdruid.*

She frowned. *Why not?*

Just tell them you're an ordinary druid. Don't use magic around them unless you have to. We need to be on our guard. Ed turned to the others. *It would be best if you two don't use magic around them either.*

I'll use my magic if I want to. Ceara raised her chin. *But I'm not sensing much from these guys other than waves of hostility.*

Your powers won't work very well on them. Lykaes have a natural immunity to magic.

Ahead loomed a village with small wooden huts. Some had no roofs, and most of them were made from the wood of the blue trees he'd seen in his memories. It gave the houses a blue hue that glimmered in the sunlight. Ed couldn't believe it. It looked just as he remembered it.

Women stood or sat brewing food or sewing, and a handful of children ran around.

The smell of grass, leather, and wood smoke reached him. It felt like coming home, yet the faces around him didn't seem familiar. They eyed him and the others with suspicion. Ed sensed their unease. He hadn't expected a warm welcome, but he hadn't expected to be greeted by so much hostility when coming here either.

"Lots of wolfies," Ceara muttered.

We need to be careful, Ed told the others. *Don't mention Ann is the archdruid. These people are very mistrustful of magic.*

How did you remember Marcus? Ceara wanted to know.

I still don't remember everything from my time here, but I recall bits and pieces.

You remembered enough to help us find the way here, she pointed out.

Why do they hate magic so much? Ann asked, glancing around uneasy.

No idea. Ed searched through his fragmented memories in the hopes of finding an answer, but nothing came to him.

How will they react to having another shifter among them? Jax asked.

Ed shook his head. *I don't know how they will react to any of us being here. I still don't remember the circumstances of my disappearance.*

Maybe someone didn't want you here, Ann remarked. Her eyes narrowed, and he felt her magic reach outward as she scanned the surrounding lykaes.

Ann, they might sense... His heart pounded faster.

Shush, act natural. They won't sense me.

How do you know that?

Because I'm being careful. I can't hear their thoughts.

Ceara, you try, Ann suggested. *I want to know more about what we're dealing with here.*

Ceara's eyes flashed with white light and her brow creased. *They don't like magic, they're afraid of it. It has something to do with the land. I can't sense much else from them.*

Ann glanced around. *This place seems familiar to me too. I think I came here once with my father.*

When? Why would Darius come here? Ed's eyes widened. He thought he would have remembered if Darius ever came here. Had he and Ann met before he ended up on Trin? His mind raced with even more questions.

I don't know. Perhaps he tried to form an alliance with the lykaes? Ann shrugged. *I must have been young when I came here, I don't remember much about it.*

The conversation fell silent as Marcus disappeared into a larger hut.

Ed gripped Ann's hand tighter. He sensed the presence of the alpha inside, and his nerves grew. What would his father say or do after all these years? Would he even want to see him? Ed remembered he'd been a strong, stern man.

The light blurred, and a man with long black hair and piercing brown eyes appeared in front of him. "Rohn?" He frowned. "Are you really my son?"

"Father?" Some of Lucien's hair had grey flecks running through it.

Odd, lykaes don't age once they reach adulthood.

Lucien pressed his forehead against Ed's, staring into his eyes. Ed felt Lucien's beast scan him, and his own beast came out to meet it. Ed's eyes flashed.

"It is you." Lucien grasped his face and clapped him on the back in an awkward hug. "By the gods, you live."

Ed returned the awkward embrace. "Yes, it's me."

He didn't know what to call Lucien. The word 'Father' sounded strange on his tongue. He'd never had one growing up with the Valerans. He'd only had his foster mother, Flora, and her partner, Sage.

"How can this be?" Lucien asked. "I thought you were dead."

"It's a long story, but I'm here now."

A dark-haired woman in a long blue smock moved around Lucien and threw her arms around Ed. She shared Lucien's dark eyes. "Rohn, I knew you'd come back to us." Tears dripped down her cheeks. "I have been praying to the gods for this day to come."

She felt familiar, but he couldn't place her.

"Who are you? Are you my mother?" He'd tried more than once

to picture what his biological mother looked like, but every time he thought of his mother, Flora always came to mind. She'd been a mother to him in every way that mattered.

The woman frowned. "I'm Lia. I'm Lucien's twin, your aunt. But I raised you as my own," she said. "Don't you remember me, Rohn?"

"I don't remember much of my life here," he admitted. "My name is Edward now. Edward Rohn."

"Edward? Why would you have a different name?" Lucien scowled.

"Until recently, I had no memory of my life before I disappeared," he said, taking Ann's hand. "This is my wife, Ann, and these are my adopted siblings, Ceara and Jax. We travelled through the mist to come here."

Lucien eyes narrowed as he stared at Ann. "Wife? I smell magic on you. I don't allow—"

"Ann is a druid." Ed wrapped a protective arm around her. "She is no threat to anyone. I won't have her thrown out. These people are my family and should be treated as such."

"Rohn has come home to us." Lia touched her brother's arm. "We should welcome him and his friends."

Lucien forced a smile that showed too much teeth. "Of course, any friend of Rohn's is welcome here. We must have a feast tonight to welcome you home, my son. This is cause for celebration." He wrapped an arm around Ed's shoulder, pulling him away from Ann. "Come, boy, I want to hear everything."

Ann followed him inside the hut. Jax and Ceara held back outside as Marcus went over to speak to them.

We'll take a look around and see what we can find out, Ceara said. *Ann's spell to find that dragon pointed us through the mist.*

Be careful, Ed told them. *And they're wyverns, not dragons.*

Inside the hut, Lucien had food and wine brought in for them. "Rohn, you must tell me, who took you? Was it Ranelle? One of her people?" Lucien's dark eyes flashed. "If it was her—"

Ed's brow creased as he searched his mind for a memory of that name, but nothing came to him. "Who is Ranelle?"

Lucien's lip curled in disgust. "She and her people live close to our lands in Mirkwood. Her people have been our enemies for generations now. We call them outlanders."

Ed's eyes widened as he remembered the words of his dream, *"War is brewing in your homeland. You must go there and try to create peace between the two races."*

He had no idea what he was meant to do whilst he was here. He wasn't a diplomat, he was a warrior, one of the Black Guard. Even during his time in the Black, he had fought in battles, but never outright war like the realm wars that had taken place over the last few centuries. If the lykaes and this other race were at war, what good could he do?

"I don't remember much about what happened that day. I'd hoped you could tell me." His heart sank. *So much for getting answers.*

"You were hunting in the woods with Marcus. He said something attacked you," Lia answered. "We searched, but we found no trace of you."

"I slaughtered Ranelle's people and tore down every enemy I could think of, but I never found who took you from me," Lucien growled. "What do you remember from that day?"

"I remember running through the woods, fleeing from something I couldn't see," Ed told them. "I jumped into the sea, and that took me through the mist. I don't remember much of what happened before that. I have no idea who or what chased me."

"Impossible! No one but those who wield magic can pass through the mist. Those mists are toxic, they have been there for centuries," Lucien snapped. "Someone must have forced you out. It must've been Ranelle and her magic."

"Ranelle wouldn't have a reason to harm Rohn," Lia protested, touching her brother's arm. "Why would she ever harm him? She is—"

Lucien glared at his twin and let out a low growl. "Because that bitch will do anything to strike at me and my pack."

"I don't know how I got through. I almost drowned, but Ann saved me." He squeezed her hand and smiled at her. "I ended up on an island called Trin. There, a woman named Flora took me in and raised me as her son. That's how Ann and I first met, and how Jax and Ceara became my siblings."

"Did you truly not remember any of us?" Lia touched her cheek. "You were ten winters old when you disappeared. Surely you must remember something?"

Ed shook his head. "No. Most of my life before Trin is a blur."

"Trin is the druids' isle." Lucien scowled. "Did they use magic to take you? That bastard Darius came here not long before your disappearance." Lucien's jaw tightened. "I should have known he had something to do with you disappearing."

Ann stifled her gasp by taking a sip of water from her goblet. *Spirits, do you think he knows who I am?*

Ed heard her heart rate pick up. "Flora, my foster mother, was a druid. I grew up with them. They gave me a home and a family."

He squeezed Ann's hand. *How could he? Your glamour is in place. Relax, we need to act like we don't have anything to hide.*

Turning his attention back to his father, Ed shook his head. "And I doubt the archdruid had anything to do with it. Why would he take me?"

Ann nodded in agreement. "From what I know about the old archdruid, he didn't have any dealings in Lulrien." She sipped more of her water. "Why would Darius come here?"

Lucien gave a harsh laugh. "He came to make a deal with us, and then went back on his word, the bastard. I should have known better. He, of all people, could never be trusted," he snapped. "It must've been him who took you."

"What reason would he have had to take me?" Ed raised a brow. "The archdruid never harmed me. In fact, I joined his Black Guard and served him until his death."

Lia touched Lucien's shoulder. "We should be grateful someone took Rohn in and cared for him all these years."

"You should have been with your true family," Lucien growled. "I will find out who took you."

"Lucien, what's done is done," Ed said. "I came back here to find out more about you and your people. Let's put the past to rest and move on. Look to the future."

"How did you know to save him?" Lia asked Ann. "Weren't you only a child yourself?"

Ann shrugged. "I just knew. I felt like he needed me, so I saved him. We've been close since then."

"Why come back now?" Lia asked Ed. "It's been so long."

"I wanted to find out where I came from." It sounded a reasonable enough excuse. In truth, he didn't know if he would've ever come back here if the council hadn't ordered him to. His origins had never mattered to him before now, he had a family and a life of his own. It didn't matter if they were rogues, Ed wouldn't trade his family for the world.

"You haven't lost yourself to the primal rage at least," Lucien remarked.

"What's that?" Ed frowned. The words tugged something in his fragmented memories but gave no explanation as to what they meant.

"Primal rage is where a lykae loses himself to bloodlust. He can do nothing but kill," his father replied. "When a lykae gives into the rage, it can consume them. They lose their soul and must feed their insatiable desire for blood. How could you—?"

"I'm relieved you haven't lost yourself to the rage." Lia smiled, interrupting her brother. "Now you are of age, it's hard for lykae males to control themselves, specially if they don't have their k'ia."

"What's a k'ia?" Ed asked. His beast had used the word, but he still had no idea what it meant.

"A k'ia is the light to our darkness," Lucien answered. "The half that completes us. Lykaes need their k'ia, or they lose themselves to the primal rage."

"How does a k'ia help a lykae?" Ann said.

"A k'ia calms a male lykae. It's the same for females, but they rarely lose themselves to the rage," Lucien explained. "A k'ia's light tames the beast and helps us stay in control of the darkness within us."

"Have you lost control?" Lia asked Ed.

"Once. The beast is becoming more unpredictable, I think it's sick of being locked away," Ed said, surprised his beast had stayed silent throughout this conversation. "It's hardly surprising after all these years. I never knew about my lykae nature until I started changing a few months ago."

Lucien and Lia stared at each other.

"What?" Lia asked. "You can't have only started turning months ago, you were born a lykae."

"Yes, but I had never turned or showed signs of it until I was captured and tortured by a demon." Ed shuddered at the memories, thankful he didn't remember much of that time either. He'd been so enraged when he'd first turned into a beast that his mind had blocked most of it out. The torture Orla had subjected him to probably hadn't helped either.

"That's impossible. All lykae turn when they come of age. It's at about thirteen years—sometimes younger," said Lucien. He glared at

Ann. "Did you use magic to repress his true nature?"

"Of course not," she snapped. "I was only a child myself when we first met. I always knew he was different—stronger and faster than other men—but he didn't change until he was captured by the demon. I'd never use magic to alter him."

"Ann is the one who helped me find my way back here. Without her, I would never have remembered," Ed said. "She helps me calm the beast. I came back to learn how to fully control it, can you help me with that or not?"

"We can teach you our ways and what it means to be lykae," Lia answered. "There are methods to help control the rages. We can teach them to you, but it can take years to learn to do it."

"Learning to tame one's beast can take a lifetime," Lucien said. "I am amazed you haven't lost yourself to the rage before now. Magic must've been used on you. You should have turned when you came of age—someone must have prevented that from happening."

Ed frowned. He'd thought coming here would be the solution to taming his inner beast once and for all. He hadn't expected it would take *years*. Ann pulled her hand from his and looked away. They might have to be apart for far longer than he'd anticipated. Ed knew she couldn't stay here forever.

It doesn't matter, he told her. *I already told you I'll never leave you.*

Ann didn't say anything.

"There is one thing you should know," Lucien said. "A lykae can only be with another lykae. We can't mate or bond with anyone but our own kind."

"Ann is my wife, and I won't be separated from her." Ed gripped her hand tighter. "She can stay here with me."

"Haven't you heard a word I've said? The bond between you isn't real." Lucien's lip curled in disgust. "Whatever feelings you have for the druid must end. I can't allow anyone with magic to live among my pack, it's forbidden. We are your true family, your people. Time to put aside whatever nonsense you learnt in the outside world."

Ed shot to his feet, feeling his beast clawing at the cage of his mind. Anger heated his blood. "Surely you can make an exception for my wife? I won't give up my old life, or my family."

"Why do you hate magic so much?" Ann asked Lucien with a glare. "There's magic throughout this land. Even you must feel that."

Lucien glowered back at her. "Magic cost me both my brother and my own k'ia. That's why it's forbidden. It brings nothing but death and destruction in its wake."

"You mean my mother?" Ed's expression turned grim. "What happened to her?"

"That's not important. I always taught you the dangers of magic."

"Then why do I possess magic?" Ed demanded. "I learnt and use druid magic."

Ann knew full well Ed could still use magic. Although it had been unreliable since his lykae nature had emerged, she and Ed had both used magic back at Trewa to restore the ancient stones.

I think your father is hiding something, Ann remarked. *He must know you had magic.*

"That's not possible," Lucien insisted.

"It doesn't matter," Lia spoke up again. "I see no reason why Rohn and his wife can't stay here."

Lucien shook his head. "I still fail to see how you could be bound to each other. A fasting spell wouldn't work." Lucien rose and frowned at Ed. "Have you fed on blood?"

"Why?" He gripped Ann's hand so tight she winced and he loosened his grip.

"Lykaes are forbidden from taking blood unless they're mated," Lia answered. "It makes the primal rage much more likely to take control."

"Doesn't blood heal us?" Ed asked.

"Yes, but if you fed on blood you'd be more likely to lose your soul." Lucien glanced between them.

Ed motioned to the lines that marked his and Ann's wrists. "As you can see, we are already bound. Ann will stay here with me, or I'll leave."

CHAPTER 7

Ann stormed out of the hut. After hours of listening to the other lykaes talking about Ed's future with the pack and how he'd learn to be in complete control of his beast, her head spun. All of the things they talked about excluded her. How could she be part of his life now? She'd never fit in here. She wasn't a lykae, and she wouldn't stop being a rogue either. Her heart twisted at the thought of not being able to see him anymore. How long could she stay here?

Darkness had fallen as the other lykaes got ready for the feast. Jax and Ceara sat chatting with Marcus and his men, laughing.

Great, they seem to like everyone but me since I have magic. Never mind the others have magic too. Ann crossed her arms and sighed. *They don't even know I'm the archdruid and I'm still ostracised.* She didn't want to leave Ed with these people, but at the same time, she'd be glad to get away from this place.

Ed blurred in beside her. "Hey, what's wrong?" He put his hands on her shoulders.

"I'm fine." She shoved him away. "Maybe I should go. No one wants me here."

"I want you here." He took her hand. "I don't care what Lucien says. We have a job to do."

Ann shook her head. "*You* have a job to do here. My job is stopping my brother, remember?" She drew her hand back, having him touch her would only make things harder. Maybe she should leave now before she got in any deeper. "I doubt the council meant to include me in this. You shouldn't let your feelings for me get in the way of your mission here."

"We're partners. We work on things together, like we always have. We know Urien is after something here in Lulrien. It would be a big coincidence if that and whatever trouble is brewing here weren't connected." Ed ran a hand through his long hair. "I'm not letting my feelings for you get in the way. I want you here because we work better together than we do apart."

"Ed, how long do you think I can stay here? We can't start anything." She drew back, and her heart twisted with pain.

"Maybe I won't stay then."

Her eyes flashed. "Don't be daft, you came here for a reason. You have family here, real family."

"Family isn't always blood. You and my siblings are more

important to me than any of that."

"Haven't you ever wanted to be with your real family again?"

Ed shook his head. "I don't even know these people. You and the others *are* my real family."

"Stay, get to know them. You have a chance to live a normal life again, away from…"

Ann trailed off as Marcus came over with a redheaded woman and Ed tensed. She was beautiful, with crimson red hair that fell past her shoulders, hazel eyes, and pale, freckled skin. She looked taller and curvier than Ann would ever be.

Do you know her? Ann asked.

Yes, she was at Urien's meeting of the leaders a few weeks ago. She helped Jax and I get inside the palace, Ed explained.

Ann winced. *Shit, she might know who I am.*

Relax, she'd have no way of knowing.

"Rohn, this is Jessa, one of the females of our pack." Marcus put a hand on Jessa's shoulder, and Ann noticed the redhead tense too.

"Is she your lifemate?" Ed asked Marcus.

Jessa laughed. "Gods no, I'm not bound to anyone. We don't use the term lifemates here, our mates are our k'ia—the other half to our souls."

Ann refrained from rolling her eyes. Even her own people believed in all that lifemate nonsense. She doubted anyone could promise to love and be with someone for an entire lifetime. A romantic partner was different than family.

"We were supposed to—" Marcus said, and Jessa glared at him, before giving Ed a dazzling smile.

"It's good to have you home, Rohn."

Ann— Ed began.

She closed her mind to him, refusing to listen as she turned to go.

Before she could leave Ed wrapped an arm around her, pulling her against him. "Thanks, Jessa. It's good to see you. This is Ann, my wife."

We need to talk, he said to Ann, who had opened the link again with the intention of arguing with him.

Refusing to reply, Ann reluctantly turned to the redheaded beauty, leaning into Ed as he wrapped his arms round her. She caught the hunger in Jessa's eyes.

"I heard you were at the meeting of the leaders a few weeks ago." Ann hadn't seen Jessa at the meeting, but then she'd been focused on Urien and stopping him at the time to pay much attention to who had been there. Did Jessa know who she really was?

"Yes, Lucien sent me to investigate. We heard a new archdruid had come to power." Jessa's smile didn't reach her eyes. "I went to see if the rumours were true." She shuddered. "The new archdruid is even worse than the old one. She murdered their parents, and she's feuding with her elder brother over the throne."

Oh, believe me. The throne has nothing to do with it. It's gone, Ann thought. *I couldn't care less about that. I never wanted to sit on the throne. I just want Xander back.*

I think she does know who I am, she said to Ed. Her heart pounded in her ears, and she wondered if she should transport away while she

85

could.

She won't do anything. Even if she does, no one will force you to leave, Ed said. *Not if I have any say in it.*

"Jessa was our friend when we were children. In fact, you were promised to her," Marcus explained, glowering at Jessa.

"What?" Ann gasped. "He was only ten years old when he came to Trin. Isn't that a little young to be betrothed?"

"Lykae children are often promised to each other. The sooner a lykae finds their k'ia, the better." Jessa grinned at Ed.

He tightened his hold on Ann.

Ann smiled sweetly and gave Ed a quick kiss on the cheek. "It's too bad we are bound." She turned her wrist to show the spot where the intricate fasting lines flickered in the firelight.

Marcus and Jessa both gaped at her.

"That's—" Jessa protested.

"Not possible?" Ann asked. "We've been married for a while now, and nothing can change that." It surprised her how easily the lies rolled off her tongue. *Spirits, why did I say that? What is wrong with me?*

"Let's get back to the celebrations, shall we?" Ed suggested.

He took Ann's hand and led her away. *I thought you said—*

Ann waved her hand, conjuring a ward so none of the lykaes would overhear them. "Never mind what I said," she hissed. "I couldn't stand the thought of them trying to betroth you to her."

"Ann, you need to be careful around these people." Ed hissed.

She nodded. "Like you said, we should play along so we can stay together a little while longer."

"You're jealous of Jessa."

"That's ridiculous." She put her hands on her hips. "Why would I be?"

Ed sighed. "Can we forget the k'ia nonsense and everything else for tonight?"

"Do you really want to stay here? You don't know these people. I sense danger here."

"I have to." He touched her cheek. "You'll always be a part of my life. That's never gonna change."

Ann hugged him, resting her head against his chest.

"Whatever this thing is between us, don't we owe it to ourselves to find out what we could be?" Ed murmured, running his fingers through her hair. "We've been dancing around this for years now, pretending we don't have feelings for each other."

Ann glanced up at him. "How? How can we? I'm still a rogue with a high price on my head. I can't risk staying here without putting you and anyone else in danger."

She pulled back, but Ed gripped her tighter.

"I'm not giving you up," he repeated. "Not for them, not for anything. You are the most important thing in my life, and always will be."

Ann felt the hard, disapproving gazes of the other lykaes around her. "Okay, let's see how it goes. We'll take things slow for now." Her own words surprised her. Could she contemplate having a real relationship with him that went beyond mere friendship?

He gave her a quick kiss. "Come on, let's dance."

She laughed. "You hate dancing. I've always had to drag you onto the dancefloor to get you moving."

They danced, laughing as they went. Ceara and Jax joined in. Jax always did enjoy showing off his dance moves, even among a village full of potential enemies.

The lykaes knew how to celebrate and insisted Ed and the others try their alcohol as they gathered around a large fire in the centre of the village.

"No one but lykaes can handle our ale," Marcus said. "Rohn, you try some. All of you can have a taste."

Ed took one of the tankards Marcus offered and sipped, coughing after he swallowed.

Ann laughed along with the lykaes. He'd never been good at holding his drink.

"Let me try." Jax grabbed a tankard of his own. "Ed never could handle the hard stuff. I used to drink the rest of the Black under the table."

"This I have to see," Ceara scoffed. "Bet you'll choke on it, bird boy."

"Alright, sister, you try," Jax retorted. "Bet you can't handle it either. You never could handle more than three normal ales."

"Jax, you should know by now that challenging her isn't a good idea," Ann remarked.

Ceara rolled her eyes and grabbed a tankard of her own. "Hey, if bird boy here can handle it, so can I."

"Drink more than a mouthful," Marcus insisted.

"You two better not be hung over tomorrow," Ann told them. "We still have work to do." *Like tracking dragons.*

"We can't turn down a challenge." Jax clinked tankards with Ceara. "Cheers, sister."

Both he and Ceara threw back their tankards, gulping down the brew. They both doubled over coughing and gasping for breath. Tears streamed from their eyes, and all the lykaes broke into hysterics.

"Care to try some too, druid?" Jessa challenged.

Ann gritted her teeth. She didn't know why this other woman was so threatened by her.

Ann, ignore her, Ed said. *She—*

Before he could finish, Ann grabbed Ed's tankard and gulped down the ale. It burned her throat as it went down, but she smiled. "You're all such babies." She laughed.

The other lykaes all stared at her in stunned amazement.

"Excuse me." She got up and walked away.

Her head spun, so she drew magic to stave off the effects of the ale. Alcohol always dulled her senses, so she avoided it whenever possible. Better to be on alert than caught off-guard, especially in an unknown land full of potential dangers.

"You and Ed looked cosy," Ceara remarked as she followed Ann. Ann conjured a ward around them in case the lykaes overheard them. "At least you finally stopped denying your feelings. It's about time too."

"If you say, 'I told you so,' I'll pour that ale all over you," Ann warned.

Ceara smirked. "You should hurry up and jump into bed with him."

Ann's mouth fell open, and she prayed the wards she'd conjured blocked the lykaes from overhearing Ceara's side of the conversation. "Ceara, keep it down! We're surrounded by people who will gladly rip us apart."

The Gliss snorted. "I'd love to see them try." She gulped down more ale. "But seriously, you should grab onto him before that redheaded bitch digs her claws in."

"You're worse when you're drunk." Ann scanned the area with her mind. Just because they were on the other side of the mist now didn't mean that Urien would stop sending things after her.

"Maybe I'm fed up with all the tension and frustration between you two," Ceara said. "Just sleep with him and get it over with."

Ann couldn't decide whether to laugh or gasp at that. "I'm not going to...we can't. Don't ask why."

"Oh, I heard what Papa Wolf said too," Ceara scoffed. "You and wolfy belong together. I've known it for years. I Just don't know what's holding you back." She took another swig of her drink. "He kissed you this morning, so you can't deny there's nothing between you now. I saw it with my own eyes."

Ann rolled her eyes. She'd known Ceara would bring this up eventually. "I told you, it's complicated." Ann crossed her arms and pulled her cloak tighter around her. It made her miss her long leather cloak that she'd left back at the vault.

"No, it's not. You want him, he wants you." Ceara slurred, stumbling.

"I won't take the risk."

"Love is a risk, Ann. Don't make the same mistake I did. I chose the wrong brother, and I've regretted it ever since."

Ann frowned, surprised by Ceara's sudden admission. Ceara rarely ever talked about her relationships with Xander and Urien and choosing her older brother. "Wait, what...?"

A chill ran across Ann's mind as she sensed another presence.

Someone's watching us. She spun around searching for the person and caught sight of movement in the trees. *Sod Lucien's no magic rule.*

Light flashed around her as she transported. She reappeared where she'd felt the other presence. Whoever had been there had vanished.

She scanned the area with her mind but found nothing. Who would be watching them? And why?

Ann scanned the area deeper, searching for any traces of energy to indicate who or what had been watching them. None remained. That seemed odd. All Magickind left traces behind unless they didn't want to be seen or found. But who could know they were here? Ann, Jax and Ceara all had their glamours firmly in place. Urien might know Ed was a lykae, but she didn't think he would guess they had come here—or did he know more? She still had no idea what artefacts he'd found back at the palace, or what new connections he'd forged during his short time ruling Caselhelm.

Jessa and Marcus were chatting with Ed and Lucien, so that

counted them out. She'd need to be even more on her guard now.

Ed appeared beside Ann as she moved around the perimeter of the village. "Where are you going?"

So far, she had found no sign of who or what had been watching her and Ceara earlier, but she doubted it was the strange entity that had been stalking them before, she would have sensed. The idea of being watched by some other unknown threat set her on edge.

"I need to clear my head, so I'm doing a sweep. Being on the other side of the mist won't stop demons from coming after us. You should be with your family."

"I have time to be with them later. I haven't been able to find out much about Ranelle or her people." He took her hand. "I feel like you're avoiding me."

Ann shook her head. "You saw what your father and the others are like. They're barely tolerating my presence as it is." She wrapped an arm around him. "I wouldn't avoid you, you big lug," she said. "Always and forever, remember?" It felt good reciting their childhood promise to always be best friends, and always be there for each other. Maybe they could be more than that now.

Hand-in-hand they moved away from the village. Ann scanned the area with her mind, feeling energy pulse through the land. It felt as if the earth itself were running with power here. "I'm beginning to understand why your people made their home here. This land is…"

"Pure magic. Yeah, I feel it too." Ed nodded.

"Given how much they claim to hate magic, though, it's strange. I sense that hatred goes back a long way."

"I heard them talking about Ranelle's race. I think there's a feud between them that goes back for generations," Ed said. "Lucien warned me not to go near them, that must be why the council sent me here."

"I've been thinking about that. Lucien claims the lykaes don't have any magic, but your magic must come from somewhere." She glanced back to make sure no one had followed them. "Where's your mother in all this?"

Ed shrugged. "I've wondered that too. I thought Lia was her because she's the only woman I remember raising me before Flora."

"Flora would be happy you came here." She smiled then sighed. Her heart still ached at the thought of her aunt, who'd died at Urien's hand a few months earlier. She'd always encouraged Ed to find out more about his forgotten past.

Her thoughts drifted away from Flora to their current predicament.

"What's wrong?" Ed asked.

She shook her head. "Nothing."

"Ann, I can sense your emotions. You're disappointed, why?"

She drew her hand away from him. "Stop that. I should be able to express my own emotions."

"You've done it to me more than once," he pointed out. "I can do the same."

Her eyes flashed. "That's because I usually know what you're feeling before you do." She sighed again. "I'm just…frustrated by everything. This. Us."

He grinned. "I like it when you say us. But…it's deeper than that. You're disappointed with me. Why?" He frowned.

"I never said that." She turned away. She didn't want to discuss her feelings anymore.

Ed blurred in front of her. "Why are you disappointed with me? Come on. Like you said, we used to tell each other everything."

Her fists clenched. "Fine. Why did you never tell me you had feelings for me before now?"

Ed flinched. "Because back then—before your parents were killed and we went on the run—I knew I could never have you," he said. "So I kept my feelings for you hidden. I never gave into any desire I had for you."

"That was five years ago. You could have told me long ago."

"It never seemed like the right time." Ed rubbed the back of his neck. "I never told you because I was scared I'd lose your friendship. I couldn't do that." His eyes flashed. "Why didn't you tell me you had feelings for *me*?"

She avoided his gaze. "I was scared to. You disappearing made me realise how much you mean to me." Ann shook her head. "Not that it matters now."

"It does matter." Ed stroked her cheek. "Time and distance doesn't change how I feel about you, I know that. Shouldn't we at least give it a chance? Find out if we can be more than friends?"

"What if it doesn't work out? What if you find your true k'ia?" she asked. "We'd be walking down a road we can't come back from."

"You are mine." He pulled her to him and kissed her.

She gasped. This kiss felt raw, filled with a hunger she'd been denying for years. Ann wrapped her hands around his neck, deepening it. In that moment, nothing else seemed to matter, there were no rules, no insistences they weren't meant to be together.

Ed pushed her back against a tree, his lips trailing down her neck.

Her breathing became ragged. "What happened to slow?" she gasped.

Ed's eyes burned deep emerald. *Can't help it. I want you so damn badly. Do you want me to stop?*

Don't you dare. She pulled him in for another kiss.

His eyes burned brighter, and his fangs scraped her neck.

"Ed, no," she cried, shoving him away so hard he stumbled. Her chest rose and fell as she breathed hard.

Ed's eyes returned to normal. "I'm sorry. You know I'd never—"

"I know." She ran a hand through her hair. "How are we supposed to have a relationship if we can't even touch each other?"

"We'll find a way to make this work. If there's one thing I do have faith in, it's my feelings for you."

CHAPTER 8

Urien paced up and down his chamber. So far, Ranelle hadn't found anything—or so she said. He'd have to find out for himself later, but first, he had much more pressing concerns.

Arwan materialised in a flash of light.

Urien had no idea why the elder had demanded the sudden meeting. Although they seemed interested in finding the door to the underworld, Urien knew the elders wanted something much more than that.

"I'm close to finding—" Urien began.

Don't bother lying, Xander remarked. His voice had become much fainter over the past few days. Was he getting weaker? Urien hoped so. He'd rather have this body to himself.

"I'm not here because of that. The Crimson have a new task for you," Arwan said.

Urien's eyes widened. "What task?" He'd agree to anything if it earned him more favour among the gods.

"The others are tired of your sister. We're worried about the damage she might do in Lulrien, especially if she somehow manages to unite the two races."

Urien scoffed. "How could she?"

"One thing we've learnt in our years of watching her is we shouldn't underestimate Rhiannon," Arwan said. "Neither should you. We want you to set a trap for her."

Urien frowned. "How?" He had tried to trap Ann before, during the meeting of the leaders, but she'd made him look like a fool.

He wouldn't make that mistake again, even if she had helped him to rid himself of his wretched mother.

"That's for you to decide." Arwan crossed his arms. "You know we don't directly interfere—not unless we have to."

No, you get others do your bidding, Urien thought.

You agree to their every demand, Xander remarked.

Urien raised his mental shield higher and his temples throbbed like a hammer hitting against hard metal.

"My sister won't fall for a trap again." Urien ran a hand through his hair, and a clump of it fell away. He stared at it in horror. "What the…?"

"I'm sure you'll think of something," Arwan said. "If you trap your sister, we'll rip her power from her. You will become the next archdruid—our chosen one here on Erthea—with all the authority and privilege that comes with it."

Urien stared at the clump of his—no, Xander's—hair. Arwan didn't seem to notice his distress—or didn't care. "You know I want that more than anything." He gritted his teeth as the pounding in his head increased to a staccato. "But how—?"

"You'll figure something out, boy. It's not our way to tell you every little detail," Arwan scoffed. "We've given you this task, and we expect you to follow it through." He raised his hand, and a young Ursaie woman with long brown hair, black horns, and glowing golden eyes appeared. She wore a simple blue gown and looked much better cared for than Urien's own slaves. "This is Ryn, one of my personal slaves. I'm giving her to you as a gift. You can use her for blood magic if you need to, but no harming her beyond that. Don't think of bedding her either."

Urien rubbed his blurry eyes. "What are you giving her to me for?"

"For you to make use of. She's spelled to heal from any injuries." Arwan patted her head like she was a faithful dog, and smirked. "Looks like you're going to need it. I'm sure we can restore you to your former body." Arwan vanished without another word.

Ryn stood there, unmoving.

Urien doubled over, clutched his head. Bile rose in his throat. He coughed it into an empty goblet that sat on the table. "Gods below, what's happening to me?" he muttered.

"Do you need help?" Ryn asked in a thick accent.

"No, get out," he snapped, motioning toward the door.

He wouldn't call his own people to help either. No point in letting them see his weakness. It had been hard enough convincing them to trust him—they'd all been so damned loyal to his mother.

Xander, what's wrong with us? Urien demanded.

No reply came.

He lowered his mental shield. Xander didn't say anything, nor did Urien feel his presence. "Xander, wake up. I need your help," he growled.

Nothing.

Xander, answer me, he snapped. *Or I'll pull another slave in here and bleed them dry. You don't want that happening, do you?*

Xander still remained mute.

Why can't I sense him? Urien thought. *Why now, when I need his presence?*

He heard the door creaking open and stumbled across the room. He couldn't afford to be weak, not now the elders had shown him such favour. He'd find a way to fix it and get back into his own body.

"Wait…" he hissed. Damn, what was her name? "Girl, come here."

Arwan had said she was a gift. Urien knew better. Arwan had sent his own spy to watch over Urien's every move.

Urien decided to make good use of her and turn her into a new blood slave. Usually, he killed his slaves—death provided much more potent magic. But Arwan had said she was spelled to heal. Urien would bleed her dry if he had to. Gods below, he didn't want this getting back to the elders.

Ryn hurried over to him. "Yes?" she said, her accent dulling the 'Y' into a 'Z' sound.

Urien grabbed for his bedpost to remain upright. "Pick the blade up off the table and slice it across your arm," he ordered.

"Why?" She sounded confused.

"Just do it," he snapped. "You're supposed to follow orders."

The room spun around him, and he gripped the post harder.

Xander, are you there?

Urien muttered words of power under his breath, invoking an old healing spell.

The room whirled, and he sank to his knees.

"My lord?"

"Come here." Urien caught the coppery tang of blood in the air and said more words of power, then everything went black.

Urien woke on his bed.

Ryn sat at his bedside. "Are you alright, my lord?"

He groaned and touched his head. "What happened?"

"You collapsed." Ryn touched his hand. Odd, why would a slave show any compassion toward him?

Neither the blood magic nor his spell had worked. Why? He'd felt the power, and blood magic made him strong. Why had this body failed?

Urien forced himself to sit up. "Too much power, no doubt. Leave me."

Ryn hesitated. "I can sit with you if you like."

Concern wasn't an emotion he knew how to deal with. People never got concerned over him, at least not in a caring way. Even Orla had shown him little affection. "Leave," he demanded.

Mother would have been able to help. He pushed that thought away. He'd wanted to be free of Orla all his life and would never regret killing either of his parents. *Maybe another elder could help. One outside the Crimson Alliance.* Perhaps the elder who'd helped him and Orla to destroy Darius?

Light flashed around him as he cast a circle to transport himself out.

Sunlight glared above, making him wince. Urien covered his eyes. "Where am I?" he groaned.

Someone cackled. "Well, I didn't expect you to land in my web, boy," said a female voice.

It didn't sound like the woman who'd helped in the past, The Morrigan.

His legs gave out, and he crumpled to the ground. "What's wrong with me?"

Another cackle. "Why are you here, boy?"

A figure moved over to him. He made out a pair of strange black eyes through his hazy vision. "I need help. Please, there's something wrong with me." He hated how pathetic he sounded. "I need…The Morrigan."

The woman laughed. "Oh, you won't find her here. Don't think she'll help you again."

"She did before."

"That was personal."

Realising how feeble he looked, Urien scrambled into a sitting position. He wouldn't lie here like a dog. "I don't know what's wrong with me." He grabbed the woman's arm, and power hummed against his skin.

"You're dying. Two souls can't occupy the same body forever," the woman said. "Your blood magic will have only sped up the process."

Urien's heart pounded. "Help me," he begged.

He couldn't believe he was begging, but he needed this to stop.

"Get away from here." She gave him a hard shove. "After everything you've done, don't expect any help from me."

Urien reappeared on the cold, hard, stone floor of his chamber. A bitter thought rolled through his mind. *I'm dying...Will my father's spell protect me from it?*

CHAPTER 9

Ann woke early the next morning, a pit of dread forming in her stomach. She still felt torn between staying here and leaving. If Lucien didn't find out who she was, she guessed she could stay awhile. Ed still lay sleeping beside her. After washing and dressing in her usual leathers, she headed outside the hut, having sensed another presence there.

Lia stood and waited for her, glancing around uneasy. Fear radiated from her mind.

What is she afraid of? Lucien?

Ann ran her hand through her hair, wondering what Ed's aunt had come here for. "Ed is still asleep if you've come to talk to him."

"May I speak with you?" Lia asked. "It's important."

Ann glanced back at the hut and sensed Ed still asleep inside. She nodded. "Is something wrong?"

Lia took her arm. "Not here. Can you take us somewhere more private?"

Ann's eyes widened and did another check around before taking hold of Lia's arm. Light flashed around them as she transported them to the woods where she and Ed had walked the night before. She hoped this was far enough away from the village to avoid anyone overhearing them. She conjured a ward around them just to be on the safe side.

Ann still sensed Lia's fear. "What do you want to talk about?" She couldn't imagine what Lia would have to say to her. Although she hadn't been as hostile as Lucien, Ann doubted she wanted her around either.

Lia glanced around. "I wanted to apologise for what my brother said yesterday about you and Rohn not being together. I saw how it upset you," she said. "Lucien is adamant about lykaes never mating with a non-lykae, but I sense how much Rohn loves you."

Ann flinched at that. "We've been through a lot together," she shrugged. "Why are you even talking to me?"

"I am the one who arranged for Rohn to cross through the mists. It's not as easy as some may think." Lia wrung her hands together. "My brother would kill me if he ever found out. Rohn needs you more than you know."

Ann's eyes widened. "Why would you do that? Surely he would have been safer here than living among my people?"

"I didn't want him growing up in the endless conflict between us and Ranelle's people." Lia glanced behind them again, as if expecting Lucien to appear. "Sending him to you was the only way to keep him safe. My brother can never know any of this."

"Then he didn't end up on Trin by accident?" Ann's brow creased. "If what you say is true, you would have needed magic to send him there. Do lykaes have magic?"

Lia shook her head. "No, we used to possess magic generations ago, but we lost it. Legend says the archdruid took our magic from us. I had help sending him through the mist," she said. "I knew he would be safer among the druids. Your father knew who he was. I'm grateful to him for keeping Rohn safe."

Ann's mouth fell open. "Blessed spirits, you know who I am? What I am?"

Lia nodded. "Yes. Your secret is safe with me."

Ann's mind reeled from this new information. "Wait, if it was dangerous for Ed to grow up here, how do I know he'll be safe now? Why are you even telling me this?"

"I needed someone else to know. I would like you to stay, Rohn needs you more than you know."

Ann shook her head. "If you know who I am, you know I can't stay here. I'm a rogue. A lot of people want me dead, not just my bastard half-brother." She crossed arms. "Besides, Lucien has made it clear he doesn't want me here."

"But you are Rohn's k'ia. You've been bound to each other since you were children. You must stay." Lia touched her arm.

"I'm his…" Her voice trailed off. His what? His friend? Lover? She didn't know what they were now. "Wait, what do you mean we've been bound since we were children?"

"Your father did something to you and Rohn to bind you."

Her eyes narrowed. "Why would he do that?" Darius had never wanted to marry her off to anyone. She had been born to be his heir, and her destiny was to become archdruid. After her parents' own disastrous marriage, she'd vowed she'd never bind herself to anyone.

Lia shook her head. "I can't answer that. I'm glad he survived in the outside world for so long. Darius said he would be safe with you." Lia brushed her hair off her face. "But I don't understand why his lykae side didn't emerge long before now."

"Like he said, it only emerged a few months ago. It was a shock to both of us," Ann said as they moved past the trees. "Did you come just to tell me I am his k'ia?"

"I came to ask you not to stray too far from him. My brother almost lost his mind when he lost his k'ia. He didn't lose his soul, but part of himself he will never recover," Lia said. "I know it will be difficult for you to stay—my brother would probably kill you if he knew you were archdruid."

"I don't understand all of this. Why would you send Ed to me? Did you make some kind of bargain with my father?" Knowing Darius, it wouldn't surprise her if he had some agenda for binding her to Ed. Although she couldn't fathom what that might be.

Lia bit her lip. "I can't answer all of your questions. Just please say you'll stay."

"I'll stay as long as I can." She needed to find out what was going on here. Something had brought Ed here, and the mystery of his disappearance fifteen years earlier still didn't make any sense. "Is Ed safe here? He wants more than anything to control his beast—"

The sound of shouting made her freeze. The buzz of several minds came to her, along with a sense of fear and the warning of danger.

"Oh no. My people are under attack." Lia sniffed, then blurred away.

Light flashed around Ann as she transported herself back to the village. She reappeared close to Lucien's hut. Lykaes and men dressed in grey tunics armed with bows and arrows wrestled with each other. Arrows whizzed through the air, coming at them from all directions.

I wonder if these are Ranelle's people. If so, why are they here?

One of the lykaes grappled a newcomer to the ground, its fangs out.

Ann hesitated. This would turn into a bloodbath if it continued, but if she used her magic, she might lead Urien straight here. Plus, Lucien might guess who she really was. That man seemed to know a lot more about magic than he should. Her magic expanded around her as she touched the minds of those fighting.

What the…? She hadn't summoned her magic, yet it shot outward. *No, stop!*

Both lykaes and the newcomers sank to their knees and doubled over in pain. They clutched at their heads as she forced the binding on them to hold them in place.

Oh bugger, what did I do that for? How did I do that? She gritted her teeth.

Lucien appeared in a blur of movement. "Witch, what the fuck are you doing to my pack?" His face was like thunder.

Ceara appeared at Ann's side. "She didn't do it, I did." She turned her attention to the men.

"Alright, children. Let's try to play nice together, shall we?"

Ann frowned at her. *What are you doing?*

Protecting you, silly. So you can stay here.

"It's Gliss, not witch," Ceara corrected. "I'm getting everyone to calm down. It's what Gliss do. We are empathetic."

Ann stifled a snort. That was far from the truth.

Lucien's eyes narrowed. "I know what you are, woman. Your magic would have no effect on my people—we are immune."

Ceara crossed her arms. "Really? How else could you explain that?" she demanded. "Ann couldn't do it. She's just a druid."

"I knew I shouldn't have let you stay here." Lucien lunged for her, his eyes burning amber and fangs out.

Ann took a step back. She didn't want to use her powers on Ed's father unless she had to. *Damn, I doubt it would take much for these people to start a war. The slightest thing would tip them over the edge.*

Ed blurred in front of her and snarled, "Don't, Lucien. If you try to hurt her, I will stop you."

"You protect her over your own kin, Rohn?" Lucien growled.

Marcus moved to Ceara's side. "Uncle, I'm sure she was just trying to help. There is no need to punish her for it."

"Enough," Ceara snapped. "I'm no threat to your people, Lucien. I just want to find out what's going on." She turned her attention to one of the newcomers and pointed to him. "You. Speak."

Ann released her binding on him.

Ed moved to Ann's side. "Tell us why you're here." He crossed his arms.

The man rose, his long black hair fell past his shoulders. Pointed ears peeked out, indicating he might be an elf, and his green cat-like eyes fixed on Lucien. He rubbed his temples. "I am Hawke, captain of Ranelle's woodland squadron. We came here seeking retribution. One of your people has been slaughtering woodland folk for weeks now."

"You came to attack my people," Lucien hissed. "Yet we've done nothing to harm you."

Hawke's lip curled. "Then why have so many of my people been going missing or been ripped to pieces?"

"He's telling the truth," Ceara told them. "I can sense it. Something *has* been attacking his people."

"None of my people have attacked yours," Lucien growled. "I should kill you for daring to enter my lands."

Ed put a hand on his father's shoulder. "Maybe we should investigate this further."

"Uncle, a lupine has been roaming around for weeks," Marcus spoke up again. "It must have been him who attacked the outlanders."

Ann frowned. "What's a lupine?"

"It's a lykae who's lost their soul." Ed ran a hand through his long hair. "It happens when they are taken over by primal rage."

Hawke glared at Marcus. "Of course you would be quick to blame a lupine. You can't even admit what you've done, can you, alpha?"

More of the lykaes surrounded them, their eyes glowing deep amber. Ann knew this wouldn't end well if things didn't settle soon.

"I think we may have killed your lupine," Ed admitted. "We were attacked on our way here by another lykae."

"We found traces of a lupine further north," Marcus agreed. "There were outlander remains there."

"You will take us there," Hawke snapped. "My—"

Ann shook her head. "That won't do any good. We burnt the dwelling down."

Hawke turned his glare to her. "Why would you do that?"

"It seemed like the right thing to do at the time. There wasn't much left to find," Ann said. *Ed, what did you do with that medallion we found?*

Ed fumbled in his pocket and pulled out the medallion. "This is the only thing we found that was left behind." He held it out to Hawke. "Here."

Lucien grabbed the medallion and let out a low growl. "This belonged to my brother. Where did you get it from?"

"We found it where the lupine stashed several dismembered bodies," Ed answered. "How could it have belonged to your brother? I thought he died over twenty years ago."

"He did." Lucien's hand shook, either in fury or shock.

Ed slipped an arm around Ann. "Now this misunderstanding is cleared up, Hawke, I suggest you and your men leave."

"You have no authority over me, lykae," the captain growled.

Ceara walked over and touched Hawke's arm. "You and your men will leave at once, okay?" Light flared between her brows. "Right, Lucien?"

The alpha scowled. "Leave, and don't you dare enter my lands again or the peace between our races will be over."

Hawke and his men retreated, and the lykaes dispersed. Ann breathed a sigh of relief. That was too close.

Jax came out of another one of the huts. "What's going on?" he asked with a yawn.

Lucien flicked a glance toward Ceara. "You'd do well not to interfere next time, witch."

"Gliss," she snapped back. "And I saved your people from a lot of unnecessary bloodshed. You're welcome, by the way."

Lucien stormed off without saying another word.

"You're welcome too," Ceara whispered to Ann.

"Thanks." Ann breathed a sigh of relief. "I didn't mean to use my magic like that."

"We need to be on our guard, remember?" Ed lowered his voice.

She shook her head. "I'm sorry. I didn't mean for it to happen. My magic just responded…" Ann didn't know why her magic seemed to be getting stronger. She'd fully trained as a druid and thought her powers had already reached maturity.

"We're lucky Lucien isn't throwing us out," Ceara remarked. "Be more careful next time. If I hadn't sensed what you were doing, we'd all be in trouble."

"Why?" Jax rubbed sleep from his eyes. "Who were those men fighting the lykaes?"

"Ranelle's people. Jax, I want you to go follow them. See where they go."

Jax groaned. "You could let me have breakfast first."

"That's what you get for sleeping with a lykae." Ceara smirked. "And drinking too much ale."

Jax scowled at her. "Hey, I saw you getting cosy with them last night too, sister. And you drank much more than me." Feathers spread over his body as he shifted into his crow form and took to the sky.

"I'm off to find some breakfast." Ceara clutched her head. "Try to stay out of trouble." She stalked away.

Ann took Ed's hand as they headed back toward his hut. "There's something I need to tell you."

A man stood at the entrance to the hut. Ann and Edward stared at him. He had long chestnut hair and dark—almost black—eyes. He wore simple clothes like the rest of the lykaes.

Ann didn't recognise him as one of the lykaes she'd met the night before, but then most of them had avoided her, so that didn't surprise her.

"Leave us," Ed snapped.

The man's eyes turned pitch black.

Demon, Ann realised too late.

The demon lunged at her, slamming her against the wall. Its fangs grazed her neck.

Ann punched him, hard. Bones cracked, but it felt like she was hitting solid rock. She yelped and used her free hand to send the demon flying with a burst of magic.

As he sprang back up, Ed lunged, his beast fully emerging. The men blurred in a whirl of claws and growls.

Ann raised her hand but hesitated. She couldn't risk using her magic without harming Ed too. *Sorry, Ed.*

She waved her hand, sending both of them crashing to the ground. She reached out with her mind, but the demon had an impenetrable shield wrapped around his thoughts.

Ann hurled a fireball at the demon, and he staggered. Ed grabbed hold of him, slashing his claws across the other man's neck.

The demon slashed at Ed, scraping its iron-tipped claws across his wrist, then hurtling him against the wall so hard it collapsed as he landed. "Fool," he hissed. "You're no match for me."

She snorted. "Thought you would have learnt you can't kill me." She clenched her fist, and he hissed with pain. "Tell my brother he'll see me soon enough."

Lucien and Lia appeared in the doorway.

"What the fuck is going on?" Lucien demanded.

"A lupine!" Lia gasped.

"Not exactly," Ann said. "That would be a demon."

Lucien shifted and lunged at the demon, slashing at it with his own claws. The demon knocked the alpha away.

"Stay back," Ann warned Lucien. "His claws are tipped with cold iron."

"Cold iron doesn't affect me," Lucien growled.

Her eyes widened in surprise. She had seen how the cold iron affected Ed when the demon had slashed him. Ann raised her hand, her eyes flashing with light. The demon snarled as she tried to force a binding on him.

Ed blurred past her, snapping the demon's neck, then ripping its head off its body, which turned to ash. Ed snarled and circled Lucien.

"Rohn, what are you doing?" Lucien demanded.

He turned his attention to Ann. "This is your fault. I should—"

Ed flew at his father, knocking him to the ground.

"Ed, no!" Ann rushed over to them and turned to Lucien. "I wouldn't threaten me if I were you. He loses control whenever I'm in danger." She touched Ed's shoulder. "Stop this. Please. He's your father."

"He wants to kill you," the beast snarled. Ed gripped Lucien's throat, making the alpha's eyes bulge.

"But he hasn't. He can't. Please let him go."

Ed growled and backed away.

"If you hurt what's mine, I'll kill you." The beast's voice came out low and guttural. He moved to Ann's side, stroking her cheek where the demon had scratched her. His touch felt surprisingly gentle.

Lucien glared at her. "He'll have to be put down. You did this, you made my son lose his soul."

"No, he's not gone. Look at him," Lia said.

"If you hurt him, I'll kill you myself," Ann warned. Flames crackled between her fingers.

"He's on the verge of becoming a full lupine," Lucien snapped.

"That's why we came here, so he can learn control. Nothing I've seen so far tells me you can do anything to help him," she said. "He's only a threat if anyone tries to harm me."

"Why would a demon come here unless you lured it here?" Lucien spat.

Ignoring Lucien, Ann reached up and cupped Ed's face. "Come back now. Give me my Edward back."

The beast hissed, turning his burning emerald gaze on Lucien, and growled.

"Lucien won't harm the druid," Lia said. "She's safe now."

"Please, Ed." Ann looked into his eyes. "Come back to me. He won't hurt me."

At once the beast retreated and Ed slumped into her arms, unconscious.

"How did you do that?" Lucien demanded. "That's impossible. He was consumed by the rage; I saw it in his eyes."

She shook her head. "The beast responds to me; I don't know why. You're lucky I was here, or he would have tried to kill you."

Lucien's lip curled. "He lost control because of you. He's blinded by his feelings for you. You—"

"Lucien, calm down. She is Rohn's wife, you can't force her to leave," Lia interrupted him. "What was that creature? How did it come here?"

Ann knew she had to tread carefully. She didn't want to risk these people finding out her true identity, or they would force her to leave. "A Fomorian demon sent by the leader of Caselhelm." She cradled Ed's head in her lap. "You may think your squabbles with Ranelle's people are important, but the demons will come here sooner or later. Nowhere in the five lands is safe from them. Ed and I work with the resistance, and part of that means hunting demons."

She and Ed had decided against telling Lucien and the other lykaes they were rogues. They'd keep their cover story as close to the truth as possible, but they didn't want to raise any awkward questions.

"The problems in Caselhelm are not my concern."

Ann took hold of Ed's wrist where the demon's claws had slashed him and held it up for Lucien to see. "You said cold iron doesn't affect you, so why is he burnt? Only people with fae blood are affected by iron. That must mean Ed isn't a full lykae." Her eyes narrowed. "There's a lot that doesn't add up from what you've told us so far. Why are you so afraid of magic?"

"Cold iron *doesn't* affect us." Lucien's eyes flashed. "Perhaps it was some new magic from the other lands. You would do well to leave this place."

Ann raised her chin. "He's my husband, I won't leave him." From what she'd seen so far these people weren't trustworthy. She wasn't about to leave Ed alone with them.

Lucien turned and stormed off.

Lia came over. "The bond between you two is strong. Don't let Lucian's harsh words come between you." She patted Ann's arm.

"Does he lose control like this very often?" She wrapped an arm under Ed's shoulder and hauled him to his feet.

"Sometimes. It seems to happen most when I'm in danger." She followed Lia inside the hut as the other lykae dragged Ed over to the bed. "Can you help him learn control?"

"I'll do what I can, but it seems you are the one who helps him control himself."

Ann shook her head. "That's only a temporary solution. We can't be together all the time," she said. "Do you know why my father bound us together?"

"Only he could tell you that."

Ann glanced outside the hut to make sure no one else was around. In the distance, she spotted something flying overhead: another wyvern.

CHAPTER 10

Ed groaned as he came awake. His head pounded like he'd been hit by a hammer. "Argh, I lost control again."

He found himself back in his hut, with its dark wooden walls and makeshift bed. The straw mattress dipped underneath his weight. Ed couldn't believe he'd lost control—in front of his father, no less. What would Lucien think now?

He'd heard Ann's conversation with Lia as well. He guessed the bond between them had been getting stronger. He'd never been able to listen in on her conversations before. Why hadn't Ann mentioned them being bound? Ed wondered if it was true at first, but he didn't doubt the connection between them. His beast had told him as much, so it had to be true.

"We killed the demon at least." Ann sighed and rose from where she'd been sitting at his bedside. "I need to go. Your father is right, I brought the demon here."

"What did Lucien say?" Ed glanced down at his wrist, now marked with three deep red scratches. His wrist stung, but he ignored the pain as he scrambled up. "Bloody demons." He frowned as a memory came to him. "I heard him say iron doesn't affect lykaes. What does that mean?"

"You must have some fae or eleven blood." Ann grabbed her pack. "He didn't say much of anything, but he's not happy I'm staying here. We need to find out whatever he's hiding."

"I'll talk to him—maybe he will open up to me if he learns to trust me." He scrambled off the bed. "Is there anything else you want to tell me?"

"I managed to avert the demon questions. Told him we're part of the resistance." She swung the pack over her shoulder. "And I spotted a wyvern flying over earlier. Ceara and I are going for a look around. I'll see you later. Your aunt was looking for you this morning." Ann gave him a quick kiss. "She came and talked to me earlier. I think she knows a lot more than she is letting on, *she* helped someone send you through the mist to Trin."

Ed's brow creased. "Did she tell you why?"

"No. Just said something about wanting to keep you safe, but I can tell there's a lot more to it than that." Ann glanced toward the door as if expecting to see someone appear. "She knows who I am, too. Said my father knew about you. I think he must've helped you

119

pass through the mist." She shook her head again. "There's a lot more going on here then we suspected. I might go and visit Ranelle."

"Why? She's the enemy."

"How else are we going to figure out a way to stop the two races from going to war?"

Ed grunted. "I can't go with you. No lykae can set foot there, from what Marcus told me last night."

"Talk to your father, or Lia. Find out what she knows. At least she seems to be on our side, she said she wouldn't tell Lucien who I am."

"Lucien?" Ed found his father outside his hut.

Lucien's brow creased. "I'm your father, Rohn. You could call me as such."

"No offence, but I don't know you well enough for that yet," Ed said.

If I hadn't been given a mission, I wouldn't stay with you, either.

Lucien sighed. "Of course."

"I was hoping we could talk more." Ed knew he had to find out more about why the council had sent him here, and why he'd been sent away. It couldn't have only been to become an overseer. Why hadn't Lia told Lucien the truth?

"I heard you and Ann talking earlier," Ed remarked. "How do I have magic?"

Lucien growled. "I don't know. It must've come from your druid."

Ed scoffed. "Druids can't bestow magic like that. It has to be passed down."

He didn't smell any magic on Lucien. Lucien smelt of earth, of the wind rustling through the trees. All magic left a scent, no matter what race someone was. Unless Lucien could mask his somehow.

"Perhaps it used to be, but lykaes don't possess it." Lucien raised his chin. "You should be more worried about control over what I saw this morning."

"I only lose control when Ann is in danger. Don't lykaes lose control when something threatens their k'ia?"

"You know how I feel about that."

"I'm not arguing about my relationship with Ann anymore," Ed said. "I would like us to get to know each other again."

"As would I, my son."

Okay, maybe I can break the ice a little.

He spotted the medallion in Lucien's hand. "I had an uncle?"

"Yes, my older brother. Lucas."

"I don't remember him."

Lucien shook his head. "He was killed when you were very young."

Lucien moved away from the hut, and Ed followed. "Killed by whom?"

"A fight broke out between our people and the woodland folk. He died during the battle."

"How did his medallion end up in the hands of the lupine?"

Lucien shrugged. "I don't know. I thought it had been lost decades ago." He slipped it around his neck. "Come, I'll show you something." Lucien shot into the distance.

Ed's beast clawed at his mind, eager to run. Houses and trees flashed by as he sped after Lucien.

He reappeared on the edge of the verge. In the distance loomed an enormous tree, so tall it disappeared beneath the clouds. Its leaves were like heavy curtains.

"This is where our land ends. Beyond is their territory," Lucien said. "You must never venture near there, they will try to kill you on sight."

"Why do our people and theirs hate each other so much?" Ed suspected it went much deeper than just a feud over land.

"We've always despised each other. We lykaes are hunters, and we don't like to share our territory."

"There must be a reason," Ed persisted. "All feuds start somewhere."

"It's lasted so long I doubt anyone remembers why," Lucien said. "I just wanted you to be aware. It won't matter to them if you're different."

"What was your brother like?" Ed went on. Maybe if he got Lucien to open up, he'd find more answers.

"Strong, proud. As a lykae should be. He tried for a truce with those damned outlanders." Lucien's eyes flashed amber. Ed had noticed all the lykaes' eyes turned amber—or red, in the case of the lupines. Why did his own eyes glow emerald?

Yet another unanswered question.

"One thing I've learnt in the Black is war never solves anything," Ed said. "Both sides end up losing."

"War has been the only way to deal with them."

"Why waste so much innocent life?"

Lucien's jaw tightened. "You must have learnt to defend what's yours."

Ed nodded. "Of course. I'm no pacifist, but I don't believe in senseless murder."

"Did your foster father teach you that?"

Ed smiled. "No, never had one. Flora was fasted to a woman. Sage was Darius' adviser."

Lucien gave a harsh laugh. "That son of a bitch never took advice from anyone."

Ed raised a brow. "You knew him then?"

"Well enough. Back then, people thought he'd be different from his tyrannical father. Of course, he wasn't. He had no intention of freeing us."

"You mean from the moon curse?"

Lucien nodded. "Indeed."

"That lupine, where did it come from?" Ed glanced over at the tree. "Marcus said lupines are rare."

"They are, but more have started appearing."

"Maybe the current archdruid will be different," Ed suggested. He wouldn't talk about Darius' successor too much. He knew Lucien would never let Ann stay if he found out the truth.

Lucien gave a harsh laugh. "I doubt it. The archdruid enforced the spells that oppressed us and many other races onto us. This one will be no different."

"She is different," Ed insisted. "She's not on the throne for one thing."

"The affairs of Caselhelm do not concern us. If you want to help, let's go hunting. See if we can find more lupines."

Ed wanted to ask more questions, but he wouldn't pass up this opportunity. "Could Ranelle's people be turning lykaes?"

Lucien barked with laughter. "I'm sure they'd love that. No, son, they can't turn us into lupines."

"How does someone lose himself to the rage?"

"Many things can cause it. Some never master control. Death, anger, and loss can all trigger it. That's why it's important to find your true k'ia."

Ed opened his mouth to protest but stopped. "How do you know someone is your k'ia?" he asked instead.

"You'll be drawn to them. It's an instinct. Your beast will know them."

"Was it like that when you met my mother?" Ed asked. "I don't remember her at all." He kept searching through the fragmented memories of his early childhood, but still hadn't found a trace of his mother.

Lucien flinched. "Let's hunt." He shot into the distance.

Ed sighed. *Still he won't talk of her. Is it pain, or is there more to it?*

Ed followed after him. The great blue woods loomed around them. *This looks like the place I remembered before I was chased. Why would anyone chase me? If only I could ask my father these things and he would answer.*

"How do we hunt lupines?" Ed asked.

"We can sense them. How…?" Lucien shook his head. "I keep forgetting you know so little about us. I don't understand why you'd forget so much."

That's a good question. Guess it was part of me becoming an overseer. His mother must've had magic, and possibly even been an overseer herself. Perhaps that was why Lucien hated magic so much.

"I've remembered some things," Ed added. "Like not feeding on blood. Plus, my beast tells me things."

"Concentrate, Rohn," Lucien growled. "All lykaes can sense each other. Did you sense the lupine before it attacked you?"

Ed nodded.

"Good. Focus. What do you sense?"

Ed inhaled, took in the scents around him. Other than the usual leaves and earth, there were no other smells. "I don't feel anything like the lupine. It felt…dark, angry. Its rage almost palpable."

"Concentrate. Don't just use your sense of smell. Our senses are much stronger than any other race."

Ed knew that well enough. When he'd first turned, it had been unbearable. Everything was so sharp, loud, and bright. He felt it then, coldness surrounded by hot rage. Ed followed the feeling. Trees rushed by as he shot toward it.

Ed reappeared in a clearing. The forest felt darker here, as if the very trees were watching him.

Light flashed as a beautiful woman appeared. Her long red hair shimmered in the light, and her emerald eyes sparkled.

Not a lupine, Ed realised, and the cold feeling faded. Had it come from her or something else? He couldn't tell.

Lucien shot in front of him before Ed had a chance to react. "What are you doing, woman?" the alpha growled.

"You're trespassing in my woodland," the woman snapped. "I came to tell you to get out." She glared back at Lucien as if not at all intimidated by him.

They fell silent as they continued to glower at each other like they were having a silent conversation. Ed didn't need to hear anything, their gaze spoke volumes.

"We were hunting lupines," Ed spoke up.

Both Lucien and the woman stared at him like they'd forgotten he was there.

"I'm Edward Rohn. And you are?"

Lucien's lip curled. "This is Ranelle."

"Why are you my woods, Lucien?" Ranelle put her hands on her hips.

"I might ask you the same thing," Lucien spat back.

"You're trespassing on my land."

"This area is still *lykae* land," Lucien retorted. "And if there's a lupine around, I'm within my right to hunt it down."

"Another lupine?" Ranelle arched a perfect eyebrow. "Are you driving all your people to madness?"

Lucien gave a harsh laugh. "No. I'm sure your people would—"

Ed stood there for a moment, unsure what to do. He was supposed to be bringing them together, not letting them argue like this.

"Lucien, maybe we should go." Ed put a hand on his father's shoulder. "We don't want to intrude, Ranelle."

"*You're* not intruding, Rohn." Ranelle turned back to Lucien. "Your son has much better manners than you."

Ed furrowed his brow. "Wait, how do you know who I am?"

Ranelle and Lucien fell silent, glaring at each other.

"I am a member of the council. It's not hard to recognise you, given that you spent years with the—"

"The former archdruid," Ed interrupted. "Not anymore, though. I'm married, and travel with my family now. My days in the Black Guard have long passed." He didn't want Ranelle to mention Ann, or Lucien might figure out who she was. "We are sorry for trespassing on your land. Lucien—"

Lucien turned his glare toward Ed. "Why are you apologising to this woman?"

"Because she's your enemy, not mine," Ed stated. "If you stop accusing each other, maybe you can come to a peaceful settlement."

Ranelle laughed. "It's far too late after everything he's done."

Lucien's eyes flashed amber.

"Ranelle, would you mind if I hunted around for lupines?" Ed asked her. "My father can leave."

"What?" Lucien seethed.

Ranelle gritted her teeth. "You may. But I want him gone." She glared at Lucien.

"Thank you." Ed bowed his head.

Lucien, maybe you should go. Ed had no idea if Lucien would hear his mind speak, Ed had learnt how to do it growing up with the druids.

Ranelle crossed her arms, expectantly waiting to see what Lucien did next.

"Don't go too deep into Mirkwood. There are other things there besides her people," Lucien warned. He disappeared in a blur.

Ed breathed a sigh of relief.

"I'm glad you're not like him," Ranelle remarked.

Ed frowned. "Have we met before? You seem so familiar."

Ranelle smiled. "We met when you were a boy."

He shook his head. "I don't remember much of growing up here."

Damn, why did I admit that to her? She's a stranger.

"Do you know what I am?"

Ranelle nodded. "You're lifemate to—"

"I meant about me being an overseer." Ed covered his mouth. He didn't detect any threat from this woman, yet he didn't trust her. *Why do I keep blurting everything out?*

"Be careful who you tell about that," Ranelle said.

Ceara, where are you? Ed called.

With Ann, trying to avoid being hit by bloody trees!

Get Ann to send you to me. Hurry!

Why? Ann asked. *What's wrong?*

Just send Ceara. Please.

Was Ranelle compelling him to talk with magic? If so, Ceara should sense it with her empathic powers.

Ceara appeared in a flash of blue light. "Hey, what's wrong, wolfy?"

"Please excuse me." Ranelle said and vanished in a flash of light.

"What's going on?" Ceara frowned. "Who was that?"

"That's Ranelle. I think she compelled me."

"To do what?"

Ed shook his head. "I don't know. Do you sense anything from me? Am I under compulsion?"

Light flared between her brows. She directed it at him. "You know my magic has a limited effect on you."

"Concentrate. I need to know."

"Nope, I'm not sensing anything."

"Things around here are getting stranger."

CHAPTER 11

Ann appeared at Ed's side a few moments later. "What happened? I felt your panic."

"I'm off to find bird boy," Ceara said. "See you back at the village."

"Jax isn't at the village," Ann pointed out.

"No, but there are lots of shirtless men there." Ceara grinned. "Hurry up. Unless you want me here while you frolic around the woods?"

Ed sighed. "We're not frolicking."

"No, you're admitting being an overseer to the enemy," Ceara replied.

Ed gaped at her. "How do you know that?"

"I've always known. Heard Mum talking about it to Sage once. Just wondered how long it'd take you to remember it."

"What else did Mum say?"

"Not much. Just how you were sent watch over Ann. Something about a bond. That part is obvious."

Ann waved her hand, and Ceara vanished in a flash of blue orbs.

"What happened?" Ann repeated.

"I met Ranelle. Lucien and I were hunting for lupines. She appeared and said we encroached on her territory. It's strange. They seemed to be fighting over more than land."

"A lot about this place doesn't make sense," Ann remarked, pushing a leafy curtain aside. "Let's look around."

"Maybe we should talk about our bond."

Ann winced. "We don't know there is one yet." She pushed through the trees.

"Why are you so afraid?"

"Because I'm…We don't know if this bond is real, so let's not jump ahead of ourselves."

Ed caressed her cheek. "You're not gonna lose me, if that's what you're afraid of."

"I'm not—" she protested and sighed. "Not afraid of that."

"The others can handle things back at the village." Ed took her hand.

"Jax is searching the skies for wyverns," Ann replied. "Ceara will…be watching the lykaes."

Ed chuckled. "Oh, I'm sure of that."

"It's hard not to watch half-naked men." She grinned. He scowled, and she laughed. "I only said watching."

They pushed through more trees together. "I'm glad to get out of the village," Ed admitted. "I feel suffocated there."

"Maybe we should talk to Ranelle, or the council. Find out more of what they expect you to do here."

"You hate the council."

"True, but only because they refused to help after my parents were killed." Ann had vowed never to talk to the council again after that. "My father said they are fools."

"Maybe lupines are part of the problem here. Perhaps Urien is looking for them."

"Lupines wouldn't help him much. He has wyvern, he'd want something more powerful than them." Ann raised her hand so that the trees moved aside. "Do you sense anything?"

"No lupines."

Ann scanned the area with her mind. The air crackled with magic. "It's odd Lucien hates magic so much— it's in the very air all around us here."

The trees grew denser, casting eerie shadows around them as shafts of light sparkled through the heavy black canopy overhead.

"Lulrien was said to be one of the more powerful realms. I'm surprised no one took it over."

"The mists probably stopped them."

"We got through," Ed pointed out.

Ann hesitated. "What if the bond between us is real?"

"It is. I've always felt like we were meant for each other," Ed smiled.

She bit her lip. "But what if it's the only thing drawing us together?"

Ed shook his head. "That's not how bonds work."

"Think about it. We have no idea how or why my father bound us together," Ann said. "Or how it might affect us."

"I know how I feel. Do you?"

"I'm worried this bond is influencing us. Maybe you'll find your real k'ia, then I'll be obsolete."

Ed laughed and kissed her. "You'll never be obsolete to me, love. There's no one else for me."

Ann winced at the endearment. Every time they got close, she felt more of her resolve slipping away. "I still want to know more about this bond. Lia wouldn't tell me much other than that someone on this side of the mist must've been involved."

"More unanswered questions. I never thought coming back here would be so confusing."

"I wanted you coming home to be better." She touched his cheek.

Ed chuckled. "I don't need a place to call home. You're my home, always have been. I don't need walls or doors."

Ann smiled and took his hand. "Come on, we're supposed to be looking around. I've always been curious to see what Lulrien is really like."

"Most of it is forest, from what I remember."

Ann scanned the area deeper with her mind. It was hard to see anything beyond the trees.

"Archdruid?" a voice whispered.

Ann stopped dead. "Did you hear that?"

"Hear what?"

"Archdruid?" the voice said again.

"That. If it's that shadow thing, I will find a way to vanquish it."

She made a move forward, but Ed stopped her. *Do you sense it?*

No, but I'm worried it might lead us into a trap. He gripped her hand tighter.

Ann threw her hand up to cover her face as a heavy curtain of leaves covered her. She drew it back, revealing a small glade behind it. A small figure stood there, appearing no taller than a child. Her long dark hair fell past her shoulders, and her clothes appeared to be made from leaves.

"Welcome, archdruid." The girl beckoned them forward.

Ed tightened his grip on Ann's hand. *I can't sense what she is.*

"Hello. Are you lost?" Ann asked.

Don't be fooled by her appearance, Ed said. *Ceara said she sensed fae when we passed through the mist. I think that girl is fae.*

"No, I'm here to welcome you to Lulrien." The girl held out her hand. "Come. Everyone is so excited to see you."

Ann glanced at Ed. Although she'd learnt of the fae—of which there were hundreds of different kinds all over their world—she'd never met many of them.

The druids and the fae had been close allies—even kin once. That had changed over the centuries. Many of the fae were forced to abandon their territories thanks to laws set by the elders and former archdruids.

"Welcome me?" Ann frowned.

"Yes, my people are eager to meet you."

Ann, this isn't a good idea, Ed said. *Your grandfather despised the fae. I can't imagine why they'd want to welcome you.*

I know the history my family has with them. Ann cast her senses out, but there was no warning on the air, and the trees didn't seem aggressive either. *We should check it out.*

Ed scowled. *Why? I'd rather not walk into a trap. My father told me to be wary of the forest too.*

I'm curious, she admitted. *Most fae I've met haven't been as hostile toward me as other races are. Let's look around. I'll transport us out if it is a trap, or you can use your speed to escape.*

Ed's eyes blazed bright emerald, and the girl flinched. "If this is a trap, don't try anything," he growled.

"It's not. We want to welcome you as friends." The girl trembled.

"Okay, lead the way," Ann said to the girl.

Try not to scare anyone, she told Ed.

He snorted. *I don't scare anyone.*

In your beast form you do. Apart from me, that is. She flashed him a smile.

They moved through the small clearing. More branches and heavy foliage covered their way. The girl sang something in an odd language, and the branches and leaves moved aside.

Ann scanned the girl with her senses. She felt like the forest, old, strong, and powerful.

Do you see a glamour on her? Ann asked Ed.

With his keen eyesight, he might have detected a glamour even if she couldn't.

No, none. Ed gripped her hand. *Say an anti-glamour spell.*

What if we offend her? My father always told me never to annoy the fae.

The fae were one of the oldest Magickind in their world. They'd been around since before the dark times, when a lot of Erthea had been destroyed.

"Briseadh an glamour." Light sparkled over the girl, who seemed unaware of the spell. Ann had felt Ed's power join with hers. It felt almost as natural as breathing.

The girl passed straight through the foliage and disappeared.

"This doesn't look good," Ed remarked.

"Don't worry. I'll save you if something does go wrong."

"That's not the only thing that worries me, love."

Again with the "love". Ann didn't wince this time.

"I think we're supposed to walk through it," Ann said. "Let's go."

Together, they walked through. Ann kept a tight grip on Ed. As curious as she was about the fae, she wasn't stupid. She'd still be on her guard on the other side.

The trees loomed even taller than Ranelle's great tree. Sprites zipped over their heads.

"This is beautiful," Ann breathed.

"I haven't seen a glamour yet," Ed said.

"We're exploring places that have been cut off for centuries. Try to be a little more enthusiastic."

Glowing balls of light danced around them. Dozens of colours blurred together in a sparkling rainbow, and a cacophony of sound.

One ball of light landed on Ann's shoulder, and she realised it was a winged sprite.

"Welcome, archdruid." A short old man with gnarled skin said as he hobbled forward. "And Rohn, overseer."

Ed's eyes narrowed. *How do they know what I am?*

Ann shrugged as her skin tingled. She gasped, realised her glamour had faded. "What the—?"

More creatures came out from the trees, brownies, leprechauns, and all other manner of fae. Ann doubted even Ed could name all of them.

Every one of the creatures sank to their knees and bowed their heads.

"Why are they bowing?" Ann hissed.

Ed shook his head. He seemed as just confused as she felt. *I've never known them to get like this around anyone.*

Three sprites flew down and dropped a crown of white roses onto her head.

"Would someone please tell me what's going on?" Ann asked.

A woman materialised. She had long white hair that shimmered against her opal skin as she stepped forward and bowed her head. "I'm Ninia. We've all come to welcome you, archdruid."

"Why?" Ed stepped between Ann and the woman.

"It's been centuries since the archdruid came here. We're glad to have you and your lifemate."

"He's not—" Ann protested. "I'm surprised, given some of the past animosity between the fae and former archdruids."

Ninia smiled. "You're different. You fight for what's right and just."

"You expect us to save you from something, then?" Ed arched an eyebrow.

"Excuse my husband." Ann moved around him, wondering why she had called him that.

"Darkness is coming to Lulrien. That's why you're here, yes?"

Ann and Edward glanced at each other, uncertain.

"Something like that," Ann said. "Ninia, is there someone here we can talk to? An elder, or someone in charge?"

"Yes, we'll take you to see her later. First, we will have a feast to celebrate your return to Lulrien."

"No, we won't be staying long," Ed said. "Take us to your leader now."

"She's not here," Ninia replied.

"Ed, we should stay a while," Ann suggested.

You can't be serious, Ed protested.

They're a lot friendlier toward us than both the lykaes and Ranelle's people, she said. *Maybe we can learn something from them.*

Ed sighed. *This isn't why we were sent to Lulrien.*

You don't know that. Let's stick around.

The fae parted and led them into the village.

"Rhiannon?" another voice called.

Ann glanced around, but no one appeared to have said anything. More eyes watched them from the trees. But she still felt no threat from them.

"We'll have food and wine brought for you," Ninia said.

Ann sat down on a fallen tree.

I still think this is bad idea. Ed sat next to her.

"Ninia, what do you know about the dark presence you mentioned?" Ann asked.

The laughter and dancing around them died down for a moment, and Ninia hesitated. "It comes from below. You will defeat it."

"But you must know what it is?" Ed persisted. "And why it's a threat?"

"Rhiannon, I need to talk to you," the voice said again. "Come to me at the stone."

"You hear her, don't you?" Ninia appeared by Ann's side.

"Who?" Ann frowned.

"She wants to talk to you. Just you."

Ann glanced at Ed, who'd fallen into conversation with the old man.

She rose. "I'll be back."

139

Ed nodded. *Be careful.*

Ann followed after Ninia until they reached a huge standing stone.

"Touch the stone and you will go to her," Ninia urged.

She hesitated, but Ed seemed less on edge now.

"Come, Rhiannon," the voice said.

"You are safe within our borders, archdruid. You have my word," Ninia said.

Ann touched the stone. A buzzing sound echoed around her, and light blinded her.

As it faded, she found herself surrounded by more lush greenery. When she turned around, the stone, Ed, and all the fae had vanished.

"Fuck!" She growled. "I should have known this was a trap."

"Don't be so dramatic, girl." The familiar woman hovered off the ground. Her long black hair was draped around her like a cloak and her coal black button-like eyes stared out of her translucent face. "Welcome to the heart of the forest."

"Oh, for the love of spirits, why are you here?"

"Because I need to talk to you," the seer replied.

"Nothing you say ever proves helpful. Send me back." Ann crossed her arms.

"You're so much like your mother." The seer cackled.

Ann snorted. "I'm the opposite of my mother. She was…"

"I didn't mean your father's wife."

"Don't go there," Ann warned. "I don't have anything to say to you."

"I brought you here to listen, not talk."

"Okay, if I'm listening, why not tell me your name first?" She had never bothered to mention her name on previous occasions.

The seer tapped her chin, thoughtful.

No doubt trying to think up a fake name.

"Hmm, call me Domnu. That's what the fae call me."

"Fine. Talk." Ann sighed.

"I need you to listen to me this time. Take heed."

"Why? You never tell me anything helpful," Ann snapped.

"I warned you the house of Valeran would fall."

"Yes, but you failed to tell me how it would happen, and I couldn't stop it." The toadstool Domnu hovered over burst into flame.

"Your powers are getting stronger. But then you always were a *fae dóiteáin.*"

Ann's eyes widened as she recognised the words in the druid tongue. "A fire fairy?" She shook her head. "I'm a druid."

"Oh, you're much more than that," Domnu said. "But I brought you here to discuss your brother. He's working in Lulrien, and he has no idea what he is getting into."

"Enlighten me then."

Domnu's strange eyes shimmered with power. "What lurks below shall come above. The darkness once locked away shall return."

"What does that even mean?" she asked. "Why do you have to be so damn cryptic?"

"I'm telling you what I've seen," Domnu retorted. "It's for you to find out the rest."

"Why not give me a straight answer?"

Domnu laughed and hovered upside down, her hair billowing around her. "Where would be the fun in that?"

"Okay, thanks for the warning—a lot of good it does me." She turned to leave. "Thanks for nothing."

"Don't you have more questions?"

"As if you'd give me anything but vague answers." Ann scanned the trees in search of the standing stone but found no sign of it. Where had it disappeared to? Maybe she could transport back to Ed. Blue light sparkled around her.

"I can answer some things."

Ann reluctantly let her body reform. "You lead the fae here?"

Another cackle. "Ancient one, no. The fae are leaderless. They were governed by the council too once, but they keep to themselves now."

"Why do they think I can help them?" Ann turned around again. "I'm surprised they don't hate me after what my grandfather put them through."

"You're different from him. You give the fae hope."

She snorted. "I don't see why. I'm just one person."

"You are different from all your ancestors, that's why."

Ann wondered why Domnu was speaking to her like this. The seer usually told her vague nonsense then disappeared. What had changed?

"What's the entity that follows me around?"

Domnu laughed. "That I can't answer, but you'll find out soon enough."

And we're back to vagueness.

"How do I get back to Ed?" The stone still hadn't reappeared.

"Aren't you going to ask about him?"

Her brow furrowed. "What about him?"

"You must want to know more about your bond."

The bond again!

"Alright. All seeing one, why am I bound to Ed?"

Domnu rolled her strange eyes. "I thought that would be obvious."

Ann shook her head. "No, it isn't. Please let me go back now."

"You can find the answers to your bond. Bonds don't form unless they're meant to." Domnu turned back up the right way. "You may need it sooner than you think."

"I don't even know what I feel for Ed. There's an attraction between us, yes, but he wants more than that."

"What are you so afraid of?"

Ann looked away. "Of being hurt, I guess. Of not being able to love him back," she said. "My parents despised each other. My father had a different woman in his bed every night. I don't want that." She shook her head. "That's why romantic love is pure nonsense."

"You don't know the full history of what happened between your parents."

"Why did I even tell you that?"

"Perhaps you needed someone to talk to besides Edward or your rogues."

"No offence, but you're not someone I'd trust with my problems." She ran a hand through her hair. "I don't know how to stop Urien. How do I undo my father's spell?"

"That I can't answer. They used dark magic to create it."

"They?" She frowned. "Who helped Papa with the spell?"

"All in time."

Ann found herself back in front of the standing stone. "Thanks," she murmured.

She scanned the crowd for Ed and spotted two nymphs dancing around him. She cleared her throat as she approached, arms crossed. "Having fun?"

Ed untangled himself from the two gorgeous women. "Not exactly," he muttered.

Spirits, I thought they'd never leave me alone.

Ann laughed, and Ed asked, "Where did you disappear to?"

She told him about seeing Domnu. "She gave me some of her usual cryptic nonsense."

"Can we go back to the village now?" Ed asked.

Ann took his hand and drew him aside. She gave him a passionate kiss.

Ed's eyes widened. "What was that for?"

"At least now we're together I can kiss you whenever I like." She gave him another quick kiss. "I'm glad we're together, I don't know if

I could face Urien without you. I just wanted to say, no matter what happens, we can get through anything together."

Ed grinned and wrapped his arms around her. "I'm glad you're with me too."

CHAPTER 12

Urien watched the life fade from the eyes of the Ursaie slave he'd stabbed through the heart. Light radiated from her body as her power flowed into him. He'd hoped killing might ease some of his suffering, but still the blood magic refused to do any good to his dying body. Ryn's blood hadn't helped either. No matter how much he took from her, she still healed and he still felt himself getting weaker.

Finally, everything had been going well. Most of Caselhelm was under his control, and his army grew stronger, especially now he had the wyverns at his disposal. Why did this damned body have to wear out? He hadn't seen his own body since Ann had ripped his soul from it five years earlier.

Urien moved over to his desk. On it sat an old scroll that he'd found in a secret compartment in Darius's hidden chamber. He scanned the scroll again. It had taken a while to translate the ancient druid tongue, but the scroll spoke of a doorway into the underworld. Legend said some of the worst of Magickind had been locked away during one of the very first realm wars. Among them were his mother's race, the Fomorians. Only a handful had survived over the centuries, forced to interbreed to avoid extinction. Since then, what remained of their race had become weaker and far less powerful. Once, the Fomorians had been the scourge of Erthea, spreading terror throughout the five lands. Urien would find what remained of his brethren, and the five lands would all bow to him.

"Get rid of that body, would you?" he called to the guard outside his study. A pool of blood surrounded the dead Ursaie. He hated how messy blood magic was, but it served its purpose.

Light flashed around him as he reappeared inside Ranelle's chamber. Ranelle jumped at the sight of him. "My...my lord." She bowed her head.

Good, she finally seemed to be learning her place. At least she hadn't tried to kill him since their early encounters. "I came to find out what progress you've made."

Translating the scroll had been the first problem, but once deciphered, he'd determined the doorway to the underworld would be here. He tasked Ranelle and her people with finding it.

It made perfect sense, that was why the mists had cut Lulrien off from the rest of Almara.

Ranelle sighed. "We're still digging. We haven't found anything."

"What's taking so long?" Urien demanded. "You've been digging for almost a month."

"Maybe you misread the ancient texts. My people don't remember any such battle taking place here." Ranelle tucked a look of hair behind her ear. "I would know. They would have warned us."

Urien snorted. "No, it would have been erased from history. They wouldn't have wanted anyone to find the doorway again." He yanked her chamber door open. "Take me below ground. I want to see the progress myself."

Ranelle hesitated. "I already told you—"

"Take me there. Now." He pulled the Arcus stone from his pocket. "Do I have to use this?"

Ranelle flinched. He knew how much she feared the stone's power, despite her outward resistance.

Don't harm her, Xander's voice whispered in his mind. *Haven't you hurt enough people already? You have so much blood on your hands.*

Ah, I'm surprised you're still there, brother, Urien remarked. *These are your hands, not mine. Everyone I've killed or harmed will remember your face. Think of that.*

Xander fell silent again.

Urien grabbed hold of Ranelle's arm. "Take me below ground," he repeated.

She sighed and shut the door. "Fine, but I don't want anyone to see you, word might spread back to the lykaes and your sister." She motioned for him to follow. "Come, I will take a different route down there."

She touched a knot on the wall, and it swung open with a groan, revealing a stairwell.

Urien followed behind her. He kept a firm grip on the Arcus stone. As much as he liked Ranelle, he wouldn't put it past her to try something. She'd do anything to protect her people. That much he knew for certain.

Ranelle conjured an orb of glowing emerald energy to help them see their way. It cast dancing shadows along the walls of the tree.

He didn't like having to walk behind her, but the staircase proved too narrow to walk beside her.

They descended lower and lower. It became even darker, so dark the orb barely illuminated anything.

"Are we there yet?" Urien demanded. He had checked on their underground operation a couple of times but had been using the projection orb back at the palace, not in person like this.

"Almost." They reached another doorway. She twisted another notch, and the wall slid aside. The smell of smoke hit them and sweat broke out on Urien's forehead from the searing heat.

They moved down a wide tunnel dug deep into the earth. Ranelle led the way, the green orb hovering above her.

Urien waved his hand and muttered, *"Soilsigh."* The orb burned brighter, illuminating the tunnel.

The further they moved down it, the hotter it became. The tunnel widened into a much larger cavern that had been blasted out of the bedrock.

Around them, several wyverns moved about while a couple of

guards stood watching them. Some of the beasts would dig, while others breathed fire to blast through the hard rock. Above them were the branches of the great tree that Ranelle's people called home, its roots curled like a net of blackened and burned threads. He remembered Ranelle had been worried all this digging might affect the tree's health and growth.

Urien couldn't care less what happened to a worthless tree. All he cared about was finding that damn door, then the elders would help him find his missing body. Ann had hidden it too well for him to even sense it.

"This is how far you've dug?" he scoffed. "We're barely five miles below ground."

"The work is hard, and the workers are tired," Ranelle said, her eyes flashing. "I told you it would take time to get through."

Urien shook his head. "This is unacceptable. I'll never find the door at this rate," he growled. "Why haven't you pushed them harder?"

"The poor creatures are working as hard as they can." She raised her chin. "Wyverns are not supposed to be kept underground."

"You're not pushing them hard enough." He yanked out the Arcus stone. "Seems I've been too soft on you." He turned his attention to one of the smaller wyverns, a green coloured thing with a serpentine body. Much smaller than the other hulking beasts crawling around down here.

"No!" Ranelle grabbed his arm. "They're working as hard as they can. You can't push them any harder."

"Hard isn't good enough." The ancient jewel vibrated with power.

The small wyvern struggled as the stone let out a high-pitched wail. The beast tugged at the chains that bound its legs to the nearby wall, making the metal groan in protest.

Urien revelled in the animal's pain as the stone's power vibrated through his body. "Dig faster, dig deeper!" he cried. "You worthless beast."

Ranelle made a grab for the stone. Urien raised his other hand, sending out a burst of lightning. His head throbbed from having to use power, but he ignored the pain.

The bolt struck Ranelle in the chest and sent her crashing across the cavern. She landed a few feet away, writhing in pain.

The wyvern reared up on its hind legs and charged at Urien.

"Stay back," he growled.

No! Xander yelled, and Urien's hand trembled. He couldn't believe it, Xander couldn't take control, this was his body now.

The wyvern spotted his moment of weakness, and metal clanked as it pulled free and the bolts on the wall snapped. The wyvern snapped its jaws and knocked Urien to the ground.

Urien screamed as the wyvern's claws slashed through his tunic, ripping through his flesh. He looked down, horrified to see blood blooming over his torso. *Gods below, how am I going to heal from this?*

He gripped the stone tighter. "I'll kill you for this," he growled.

"Go," Ranelle called to the wyvern.

One of the guards came at Urien with a sword. "Hurry, get out of here," he said to the beast.

The wyvern hesitated, glancing between Ranelle and the guard.

Break its legs, Urien commanded the stone. He fired a lightning bolt at the guard, who dropped to the ground in pain.

The wyvern collapsed as its bones snapped. A second guard charged at Urien as the wyvern screamed in pain, no longer able to move its legs.

"Stop," Ranelle begged. "Please don't hurt him." She crawled toward the wyvern. "I'm sorry, this is all my fault."

The guard dodged the bolt Urien hurled at him and stabbed a knife through Urien's shoulder.

Urien hissed with pain. "Go," the guard said to the crippled beast. "Hurry."

Still struggling, the wyvern crawled across the tunnel, flapping its massive bat-like wings.

Urien struck the second guard dead. He scrambled up, ignoring Ranelle, and hurried up the opposite tunnel, but it was too late. The wyvern had escaped.

Urien shook as he made his way through the underground tunnels, injured after the fucking wyvern had attacked him. He needed time to calm himself. He stormed out of the tunnel and into the dense forest. His wound wouldn't heal, but he'd stemmed the flow of blood with a spell. *I've got to find my own body.*

Only his mother had been able to transfer spirits from one body to another. Urien hoped the elders were able to help. He'd have to find a way to trap his sister and hand her over to them.

Ranelle had seen his weakness. That made him all the angrier. Why wouldn't Darius' spell heal him?

It must be weakening, he realised. *Ann has been tampering with it. Now I'm no longer protected as I once was.*

He muttered an oath. Damn, the one thing he had wanted gone was now something he needed to survive.

He heard voices in the distance, and Jax and Ceara strode into the clearing.

"Are you sure this is the right place?" Jax asked.

"Yes, bird boy, this is the place where I sensed the bad energy."

"I don't see or feel anything." Jax shook his head.

"The wyverns have to be coming from somewhere, we are going to find them."

Urien ducked behind a tree. The last thing he needed was to be caught by them, he felt weak and doubted he'd be able to hold them off if they attacked him.

"Alright fine, I'll take to the air." Jax shifted into his crow form and took off.

Ceara glanced around. Would she sense him there?

Urien's heart pounded harder. *"Tog ceo tocsaineach,"* he chanted the words of power, mist drew in around Ceara.

"Holy spirits, where did that come from?" She waved her arm as if it would make the heavy fog dissipate.

Urien suppressed a laugh. The mist concealed him, and better still, Ceara would suffer with its effects and forget she ever felt anything here. He'd keep the secret of the underground tunnels a while longer.

He stumbled away, knowing he would have to find way to stop his sister sooner rather than later.

CHAPTER 13

"Any sign of the wyvern?" Ann asked as she appeared in the forest Jax had called her to in a flash of light. After being with the lykaes a few days, they still hadn't had much luck finding anything—until Jax had finally spotted a wyvern. She'd been annoyed at having to leave the vault again, she needed to focus on saving Xander.

Jax swooped down beside her and shifted back into human form. "Those things fly a lot faster than I can. I lost it." He rubbed the back of his bald head. "It disappeared before I had a chance to see where it went."

"I couldn't track it either." Ceara sighed. "Dragons are beyond my powers."

"There's a lot more going on here than meets the eye," Ann replied. She paused, wondering how much to tell them. "Lia told me someone sent Ed through the mist when he was a boy, and my father bound us together." She held up her hand when Ceara and Jax opened their mouths to speak. "No, I don't know why."

"I followed the elves again. They disappeared into a giant tree," Jax explained.

"Tree?" Ceara scoffed. "How do you know they're elves?"

"They have pointed ears, and the elves in Asral used to live near trees too."

"I'm going for a closer look. Remember, we work for the resistance and we've been tracking demons and creatures who came through the mist. Don't mention we're rogues, or Ed."

"Speaking of wolfy, if you're bound, does that mean you're really married?"

Ann pushed through the trees as the giant green leaves slapped her face. In truth, she didn't know what it meant, nor was it a pressing concern. Helping Ed and stopping Urien doing whatever he was up to was much more important.

"No, I doubt my father would have forced me into marriage," Ann finally answered. "It means Ed and I are linked, that's all."

"A bond means marriage—it's like a soul bond," Ceara said.

"That would explain a lot," Jax agreed. "You and Ed have always been connected."

"Jax, shift and go keep an eye on things above," Ann said. "We have no idea what we'll be walking into once we reach Mirkwood."

Ann scanned the area with her mind. The Erthea lines running through the ground hummed with energy.

Jax shifted back into his crow form and flew off ahead of them.

The land here seemed potent with magic. Before the dark times that had almost wiped Erthea out, Lulrien had been a bustling place from what she'd read in the ancient texts.

"You should find out what this bond between you and wolfy is," Ceara remarked.

"Later." Ann's senses prickled as something moved through the air.

Ann, I see a dragon, Jax called.

Follow it. Ann scanned the skies but saw nothing. She raised her hand, using the air current to scan the area further.

It's heading off in the opposite direction.

Hurry up and fly after it, Ceara said.

Ann ran, pushing her way through the dense trees.

Ceara stumbled behind her. "We'll never catch up with it this way."

"I'll transport us." Ann said.

Ceara shook her head. "No, someone needs to find out more about Ranelle's people. I'll do that, you track the dragon."

She frowned. "Are you sure?"

"Yes, I want to know more about them. They are hiding something too, and my powers work on them."

"Be careful." Light flashed around Ann as her body turned into glowing blue orbs. She shot skyward. Moving like this instead of from one place to another took more energy.

She spotted Jax and hurried toward him. In the distance, a dark, winged creature glided across the top of the trees. It didn't look as big as the dragon they'd encountered back at Trewa. Its bat-like wings flapped as it skimmed over the giant blue trees.

I don't know how long I can keep up with this thing, Jax squawked.

Ann reached out, her hand becoming whole once more as she grabbed hold of him. Jax's body turned into orbs as well.

Whoa, I don't like this, Jax protested. *Let me go. I can fly.*

Just hold still and hang on. I'll get us to that damn thing. After a month of tracking dragons on and off, she wasn't about to let this one get away. The orbs shot after the dragon and got on its tail.

This dragon didn't fly smoothly or gracefully. Its flying seemed haphazard, and it too, wore a metal collar with glowing runes, just as the one they had encountered before had.

Ann followed it miles over the forest. The dragon's wings kept skimming the trees. She didn't know how much distance they'd travelled and guessed it must've been many leagues.

I think it might be hurt, Jax remarked.

Ann moved closer to it. Her body ached from being incorporeal for so long. *Maybe we need to entice it down.*

Be my guest. I'm not getting fried, Jax replied.

As if on cue, the dragon swung its head around and sent a column of fire shooting straight at them. Ann ducked, forcing her glowing orbs to go into the neutral plane, but it was too late. The fire struck like a bolt of lightning.

Jax slipped from her grasp and fell.

Ann's body reformed as she began her descent into freefall, and Jax yelled out as he shifted into human form, rolling head over backside as he continued to fall.

Ann called on her magic, but her body refused to transport out again. The ground reached for her, and branches hit and stabbed her as she descended.

The dragon surged after them. Its jaws snapped at her, getting ever closer.

Ed! she screamed. The ground was about to swallow her up.

Strong arms caught hold of her as the landing knocked the air from her lungs.

"You alright?" Ed touched her cheek.

"I am…" She gasped. "Dragon!"

The dragon lunged toward them again.

Ed launched himself out of the way as Jax crashed to the ground, and the dragon sent out another column of fire straight at them. He kept hold of Ann with one arm, using his free hand to deflect the flames.

"Pléascadh dóiteáin." Ann chanted words of power to summon fire.

She didn't have the energy to use her own fire power, but she could summon it with a spell. It exploded on the ground in front of them, but the dragon just roared in fury. "I guess druid fire doesn't affect dragons," she murmured.

159

"It's a wyvern," Ed corrected, deflecting another blast.

Ann glanced toward Jax he lay on the ground, unmoving. Light flashed over him—a sign of his stone magic. *Jax, you okay?*

He leapt up and stepped in front of them, the flames surged against his skin. Ann raised a hand to shield her face as the fiery heat washed over them. *Do something. I can't hold it back for long,* Jax told them.

Ann gripped Ed's hand. *Maybe we can use our powers together to—*

"No, we're not killing it." Ed set her down and moved past Jax. Ann stumbled as her legs almost gave out.

What in the spirits' names is he doing? Jax demanded.

Ed kept his hand raised, ready to deflect more flames. His eyes flashed with emerald light.

The wyvern circled him in an angry dance.

Jax moved to Ann's side. "Are you hurt?" he whispered.

She grabbed his arm for support. "I'll live. I think he's communicating with it—or trying to." Ed had talked to the other wyvern that they had encountered at Trewa. He said he'd felt a connection to it, but had no idea why.

Ed's eyes flashed brighter. "I know you're hurting," he said. "But we won't harm you."

The wyvern reared up on its hind legs, about to charge. It let out a roar, then crashed to the ground. The earth beneath them trembled from the force.

The beast moaned, and Ed moved over to it.

"It's injured," Ann said as she joined him, noting the deep gashes on its back.

"It's been tortured. It wanted to escape, I can sense it." Ed touched the wyvern's head. "Shh, it's alright. You're safe with us."

The creature snorted out hot air.

"Poor beast," Jax said. "It's been shackled. Look at the marks on its legs."

Sure enough, deep red marks bloomed over the wyvern's front and back legs.

Light flared between Ed's fingers as he ran his hands over the dragon's side.

"You're using magic again," Jax gasped.

"I still have magic, even after I turned into a lykae," Ed muttered.

Warm light washed over the wyvern.

Overseer magic. Ann had done some digging through her father's numerous books and found some information on overseers. They had healing abilities too.

The wyvern let out a mournful wail.

"It's dying." Ed drew back. "My magic won't be enough."

Pain stabbed through Ann's chest—Ed's pain. *Looks like that bond is making itself known,* Ann thought.

She put a hand on his shoulder. "I'm sorry, Ed."

"Ask it where it came from," Jax suggested. "Maybe we can figure out where Urien is getting them."

Ed closed his eyes, touching the beast's head.

"How can he communicate with dragons?" Jax hissed. "It's not natural."

Ann shrugged. She couldn't explain it either. Not much was known about wyverns. They had disappeared centuries ago, and all magic related to them had become forgotten. Even druid lore didn't say much about them.

"Maybe his lykae side can understand them," she said.

Or maybe it's because he's an overseer.

The wyvern let out a final moan, then its eyes closed.

Ed drew back. "Someone tortured it, forced it to do things." His fists clenched. "I couldn't see who it was, but I know it must've been connected to Urien. Damn him!" A burst of light shot from his hand, exploding the tree behind them.

Jax stared wide-eyed. "Okay, you're a lot more powerful now than you used to be, brother." He glanced at Ann, giving her a questioning look.

She shrugged again. It wasn't her place to reveal Ed's overseer nature. He'd tell his brother when and if he was ready.

She didn't need a bond to feel his anger and sadness. She did the only thing she could and wrapped her arms around him. "I'm so sorry."

Ed tensed for a moment, then drew her close.

"What are we going to do with it?" Jax asked. "Hardly seems right to leave it out here."

The runes on the wyvern's collar bloomed with angry red light. It enveloped the creature's body, and what remained of the beast melted away.

Ann let go of Ed. "Damn, I could have used that collar to track whoever trapped the wyverns."

CHAPTER 14

Ed moved through the village in search of Lia. She seemed to be one of the few people glad to have him back. He didn't know what he'd expected coming back here, but hostility wasn't one of them. He felt like in an outcast—alien, even. He was so different from them.

Regardless, Ed knew he had to stay, learn control, and find out why someone thought he could help these people. He'd wanted to question Lucien about being an overseer—if anyone would know about it, it would be him—but Lucien despised even the thought of magic, so Ed had decided against it. Perhaps Lia would know more.

Ed found his aunt in her own hut. The dirt floor had a rag rug covering it, and a large pot bubbled over the fire in the corner of the room. Lia's hut was round and made from mud bricks, unlike the wooden huts in the rest of the village.

"Rohn," Lia smiled as he walked in. "Come in."

"Ann said you wanted to see me. I prefer being called Edward; my family call me Ed."

Lia's dark eyes widened, and she flinched when he said the word 'family'. "Of course, Rohn...I mean, Edward." She shook her head. "It will take time for us all to adjust to your return. You were a boy when you left us." She stirred the pot, and Ed winced at the sharp scent of something foul. "I'm glad you found happiness with your wife."

"She's not my wife—not in the lykae sense, is she?" Ed leaned back against the table and sighed. "Why did you send me away?"

Lia's hand went to her mouth. "The druid told you?"

"She didn't have to. Ann and I are connected. I overheard what you said to her." He crossed his arms. "Why didn't you want me to grow up here?"

His aunt looked away, avoiding his gaze. "Because war was brewing between us and the woodland folk."

"There's more to it than that," Ed remarked. He hesitated. Should he reveal his dream to her? He had no idea how much she knew. Although Lia seemed trustworthy, he didn't want to risk exposure. "Does it have anything to do with me being an overseer?"

Lia dropped the spoon she'd been holding. "Rohn, don't ever say that word here," she hissed. "Nothing good can come of it. You'd be wise to keep your magic to yourself as well. Our people are not like the Magickind in the northern realm, such words will get you into trouble."

Ed frowned. "Why? Is it true?" He needed answers, and she might be one of the few people able to give them to him.

"I…don't know anything about that." Lia's heart rate picked up, and beads of sweat formed on her brow, both key signs of deception.

Can I trust anyone here? He turned to go.

"Wait." Lia touched his arm. "I asked you here so I can help. Meditation will calm your inner beast."

Ed scoffed at that. "I already know how to meditate. The druids taught me."

"Our meditation will be different from theirs. That's why I'm brewing this mixture."

"To choke us to death?" He covered his nose. The stench smelt like charcoal and mercury.

Lia chuckled. "No. The smell allows us to connect with our beasts. Lucien and most of the pack may dismiss it, but I'm a firm believer in the old traditions." Lia pulled the rug aside and sat down on the uncovered ground. "Come, let's begin."

His beast growled inside the cage of his mind. It didn't want to sit and meditate, it wanted answers now. He still had so many unanswered questions. He had thought he'd get answers by coming here, yet it had only raised more questions so far.

She smiled. "Sit. You need to learn to control your beast, or you risk losing yourself to the rage like you did this morning. This can't be ignored." Lia patted the ground beside her. "Being connected to the land helps."

Ed sat cross-legged beside her. He fidgeted. How would meditation help his beast, or get him the answers he needed?

"Rohn, close your eyes and calm your mind."

Ed gritted his teeth. He didn't want to calm his mind. He wondered when he'd become so impatient, Ann had always been the impatient one. He liked to be calm, collected, and not to rush into things. His training as one of the Black had taught him that.

He let out a breath. "I need answers."

"Connecting with your true self can give them to you."

Ed closed his eyes. How could his beast give him answers? It might have answered things before, but he doubted it would help now. "Now what?"

"Open your mind. Take a deep breath."

Ed's nose wrinkled as the stench grew. *How can this help? It's awful.*

His beast growled, demanding to be let out. It wanted to run, to be free.

Ed ignored it and jumped as the ground beneath him vibrated. "What's happening?" he growled.

"You are forcing your beast back. You must let it out in order to—"

"I can't do that." Ed opened his eyes and gaped at his aunt. "You saw how I lost control this morning." He didn't want to risk losing control again, Ann wasn't here to help him rein the beast back in.

"The beast is part of who you are. You—"

"I accept what I am," he snapped.

Ann and the others had spent months convincing him to accept his lykae nature. When he'd first turned, he'd thought it was a curse and wanted nothing more than to get rid of it. He did accept it now, but it felt damned hard to control.

"All lykaes are taught to do this. You too must master control."

Ed sighed and shut his eyes. The beast's ever-present self felt stronger as he did. He reluctantly forced himself to relax and relinquish control. The beast emerged but didn't force him to shift as it usually did. Ed relaxed, letting the vibrations pulse through his body. He guessed this must be what Ann felt when she connected to the earth lines and the rest of Erthea. He'd always envied that connection she had as a druid. It was something he'd never thought he would possess.

More thoughts raced through his mind. Would this help? Could he make a difference here because of it?

"Relax," Lia said, her voice gentle and soothing. "The beast and you are part of each other. You may treat it as a separate being, but you are one and the same."

"War is brewing in your homeland," the voice from his dream whispered. *"You must go there and forge peace between them."*

How? Ed wondered. *Who sent me here? What do they want me to do?*

He remembered the conversation he had listened in on between Ann and Lia, unbeknownst to Ann. Why did Lia send him away? There might be a lot of animosity between the lykaes and Ranelle's people, but Caselhelm hadn't been without its troubles either. *"Your father came here,"* Lia had said to Ann.

Ed's mind drifted as the vibrations continued to pulse through his body.

A man with long blonde hair rode into the village on a huge black stallion.

Ed blinked. He'd never seen a beast so large. Power rolled off the man in impalpable waves like fire crackling through the air.

Spirits, that's Darius!

The archdruid looked very different from the lykaes and other Magickind in Lulrien. People here usually had dark hair, but Darius' blonde hair and piercing blue eyes stood out as he dismounted from his stallion.

Lucien came out of his hut and nodded to the archdruid. "I'm surprised to see you here," the alpha remarked.

"We need to talk," Darius said. "Can we go somewhere more private?"

Lucien placed his hand on Ed's shoulder. "This is my son, Rohn."

Light flashed as a girl appeared at Darius' side. With her mop of wavy blonde hair and her father's eyes, there was no mistaking Ann even at this young age. She looked as Ed remembered her when they met on Trin. They had both been around the same age then.

Darius's eyes widened. "She's not supposed to be here," he muttered. "Rhiannon, you—" He sighed and caught hold of her as she swayed on her feet.

Darius picked her up. "I told you not to use magic. It weakens you."

Darius lowered his voice. "Lucien, this is the light of my life, my daughter Rhiannon."

Ed blinked as the memory faded. So, they *had* met before. "Lia, do you know why Darius came here all those years ago?"

Lia shook her head. "I presume you talked to your father about our curse?"

"He mentioned it, yes."

"Every full moon, we're forced into our beast forms. The rage becomes harder to control. You must know that, you are bound to the moon too."

Ed frowned. The beast did become much harder to control during the night of the full moon, along with the primal rage. "I know that. The full moon is… hard," he admitted.

"That's one thing none of us can control."

Ed sighed and rose to his feet. "How long will it take for me to learn full control?"

Lia got up and returned to stirring her pot of foul-smelling brew. "I can't answer that. It's different for every lykae."

As long as I have Ann, I don't have to worry.

CHAPTER 15

Ann let out a scream of frustration as her spell fell apart. She stared at the soul removal spell she'd created over five years earlier, on the night Urien had murdered her parents.

Xander insisted the only way to get rid of Urien was to remove Darius' spell. So far, she had found nothing in the vault with any mention of it. That didn't surprise her, Darius never made it easy for her to find things.

Ann rubbed her eyes. She'd been in here for almost three hours—sneaking out during the night was the only way to get around without the lykaes noticing her absence.

She picked up another book. It read: Lykaes: Fierce and formidable creatures that can change into beasts. Known as one of the most feared races to exist since before the dark times.

Funny how this is only appearing now. Typical. Papa always used to say answers would come when needed, not before.

She read on: The lykaes are a proud, noble race, possessing strength, incredible speed, and magic from Erthea itself.

"Magic from Erthea itself," Ann murmured. "Strange, given how Lucien claims they have no magic." Reading about the lykaes had distracted her for a while at least.

She turned her attention back to a knife that had blood on it. She'd figured using an object would be a good practice target for her spell.

She muttered more words of power. *"Ní raibh an ceangal faoi cheangal anois."*

Light flashed over the dagger, then nothing.

"Damn it, Papa. What did you do?" She rose from the floor and pulled down another book from the shelves. This one was smaller than the other heavy tomes scattered over the floor. It had no title on the spine, so she guessed it might be a journal. Darius had enjoyed writing down his knowledge and the events in his life, but so far, most of it had been mindless nonsense that talked about day-to-day goings-on. Nothing helpful.

Ann flipped the book open and skimmed through. Her eyes stopped on something about binding spells, noticing it was written in

Darius' handwriting. There was no mistaking her father's sprawling penmanship.

Ann froze. Two souls can be bound together if they are both half of the same whole. Most bonds occur through a hand fasting, but some can be bound for…

Warmth flooded through her as she felt Ed blur into the vault. She jumped as he appeared beside her. The book fell from her hand and crashed to the floor with a thump. "Do you have to do that?" she grumbled as she bent to retrieve the book. "You could knock, or walk in."

Ed shrugged. "Sorry, habit." His long hair framed his handsome face. "What are you doing?"

"Trying to find something to stop Urien. That hasn't changed because we are staying with the lykaes." She put the book back on the table. "You were asleep."

"I missed you. It's becoming hard to sleep when you're not there."

"Sorry I woke you." She rested her head against his chest.

"I'm used to it by now." Ed slipped his arms around her.

It felt good to hold onto him. It didn't matter if she held on too long anymore. "Hey, don't overseers have access to magical knowledge?"

"Some, yes. The rest we learn."

"Well, oh mighty overseer, tell me how to break my father's spell." She grinned up at him. "He gave you the knowledge the night he was killed. What did he tell you about the spell?"

"Not much. He said it'd protect you and stop you and your siblings from killing each other."

"What else?"

Ed shook his head. "He didn't show me what the spell is made of, he told me how to get you out of the palace and somewhere safe."

Ann pulled back. "Nothing I try is working. I doubt my father wanted me to know how he cast it." She pushed her hair off her face. "All spells are made up of elements, like words and intentions. More complex spells have more complicated elements, but I can't find anything. I can't even bring the spell to the surface. It must mark my body or soul in some way."

"We'll figure it out."

"You've been saying that for weeks," she huffed.

"I'm not having much luck figuring out why I was sent to Lulrien either," Ed said. "Too bad Ceara couldn't get close to that tree."

Ann snorted. "Ceara won't let a few guards stop her." She grabbed a different book. "Want to help me research?"

"I have a better idea. Maybe I can get the spell to show up."

She frowned. "How?"

"Overseer magic. But it'd be better if you were naked."

She laughed and gave him a shove. "What happened to slow?"

Ed chuckled. "I'm only being honest."

"Right," she said, unconvinced. "Do it."

Ed chanted unfamiliar words of power that sounded nothing like druid magic.

Orbs of glowing white light sparkled over Ann's body, and her skin tingled. The orbs dispersed, revealing glowing blue lines that crept up her arms, along with other symbols. They were marks she'd acquired during her training, and showed how she'd worked her way up to being a full druid.

"These are all druid signs. I think Papa's spell would be different." She pulled up the hem of her sleep shirt and yanked it over her head. Lines covered her torso and chest. They were black and zigzagging with runes. "I don't recognise these marks. What are they?"

Ed frowned. "My guess would be elder magic. Something is telling me overseers are only taught to recognise it, not use it."

"I need to record these marks."

Ed picked up his pack from the floor and fumbled through it. He pulled out a small white crystal. "Jax gave me this. He charged it to capture energy." The stone hummed with power, and a beam of light shone over her chest as the stone's power roamed over her. "There, the spell is recorded."

Ann noticed another mark underneath the vines covering her chest. This one flashed blue then purple, and was in the shape of a star. It sat close to her heart. "What's this?" She motioned to the mark. "It's not a druid symbol."

The vines and blackness of her father's spell felt strongest, bound to her like a tight bodice in an endless network of knots that had no end. It would take time to lift such a powerful spell. The vines prickled against her bare skin, cold and harsh. This star mark felt warm—comforting, almost.

Ed brushed his fingers over the mark. "By the spirits," he breathed. "It's the mark of our bond."

Her cheeks flushed. "Is it a full bond, then?"

"Yes, it's a heart bond. That must be why we've been picking up on each other's emotions." Ed caressed her cheek. "How do you feel about that?"

She shrugged. "I don't know."

His touch sent a rush of desire through her. Ann pulled him close and kissed him, hard. She wanted—needed—to be close to him. She moaned as his tongue flicked against hers.

Ed picked her up, and she wrapped her legs around his waist. Ed's eyes blazed bright emerald and he pulled back, almost dropping her. "I am—"

Ann stumbled and grabbed her fallen shirt. "You won't hurt me." She pulled it back on.

Ed shook his head. "You don't know that. I've not been with anyone since I've changed."

"Good, you should only be with me anyway," she grinned.

Ed didn't return her smile. "What if we can't be together physically?"

"Now isn't the right time anyway." She ran her fingers over the mark. "I wonder why my father bound us together."

"Maybe he knew we were meant for each other." Ed drew her back into his arms.

A pang of fear stabbed her heart. "You don't think it's just the bond drawing us together, do you?"

"No, I've always wanted you." Ed kissed the top of her forehead. "Bonds don't form unless they're meant to—that much I do know."

She sighed and rested her head against his shoulder. "The bond doesn't bother me. It feels good—right, even." She shivered. "Papa's spell doesn't. He went against the laws of nature itself. I want it gone."

Ed brushed her hair off her face. "I know, but part of me is glad you're protected from death."

Ann shook her head. "It's wrong. Everyone has to die. It's the natural order of things."

"We'll figure it out. At least we've figured out what the spell looks like."

It was a start, but what would it take to undo the spell that protected her from death?

Ann strolled through the lykae village with Ceara at her side. Ed had gone off to hunt with Marcus, so she thought she'd to talk to Lia again.

Ceara coughed. "Spirits, my head hurts."

Ann touched Ceara's forehead. "You feel warm. Maybe you're sick."

Ceara brushed her off. "Am not, I'll be fine. I'm going to investigate that tree again later."

"Ranelle's guards have stopped you twice now. Maybe Jax—"

"Jax doesn't have my powers. I *will* figure out what they're up to." Ceara yawned.

"Maybe you should get some rest."

Ceara waved a hand in dismissal. "Forget that, what's happening with you and wolfy?"

Ann suppressed a sigh. "We're working on it."

Ceara grinned. "See, you *are* letting someone through that wall around your heart."

Ann rolled her eyes. "There's no wall. Maybe I should cast a spell on you to ward off sickness."

"No, I'll live," Ceara scoffed. "Listen, Ed isn't like your father, and you're not your mother either."

"What do my parents have to do with anything?" Ann crossed her arms.

"Not every relationship is destined to fail."

Ann spotted Lia surrounded by several children running around her.

Ceara slumped onto a log, and the children all stared at Ann and Ceara, ceasing all activity.

"We're not going to eat anyone," Ceara muttered.

"Go on. Play," Lia urged the children, then moved over to Ann.

A dark-haired boy came up to Ann. "Do you have magic?"

She nodded, unsure what to say given how wary everyone had been of her.

"Can I see it?"

Ann hesitated and looked to Lia, who nodded. She raised her hand, and smoke rose up from a nearby fire and billowed around them. It shifted into the shape of a galloping horse.

The boy laughed, and all the other children gathered around to watch.

"Alpha says magic is bad," said another boy.

Ann shook her head. "Magic is all around us. It's not good or bad itself, it's how a person chooses to use it that makes it good or bad. There's magic in everything on Erthea."

"What's Erthea?" a blonde-haired girl asked.

"Erthea is our world, the earth beneath our feet and the sky above us."

You really sound like the archdruid now, Ceara remarked.

I'm only stating a fact.

Be careful. Papa Wolf despises magic. He could throw us out.

I'm not leaving Ed, no matter what Lucien says or does.

"Show us some more magic," another boy asked.

Ann hesitated. How much magic did she dare use here? She'd shielded herself, but that didn't mean she wanted to antagonise Lucien further.

"Boilgeoga."

Bubbles of glowing light danced around the children, making them squeal in delight. They ran around and chased them.

A boy who looked to be about ten tugged on Ann's arm. "Show me the magic in the earth. If it's there, why can't we see it?"

Ann smiled and ran her hand over the ground. A glowing vein of white energy appeared as the earth line became visible.

The boy reached out to touch it.

"Careful," Ann warned. "It might give you a shock."

"Lia, why can't we use magic?" The boy asked.

Lia hesitated before answering, "Not all races can wield such power."

"But Rohn uses magic. I saw him."

"Run along now, Noland," Lia said.

Jessa stormed over, glared at Ann when she spotted the bubbles. "You'd better not hurt our younglings," she hissed.

"It's only a little harmless fun," Ann said.

"Harmless? Ha! I've seen what you druids can do," Jessa spat. "You shouldn't be here. You and Rohn aren't bound in our ways."

"How come Ed can use magic then?" Ceara demanded. "Lykaes must have some magical talent."

Jessa fell silent at that.

"Shouldn't you be off hunting lupines?" Ann retorted. She didn't know why Jessa's hatred of her seemed to run so deep. Was it because she was a druid, or Ed's k'ia?

"Lykaes were said to possess magic once, but we lost the ability to use it centuries ago," Lia spoke up. "Jessa, show some respect. Ann is still Rohn's k'ia."

Jessa gave a derisive snort. "She can't be. No lykae's ever bonded with someone not of our race," she snapped. "It's a good thing you can't have children at least/ I'd hate to have mewling brats running around with your tainted blood."

Ann's eyes narrowed. "What does that mean?"

Jessa gave her a cold smile. "Lykaes can only breed with other lykaes. It's impossible for any other race to bear lykae children. And it's Rohn's duty to sire the next alpha. You are giving him a death sentence as long as he is bound to you."

All colour drained from Ann's face.

"Jessa," Lia snapped.

"What? Maybe she'll see she has no future with Rohn."

"I couldn't imagine bringing a child into this world with all the evil in it anyway," Ann spoke up. "Like I said, I'm not leaving him."

"You're more selfish than I thought, then."

Ceara jumped up. "Back off, woman. There's nothing worse than a bitch trying to steal someone else's man."

Jessa snarled, her eyes flashing deep amber.

"Enough." Lia stepped between them. "Jessa, leave now."

Jessa's eyes burned into Lia. "You're a fool for allowing Rohn to stay with her. A druid, no less. Have you forgotten what the archdruid did to our people?"

"Centuries have passed since then. Go, return to the hunt," Lia ordered.

Ann unclasped her leather tunic, exposing the star mark. "For the record, I am *truly* bound to him."

Jessa's eyes widened in horror, and she hurried away.

Lia touched Ann's shoulder. "I'm sorry for that."

Ann brushed her off. "Don't be."

Even here, I can't hide who or what I am.

CHAPTER 16

After a couple weeks of living with the lykaes, Ed decided it was time to build his own hut—or cabin, as he liked to call it. He scouted around the area for a spot to start building. After gathering up a handful of logs, he drew runes, and the logs welded themselves together.

No one but Lia and Jessa seemed to be glad to have him there, and even Lucien seemed disappointed. He hated feeling like an outcast. He might be a lykae, but he didn't act or think as they did. He hadn't fit in among the druids either, but they had been kind to the orphan boy who'd been stronger and faster than them.

"You're building your home outside the village," Lia remarked as she came over.

"Yeah well, it seemed fitting. No one wants me there," he remarked.

"It will take time. You are…different in your ways and beliefs."

"It's not that, they're all worried I'll lose control and turn into a lupine," he remarked. "I can sense it. Even Lucien acts fearful around me. I came to learn control. If you can't show me how to control my beast, then I have no reason to stay."

He turned to her. She'd been a mother to him once, just as Flora had, and he felt he could trust her. "I don't feel like I belong here. Even as a boy, I know I craved something more." He paused. "You still won't tell me anything about my mother, will you?" Ed asked, changing the subject. "Who was she?"

Lia shook her head. "It's not my story to tell, but I know she loved you very much. I'll see you at the house later. We can meditate together and work on your control."

Ed grunted as she walked off. Between meditation and building the cabin, he felt bored. He was a warrior, he needed action. To be doing something other than sitting around. Marcus didn't want to let him hunt with the rest of the pack. He didn't trust him either.

"Rohn?" a familiar voice called.

Jessa. He caught her familiar scent and winced, trying not to sigh.

He liked her well enough. She'd been helping him to settle in, but he knew she wanted more from him. More than he could ever give her.

"Marcus and I are about to go and hunt. One of our scouts caught sight of woodland folk camped on our border," she said. "Are you coming?"

Ed tossed the log aside. "Marcus doesn't want me around. I don't want to cause trouble."

"Rohn, you're stronger than he is. You should take your rightful place as first prime."

First prime was the alpha's second, next in line to lead the pack if the alpha died or they challenged Lucien for the right to lead.

He did sigh then. "Jessa, I have no desire to be first prime. I'm only here to—"

Her eyes flashed amber. "No one can live between two worlds. Sooner or later you'll have to choose one."

"I already have. My place is with—"

"The druid," she spat. "How can you desire a woman like her? I know she isn't your wife, not really."

His eyes narrowed. "How could you know that?"

She shrugged. "I did some asking around during the meeting of the leaders. It wasn't hard to find out about the archdruid and her faithful bodyguard."

"She's not the archdruid, she's just a druid. I served the old archdruid for a long time, but not anymore." He knew the lie sounded unconvincing. "Let's go, shall we?" Ed grabbed his shirt and yanked it on. Maybe a hunt would ease some of his beast's tension.

Marcus growled at him as he and Jessa approached. "He's not coming with us."

"I'm part of this pack too. You might be better at tracking, but I'm faster." Ed raised his chin.

"He is Lucien's son," Jessa pointed out.

"And I'm the first prime," Marcus retorted. "I say who goes with me and who doesn't."

"Well, if I screw up and lose control, you can laugh about it later." Ed crossed his arms. He wasn't about to give in. If a hunt helped him to learn to control his beast side more, then he'd do it. The sooner he learnt to control this, the sooner he could get back to Ann and the others.

Marcus scowled. "Fine, keep up." He blurred away.

The wind whipped past as Ed blurred too, stopping in front of Marcus and leaning against a blue wood tree. "Listen, I'm not here to take your place," Ed told him. "I just want to learn control, then I'll be gone."

"Back to your druid." Marcus's lip curled. "You don't know how lucky you are to be the son of the alpha. How can you throw that away?"

"You seem to have done pretty well for yourself. Lucien treated you like his son after I disappeared," Ed said. "I'm not going to take that from you."

"You already are. Lucien will make *you* his first prime. Even Jessa is thrilled to have you back." Marcus glared at her as she blurred in beside them.

Ed sighed. "How often do Ranelle's people sneak over and camp on this side of the border?"

"They come over whenever they feel like it," Marcus growled. "We should rip them apart while we can."

"Lucien told us to observe," Jessa said. "Not attack."

"Our peace with them won't last much longer." Marcus shifted, his eyes burning hot amber.

Ed shifted too, letting the beast have control over his body. *Must run,* the beast thought.

Ed clenched his fists. *No, we're observing.*

The beast let out a low growl.

"Quiet," Marcus hissed. "They will sense us if we're not careful."

The three of them blurred, ducking behind the blue trees as they went.

Ed sniffed and caught the scent of the woodland folk. He heard four heartbeats close by.

Marcus blurred closer. "Three outlanders, and someone else with them."

Ed edged closer, the soles of his boots making no noise as he moved. "Who is it?"

"I can't say. I think it's a prisoner. I see a cage," Jessa replied from the opposite side of the trees.

"Jessa and I will attack. Rohn, you try to help the prisoner. If it's another outlander, kill them."

Ed hesitated. He never killed just for the sake of it.

"Rohn?" Marcus hissed.

He gave a curt nod and stalked along the treeline. His beast felt a rush of excitement as blood pounded through his ears. It was excited by the thrill of the hunt, the need to kill.

Keep it together, he told his beast. *We can't lose control here.*

Despite days of practising meditation and communicating with his inner beast, none of it had helped so far.

Hunt, the beast thought. *Prey.*

Ed rolled his eyes if he could have.

Three outlander men stood around a metal cage. They all had the same reddish gold auburn hair as the men Ed had seen before. Another man sat hunched over inside the cage. He had dark hair, but Ed couldn't see him clearly enough to make out what he looked like.

"He's lykae," Ed hissed to the others.

"He can't be. I don't recognise him, or his scent," Marcus replied. "I have the best nose in the pack. I would know if it was one of our people."

"If he is one of us, we need to help him."

Marcus growled. "Lucien wants us to keep the peace with those pointy-eared bastards. We should leave."

"Lucien wouldn't want us to leave a fallen brother among the enemy, would he?" Ed demanded. "We can't leave. No one should be caged like a fucking animal."

Marcus' eyes gleamed. "You're right. Jessa, with me. Rohn, get him out of there. You're the fastest."

Ed blurred toward the cage as Marcus and Jessa flew at two outlanders. Another outlander notched his bow and sent arrows whizzing through the air.

Ed dodged them, hearing them hiss past him as he blurred. He spun, lunging at the outlander. The outlander jumped and backflipped out of the way. The man landed, spun, and came at Ed with a short sword. Ed blurred, dodging the oncoming arrow, and punched the elf, sending him crashing to the ground.

Marcus grappled with his attacker, and Jessa took off as her outlander fled.

Ed's outlander sprang up, blood dripping down his face from where Ed had struck him.

Marcus howled as his elf jabbed him with a metal rod that sparked with static.

Ed dodged another blow, blurred and lunged for Marcus' attacker, yanking the elf away from his cousin.

The other elf fired arrows toward Ed.

Ed ducked as his beast took full control and caught hold of the arrows, hurling both at the elf and hitting him in the chest.

Marcus cried out as the second elf jabbed him in the neck.

Ed growled, yanking the elf off of his feet. He caught hold of the rod, staring at it as he held it in his other hand.

"This is a Gliss weapon," the beast's voice came out low and guttural. "Where did you get it?"

"I'll tell you nothing, you filthy beast," the elf snapped.

"Kill him, Rohn. They're trespassing on our lands and torturing one of our brothers," Marcus growled. "Kill him."

The beast wanted to do just that. It wanted to rip the elf apart, to taste its blood.

Ed fought for greater control. "Where did you get this?"

He glanced at the rod. All Gliss marked their weapons—Ceara had a triquetra symbol on hers—but this had no marks.

The elf drew a knife and bore down on Ed, about to strike.

In one swift move, Ed snapped the elf's neck.

"Jessa?" Marcus called.

A scream rang out in the distance.

"I'll go," Ed said. "Help our brother."

He blurred away, heart pounding as he ran.

Jessa lay on the ground, the elf dead and bloody beside her.

"What happened?" he asked. "You alright?"

Jessa blinked, looking dazed.

"Jessa? Are you okay?" Ed knelt, fighting to keep control of his beast as it caught the scent of blood.

Her lips curved into a smile. "I'm fine." She sat up, grabbed hold of him, and almost kissed him.

Ed's beast retreated at once. His fangs and claws retracted as he gasped and pulled away. "I'm…what are you doing?" He shoved her away when she reached for him again.

"You came to save me."

"I came to make sure you're alright," he insisted.

He heard another shout. His eyes burned emerald as the smell of more blood carried on the air. "Marcus."

He gave Jessa a hand up and shot back toward Marcus, who stood, clawing and slashing at the now-freed prisoner.

The other lykae's eyes burned blood red and anger rolled off him.

Primal rage, Ed realised. He'd seen the same in the rogue lykae who he'd fought before he and the others had crossed through the mists.

"Lupine," Jessa growled. "Rohn, be careful. Lupines are stronger and faster than us." Her fangs came out, and the lupine snarled, knocking Marcus to the ground.

Marcus sprang back up, and the three of them surrounded the lupine.

Ed let his beast take full control. He felt primal rage begin to heat his own blood, but he fought it back.

"I'll grant you a quick death if you surrender," Marcus said.

The lupine laughed. "You will die." He lunged at Marcus, who blocked his first blow.

Another outlander appeared and fired arrows.

Jessa blurred and leapt at him, and Ed grabbed the lupine, biting into the man's neck then ripping his head off.

Marcus lay on the ground, his breathing ragged as blood seeped down his chest.

"Shit, Marcus." Ed shifted back, forcing the beast back into the cage of his mind.

"You saved me," Marcus gasped. "You risked yourself for me."

"That's what brothers do," Ed replied. "What can I do? Do you need blood?"

"No. I can't take blood, or I risk losing myself to the rage," Marcus said. "I'll have to shift and let my beast have complete control. Rohn, if I can't turn back—"

"You will." Ed gripped his arm.

Marcus screamed and his eyes burned hot amber. Fur covered his body as it shifted into that of a true beast.

Ed backed away, stunned.

"All the outlanders are gone," Jessa called as she reappeared. "Oh, shit."

"He said he had to shift to heal."

"Shifting into our full beast forms can be as dangerous as feeding on blood," she said.

Marcus howled and advanced toward them.

"Marcus, listen to me. I know how strong the beast is when it takes over," Ed said. "But you're stronger. Come back."

Marcus snarled, his fangs elongated.

"Turn back, you bloody idiot," Jessa snapped. "We both know I'm stronger than you. Rohn and I will put you down if we have to."

Marcus doubled over as his body changed back into human form.

"You alright?" Ed touched his shoulder.

Marcus gripped Ed's forearm. "You did a good job today, Rohn. You may not fully accept your beast, but it's who you are."

"I'm starting to accept it more." He glanced down at the dead bodies. "What are we going to do with them? Won't the elves retaliate?"

"Not if they can't find them," Jessa replied. "We'll bury them."

"Wouldn't it be best to keep them? Show their leader what they did?"

Marcus snorted. "She would see this as an act of war. No, we need to get rid of these," he said. "She'd say they were justified in capturing their prisoner because he was a lupine, and lupines are a threat to everyone, since they're consumed by rage."

"Wait, I want to search them first." Ed knelt and examined each body, finding two more rods. "These are weapons used by Gliss. Why would elves have them?"

"Gliss?" Marcus frowned.

"They're women trained in the deadly arts. They have empathic powers and were trained as bodyguards to the Fomorian queen Orla. Now they serve her son, Urien Valeran," Ed explained. "They can deflect magic using their empathic abilities and are masters of torture." He rubbed the back of his neck, remembering the agony they had put him through. "They are the ones who brought my lykae side to the surface again." He frowned at the rod. "Gliss rarely ever travel, which means Urien must be on this side of the mist. I have to talk to my father."

"You think Ranelle's people are joining forces with the demons?" Marcus said. "They may hate us, but they've never —"

"It's the only explanation as to why they have these. No Gliss willingly gives up her weapons. I doubt the elves could even hold them comfortably. They cause the wielder unimaginable pain." He slipped the rod into his belt. "Let's go."

After Ed had spoken with Lucien that night, he had outright refused to do anything about investigating the elves joining with the demons and said he wouldn't attack them unless he had to. They couldn't afford another war. Ed couldn't understand it. Lucien had *seen* a demon yet refused to acknowledge what a threat Urien posed.

Ed slumped next to Marcus around the fire.

"Why can't he admit they're a threat?" Ed grumbled. "Demons are real, and no one—not even on this side of the mist—will be safe from them."

"It will take more than a couple of weapons and your word to get him to do that," Marcus replied. "But I agree with you. The outlanders are growing in number, and our numbers are dwindling, since so many of us were killed in the last war." He gulped down some of his ale. "Sooner or later they'll attack and steal our land out from under us."

"I get the impression he hates Ranelle and her people, so why doesn't he fight them?"

"I think he's disheartened after losing so many of ours. After you disappeared, it broke him inside," Marcus said. "Our fight with the elves was brutal and bloody, and it didn't bring you back. I doubt he got over losing his k'ia either."

"Did you ever meet my mother?"

Marcus shook his head. "I don't think anyone did." he said. "You don't seem keen on testing our women. You could find your k'ia. Aren't our women good enough for you?"

Ed snorted. "My heart is already spoken for."

Marcus laughed. "You're still fixated on the druid? She's beautiful, I'll grant you that, but —"

"What does finding your k'ia feel like?" Ed interrupted. He didn't want to hear about how Ann couldn't be his again.

Marcus sipped his ale. "I wouldn't know."

"The others talk about it, but how are we supposed to know who our k'ia is?"

"You desire your k'ia above all others. You're drawn to them. They're the one person in this world who's made for you." Marcus looked up at Jessa, who danced around the flames, watching Ed.

Ed noticed her staring at him, but he ignored her. He glanced back at Marcus. "Your beast will tell you, right? I mean they can't get it wrong, can they?" he asked.

"You can confuse lust with longing for your k'ia, but deep down, yes, I think you know," Marcus agreed then sighed.

"How long have you been in love with Jessa?"

Marcus shook his head. "She won't have me. I'm not what she'd choose in a k'ia, she told me so herself." He scowled. "You're the one she's meant for."

Ed shook his head. "I can't be hers. Don't tell me otherwise. There's only one person in this world who I'm meant for."

CHAPTER 17

"It's the full moon night," Ed said as he, Ann and the others sat eating dinner together. "Which means all the lykaes will be forced to change."

Ceara coughed. "What does that have to do with us?"

"It means you might want to stay in the vault tonight. Just to be safe." Ed took a bite of his meat. His heart pounded at the thought of the night's coming hunt. He didn't know what to expect yet, but the pack considered it to be a rite of passage for every lykae member.

Ceara coughed again and spat out some of her food.

"You've been coughing a lot lately," Jax remarked.

Ceara scowled at him. "I'm fine. It's a stupid cough," she said. "What progress have we made in getting into the big tree?"

"Nothing yet. Its magic still repels me whenever I try to get close to it," Jax replied. He shoved potatoes into his mouth, then swallowed. "Maybe we should introduce ourselves to the people who live there. That would be easier than all this sneaking around."

Ed shook his head. "No, not unless we have to. I don't trust Ranelle."

Ann sighed. "I'm still working on that damned unbinding spell." She twirled her vegetables around the plate. "I wish my father had written something about it as a reference."

"Why not summon your father and ask him?" Ceara said, then doubled over coughing.

"That cough sounds bad." Ed leaned forward and heard her wheezing. "Maybe I can heal you." He touched her shoulder.

Ceara shoved his hand away. "No, I'll heal myself, thanks. The old-fashioned natural way."

"I've tried summoning him, but he never answers," Ann replied. Ed gave her shoulder a squeeze.

"So, sister, what's the plan for tonight?" Jax asked. "More ogling lykaes?"

"No, we were going to meet the fae too." She shivered. "But I think I'll just get an early night." She pushed her plate of food aside and rose. "See you in the morning."

"I'll go with her back to the vault." Jax picked up his own plate of food and stood up. "See you two later."

"I'll go with them," Ann said to Ed. "I need to spend more time working on the binding spell."

"I'll come with you, then."

Ann arched a brow. "The lykaes were suspicious enough of the time we spent with the fae. You should go, the moon will be up soon." She rose and leaned down to kiss him.

Ed pulled her onto his lap. "I'll miss you tonight."

"You'll have fun hunting, or whatever it is they do." Ann slipped her arms around his neck. "You should go."

Ed kissed her softly at first, then deepened it.

Someone cleared their throat.

They pulled apart to see Lucien standing there. He wore his usual scowl. "Rohn, the moon will be up soon. We should leave."

Ed sighed as Ann made a move to get up. *Why didn't I sense him coming?*

He tightened his arms around her. "The moon won't be up for a while. It's barely dark." Spirits, why did his father have to show up now? He'd hoped to finally spend some time alone with Ann.

"Still, it's your first moon hunt. I wanted to talk to you about it." Lucien crossed his arms.

"Sit and talk then." Ann motioned to the empty chairs.

Lucien's eyes widened. He needed to learn to accept Ann's presence. Ed hoped them spending time together would make his father realise how important Ann was to him.

"I have to—" Lucien protested.

"Sit, I don't bite." Ann gave a nervous laugh.

Maybe I should go.

No, I want you here. He needs to get used to us being together.

Lucien hesitated, then sat down.

"What happens during the hunt?" Ed broke the uneasy silence. Marcus and Jessa had mentioned it, but he didn't know what would happen. "Marcus says it's different from our normal hunts."

Lucien nodded. "Indeed. Every full moon, we change into our true beast forms. We hunt and catch prey."

He glanced at Ann. "It's best if you and your friends remain here. We can't control ourselves during the moon phase."

"It's a powerful time for magic as well," Ann remarked.

Lucien opened his mouth, then closed it. "I'd rather you didn't practice here."

"Oh, don't worry, I won't be here." She flashed him a smile.

"Do you hate magic because of the curse?" Ed asked. He'd been asking Lucien questions whenever he could. Lucien never told him much.

"I…In part, yes. It hurts for us to change every full moon."

"Who cast the curse?" Ann sipped her wine.

Lucien's fists clenched. "The archdruid, of course. The bastard bound us."

"Why?"

"Because he feared our strength, no doubt. At the full moon we become stronger, yes, but it's much harder for us to control ourselves."

"Did you and my mother hunt together?" Ed wanted to know.

Lucien paled. "I…"

"I need to know about her." No one would tell him anything about his mother. It seemed like the pack had never even met her. Yet more secrecy he didn't understand.

"She was… Yes, we hunted," Lucien admitted. He shot to his feet. "Come, the moon is rising. We must go."

"I need to change first." Ed let Ann go and stood. He headed off into the other room to grab a clean shirt out of his pack.

"You still haven't left yet," Lucien said to Ann.

"Don't think you'll scare me away so easily."

Ed fumbled with his clothes as he listened. He smiled.

"I told you, it won't work between you," Lucien stated.

"Why? It's worked between us for years now."

"Before Rohn turned, perhaps, but not now. You're too different from each other."

Ed gritted his teeth. *Not again.*

Why wouldn't Lucien just accept them as a couple? They'd been here for over two weeks now and Ann hadn't left yet.

"Why are you so determined to split us up?" Ann asked.

"Because I don't want Rohn to go through the same pain I went through being mated to a non-lykae," Lucien snapped.

Ed froze and stormed back into the other room. "My mother is a non-lykae?"

Lucien stiffened. "She's gone. It doesn't matter."

"Of course it does," Ed snapped back. "Why have you never told me this?" He'd suspected his mother might not be a lykae—he had magic and could do things other lykaes couldn't.

"No good can come from this relationship," Lucien insisted. "Your mother and I tried to make it work, but it didn't, because we were two different races."

"We are *bound*." Ann crossed her arms. "It's a true bond."

Lucien gave a harsh laugh. "Bonds may seem wonderful at first. You don't have a true bond, not the way lykaes have with each other."

Ed pulled back his shirt to reveal the star mark on his chest. "Yes, we do." The mark seemed to become more visible every day he and Ann grew closer.

Lucien's mouth fell open. "How?"

"It doesn't matter. You need to accept Ann is part of my life."

He slipped an arm around her and gave her a quick kiss. "I'll see you later."

Ed followed Lucien out. "What was my mother?"

Lucien shook his head. "Not tonight, son. I've said enough already."

Ed's fists clenched. "You haven't said enough," he growled. "Why not tell me the truth?" He gripped Lucien's shirt.

Lucien blinked, surprised. "Losing your mother almost killed me. I don't want you to endure that same fate."

"I won't. Ann means everything to me."

"Do you really think you and the druid will last?"

Ed sighed. "Just because your relationship didn't work doesn't mean mine won't," he retorted. "You need to accept that."

Lucien looked away. "Enough of this. Let's hunt." He shifted into his beast form. Bone and muscle popped as his body changed into a full lykae.

Ed shifted too. His beast was happy to be free. The beast hadn't felt so much of a separate entity, more a part of himself. Being with Ann and accepting their bond had helped.

Marcus appeared at his side. "Ready for the hunt?"

Ed nodded and blurred alongside his cousin as the moon shimmered above them like a glowing orb. Every full moon since he'd first turned had been agony, but now he didn't fight the change, or the moon's call.

The pack moved as one and stalked after their prey.

Ed caught the scent of a deer and something else. Something darker. The stench of decay and the coppery tang of blood made it hard for him to concentrate. The pack hadn't attacked yet, but they only seemed interested in the herd of deer as they stalked through the trees.

Each lykae skirted around the herd of deer. The animals' eyes flicked up, and several of the deer took off in the opposite direction

Rohn, keep up, Marcus said. *It's important to make your first kill tonight.*

Ed focused on the deer, but the stench of decay overwhelmed him. *Marcus, do you smell that?*

I know how enticing the prey smells, especially during your first hunt. You need to focus.

No, not that.

He shook his head, but Marcus remained focused on the herd. The shadows of the other lykaes blurred past as they ran.

A wail carried on the air.

What's that? Ed left the pack behind him.

Trees rushed past, dark and eerie like skeletons under the silvery moon.

Ed stopped, breathing hard. The stench seemed stronger here, but where did it come from?

Ed pushed through the trees. Energy vibrated against his skin, barring his way. He reached out with his mind, and invisible energy sizzled against him.

Why would there be a ward here? This was outside lykae lands, but a good distance away from Ranelle's great tree. He blurred to get through, but the force knocked him to the ground as the ward held firm.

Something stalked through the trees behind him. Ed caught a flash of red light. *Another lupine! Where do they keep coming from?*

Had the fae sent them? Were they harbouring them? He didn't smell any fae nearby.

The lupine lunged at him, and Ed blurred out of the way.

The lupine laughed. "You're too weak to take us both on."

Great wings stirred the air, and a wyvern appeared.

Bugger! Why do there have to be two of them?

The wyvern sent a stream of fire at him, and Ed gasped mid-blur. The flames licked at his skin, but the heat didn't scorch him is expected.

He hit the ground. His body shifted back. Ed raised his hand and deflected the flame, more out of instinct than intention.

The lupine lunged at him again, its fangs digging into his neck. Ed couldn't push it off as he kept the flames at bay.

"Ed!" Ann appeared at his side a flash of orbs. She blasted the wyvern using her own power.

Ed scrambled up as Ann blasted the lupine away from him. *Ann, direct the fire toward me,* he called out.

What? She stared at him in disbelief.

Do it!

The fire came at him again. Ed raised his hand and sent the flames at the lupine. The beast howled as his body burst into flame and turned to ash.

The wyvern took to the air, vanishing into the night.

Ann helped him up, and they retreated to the vault. Ed stumbled into the main room and ripped off a piece of his torn shirt to press against his neck.

"Here, take my blood." Ann held out her wrist as he slumped onto the divan.

"No, I'm fine." He pressed the cloth firmer to stem the blood flow.

"Now is not the time to be stubborn, you big lug."

"I'll heal, it's just a bite. What if I lose control?" He didn't want to undo all the progress he'd made.

"I'm your k'ia. You won't lose control if you feed on me." Ann ran her hands over his chest. "You're not burnt anywhere. How is that possible? I felt you get hit."

"I don't want blood. Use magic like you did the night we first kissed."

Her hands flared with light as their minds opened to each other. The wound on his neck faded as orbs of light swirled around them.

"I guess being fire resistant is part of me."

Ann drew back. "What were you doing?" She sat down on the divan beside him. "I thought you were hunting."

"I smelt something—decay—so I followed it, and a lupine plus a wyvern attacked me," Ed told her. "Urien must be using them somehow. We have to find out how and why that area is warded."

CHAPTER 18

Ann went back to the spot where they had encountered the dying wyvern. So far, none of them had found any trace of where the creature had come from, and Ranelle's people having a lupine in their grasp made her even more nervous.

"Come on, let's take a look around." Ann said to Ceara.

Jax flew overhead. He'd been watching Ranelle's people since their arrival in Corenth but hadn't learnt much about them either. He couldn't get too close to their tree without its magic repelling him.

"I don't see what good coming here will do," Ceara remarked. She doubled over coughing.

Ann frowned. Ceara had had the cough for a few days now, and it seemed to be getting worse. "You sure you're alright?"

"I'm fine. I told you, no fussing over me," Ceara snapped. "It's a cough."

"It's getting worse."

Ceara waved her hand. "I'm fine, just a bit tired. What are you looking for?"

"Given how injured that wyvern was, it must've come from somewhere close by."

"We've already looked here." Ceara yawned and mumbled something Ann couldn't hear.

Jax swooped over their heads. *Still can't see anything from up here either.*

Ann scanned the area with her mind, going deeper than she had before. Something didn't feel right here. The energy deep below the earth felt cold and dark.

She moved on, then raised her hand. A glowing blue vein of energy appeared as the Erthea line materialised, leading from where the wyvern had died. A lot of Magickind could sense the lines—often without even knowing it. The wyvern could have used that as a guide. If she retraced its path, she might find where it had come from.

Ed had gone off to patrol the other side of the wood with Marcus and the other lykaes. She would have been glad to have him by her side.

Jax, follow me, she told him.

She glanced back at Ceara, who had sat down on a fallen tree stump. "Are you coming?"

"Yeah, yeah." Ceara rubbed her forehead.

206

"Maybe I should check you over," Ann suggested.

"You're not a healer."

"I had some training. If you're ill, I can—"

"No, I'm fine. Let's move." Ceara scrambled up.

Ann turned her attention back to the glowing line and followed it as Ceara traipsed behind her and fell back several paces. Her usually pale skin looked almost translucent against her long black hair.

Ann wanted to perform a healing spell to fight off illness, but knew Ceara would refuse. *Bloody stubborn Gliss.*

Ann quickened her pace. The cold feeling increased the further she followed the line.

"Wait for me," Ceara called after her.

Ann, we're close to the great tree, Jax said.

"Why am I not surprised?" she remarked. "Maybe it's time we—" Ann stopped dead as five elves surrounded them, arrows drawn. Odd, she hadn't detected them.

Jax squawked in alarm.

Jax, stay back, Ann told him. *I don't want them realising you aren't really a bird.*

"What are you two doing here?" Ann recognised the leader as Hawke, who they'd met a few days earlier. "You are trespassing in these woods."

Ann raised her hands in surrender. "We're travellers. We were exploring."

Hawke gave a harsh laugh. "I know you're staying with the lykaes. You're spying on us for them."

Ceara laughed, although it came out as more of a wheeze. "Why would we do that? We have more important things to do than watch a bunch of pointy-eared people frolicking around the woods."

"We work with the resistance. We've been tracking dragons for the past month, since one came to a druid settlement," Ann said. "We're not spies. We're staying with the lykaes because I am fasted to one."

"A likely story," Hawke scoffed. "You'll be taken before Lady Ranelle. She'll decide what to do with you."

Good, high time we met the elusive Ranelle in person.

"Time to back off…" Light pulsed between Ceara's eyebrows, and her words slurred. She stumbled, then collapsed to the ground.

"Ceara?" Ann made a move to go to her. Jax swooped lower, ready to attack.

One of the elves picked Ceara up.

"Come." Hawke grabbed Ann's arm and dragged her forward.

As much as she had wanted to see inside the tree, she hadn't expected it to be like this. Ceara remained unconscious, and the elves refused to let her near her friend.

The trees here were much taller and thicker than those she'd seen on the way. The green and blue woods that reached toward the heavens appeared higher than most buildings. It reminded Ann of the old tales of ancient man before the dark times, and their great cities of steel and stone that reached toward the sky.

Jax, what can you see? Ann asked.

He continued hovering overhead as they moved toward the great tree. *This place is impressive. The elves—if they are elves—have got a palace within the huge tree. No wonder the lykaes don't like them, I'd say these guys got the better end of the plain.*

How many elves do you see?

A lot. I can see fifty from up here, but I'm guessing there are a lot more inside. There are a few guards outside. Maybe we should call Ed.

No, not yet. I don't want to put him in unnecessary danger.

Ann scanned the area with her mind. The cold feeling she'd sensed earlier hadn't evaporated. She guessed they must be getting closer to the source. Hawke kept a tight grip on her wrist, but she'd get away from him as she had to.

I'm worried about Ceara, she said to Jax. *They won't let me touch her.*

Why not just use your magic? Jax asked. *I can provide a good distraction if you need me to.*

No, this might be our only chance to get inside this tree.

Ann noticed the guards surrounding the tree palace, and Jax swooped down toward them. A giant tree rose into the clouds. Windows peeked out through its trunk, running all the way up it, and an enormous canopy was draped over it like a heavy blue curtain, reaching down to the ground. It seemed an unusual place for elves to live. The elves she'd encountered in other territories lived in forests but weren't usually so high off the ground.

Ann yanked her arm away from Hawke as they neared the entrance to the ginormous tree. "My friend is ill. The least you could do is let me check on her."

"Your friend will be seen to once we get inside," Hawke replied.

Ann hesitated. She knew she needed to find out more about Ranelle and her mysterious people, but that didn't mean she was willing to let them do anything to Ceara.

Ann scanned the tree with her mind. Dozens of elves dwelled within, and she sensed the presence of even more minds below ground. Power hummed through the earth.

Ann, I don't like this place, Jax told her. *Something feels off.*

Ann let her mind roam deeper through the ocean of power that flowed underneath her feet. Something didn't feel right to her either, but she couldn't figure out what it was yet.

Let's see what Ranelle has to say, she replied. *Then we'll leave.*

I'll shift and come inside with you.

No, stay out here. I don't want them finding out you're a shifter. Keep looking around, I'll be fine, Ann told him. *I'll make sure nothing happens to Ceara.*

The doors opened, and Ann headed inside. Dark and red haired elves all stared as Ann made her way down the long corridor. She'd never met Ranelle before and tried to remember if Darius had dealings with her. She knew it was possible, Darius had crossed over more than once.

She followed the guards into a large hall. Its high vaulted ceiling loomed above, and knots and vines covered the walls.

Hawke and the other men led her down a long passageway. It seemed strange this entire place was built out of a tree, tree that seemed alive with magic.

Ann turned her attention to Ceara, focusing her senses on her instead. Ceara was still breathing, but Ann sensed sickness inside her body. *Damn, I knew I should've checked on her earlier and used the healing spell. I shouldn't have let her brush me off like that.*

She considered calling Ed, but he'd only rush in to help them, which would cause more problems. If she needed to escape, she could.

Hawke led them into a large hall that Ann guessed to be a meeting hall. Strange, she'd expected to be locked up.

To her relief, there were no other elves around to gawp at them.

"Wait here," Hawke said, disappearing down another passageway.

Ann moved over to Ceara as the elf who'd been carrying her set her down on a small divan. She touched Ceara's forehead and scanned her body with her senses. Sickness radiated from Ceara's body. How much had the Gliss been hiding from them? *Typical Ceara, she would never ask for help. She thought she'd fight off the sickness by herself.*

"*Leigheas agus iomlán a dhéanamh.*" Ann hoped an all-around healing spell might do the trick.

Light flashed over Ceara's body, but she didn't wake up.

"Your magic won't have much effect on her," said a voice.

Ann turned around to see a woman dressed in a sheer green gown. Her long red hair fell almost to her waist, and a gold circlet adorned her head. "I am Ranelle, Lady of Mirkwood," she said. "Welcome."

Ann hadn't expected to be welcomed, Hawke and his men had more or less arrested them and dragged them here.

"Why not?" she frowned. "I am a druid. We can heal a lot of illnesses."

Ranelle shook her head as she moved over to them and pressed a hand to Ceara's forehead. "She has the mist sickness."

"The what?"

"Some people experience sickness after they pass through the toxic mists on their way into our land."

Ann shook her head. "No, that's impossible. I cast a spell to protect all of us from any effects of the mist."

"What have her symptoms been?"

"Why should I trust you?" Ann demanded. "Your men dragged us in here for so-called trespassing."

"We can't be too cautious, relations between us and the lykaes haven't been good." Ranelle drew back from Ceara. "I can help your friend if you'll let me."

Ann's eyes narrowed. "Again, why should I trust you?"

"I'm the only one in Lulrien who can save your friend's life. The lykaes won't be able to cure her sickness. Your magic won't be very effective either, archdruid."

Ann's mouth fell open. "How…?"

"I know who you are, you need not fear me. I won't tell the lykaes your secret, if that's what you're afraid of." Ranelle glanced from Ann, to Ceara, back to Ann. "I'm one of the leaders of the council. Your power gives you away."

She gritted her teeth. The glamour her grandmother had given her five years ago was meant to shield her identity, but Ann had noticed it hadn't been concealing her so well over the last few months. Maybe it was because her powers were growing stronger, or perhaps because she'd finally accepted her role as archdruid.

"That doesn't give me reason to trust you," Ann retorted.

"Come, we'll move your friend to a more comfortable room. Trust must be earned, and that will take time. But you can believe me when I say I'm not a threat to you, Rhiannon Valeran."

Ann followed Ranelle and her guard as he carried Ceara into another room containing a large four-poster bed covered in blankets made from leaves. The guard set Ceara down on the bed.

Ann still didn't feel able to trust Ranelle, or to let her help, but she hadn't sensed any deception— not that she was easy to read. Ann scanned the mysterious woman with her mind but picked up on no thoughts.

She had met the council a few times growing up, and didn't recall ever meeting Ranelle, although the council had interacted more with Darius than her.

Ann, what's going on? Jax asked. *Are you and Ceara okay? Is she awake?*

I'm with Ranelle. She says Ceara has been affected by a sickness caused by passing through the mist. She says she can heal her.

And you believe that?

I don't know. Ceara didn't respond to my healing spell, and that works on most illnesses.

"How long has your friend been ill?" Ranelle asked, interrupting Ann's mental communication.

"A few days. She's been tired and had a persistent cough. My spell should have protected her when we came through the mist."

Ranelle shook her head. "The mist is supposed to keep everyone away so Lulrien remains hidden."

She turned to her guard. "Jurek, bring me the potion."

Ranelle turned her attention back to Ann. "Your friend—"

"Her name is Ceara."

"Ceara will need treatment for several days. It would be safer if she stayed here during that time."

Ann crossed her arms. "I'm sure I could administer the treatment if you give it to me."

Ranelle shook her head again. Vines crept down from the walls and wrapped around Ceara's body. "Hometree has healing magic. It will help with her recovery."

The vines flashed with light.

Ceara groaned and her eyelids fluttered.

"Ceara?" Ann moved to her side, but Ceara didn't respond to the sound of her voice.

"The sickness is strong in her. It will take time for her to recover. If we move her, she may grow worse."

Ann opened her mouth to protest then closed it. She'd sensed the sickness and doubted she'd be able to cure it by herself. Healing unknown illnesses took time and a lot of energy, depending on how the illness affected someone. Magic wasn't a simple cure-for-all.

"You're welcome to stay with her," Ranelle added. "Contrary to what the lykaes think, I'm not your enemy."

Ann reluctantly nodded. If Ceara had to stay here, she'd have to go back to the village and tell Ed what had happened.

Once Ranelle had left the room, Ann raised her hand, and Jax materialised in a flash of blue light.

"Finally," Jax breathed a sigh of relief. "How is she?"

"She's resting. They say she got a sickness when we passed through the mist, but I find that hard to believe." Ann touched Ceara's forehead. The Gliss' brow felt hot with fever.

"One of your father's books says the mist causes poisoning," Jax pointed out. "The guards won't chase me away, will they?" He peered out through the doorway, as if expecting someone to storm in.

"No, tell them you're with me. I need you to keep an eye on Ceara whilst I head back to the village to tell Ed what's happened and grab my things." She touched Ceara again to make sure she was breathing. "Ranelle says Ceara can't be moved, so you and I will have to stay here so we can watch over her."

Jax's eyes widened. "What about Ed?"

She shook her head. "He can't come here. Ranelle's people are on edge enough as it is."

"He won't like this."

She sighed. "I know, but this is the way it has to be. I'll be back." Light flashed around her as she transported out.

Ann reappeared back inside the hut she'd been sharing with Ed. "Ed?" she called.

He blurred in. "Finally, where have you been?" He gave her a quick kiss. "You've been gone ages."

"Ceara collapsed whilst we were out looking for wyverns." Ann returned his embrace. "She's with Ranelle's people."

Ed's eyes narrowed. "Why?"

"Ranelle said they can help. She gave Ceara something, but says she needs to stay there for a few days. Jax and I are going to stay with her."

"No, that's a bad idea." Ed said. "What if—?"

"I'm not gonna leave her there all alone." Ann picked up her clothes and shoved them into her pack. "It's only a few days. We'll talk constantly—"

A scream cut her off.

Now what? Ann dropped her pack, and she and Ed hurried outside.

Two red-eyed lupines whisked through the village, knocking down lykaes in their wake.

"Where did they come from?" Ed growled.

One lupine lunged straight toward them. Marcus appeared and knocked the lupine to the ground.

Ann froze, spotted a wyvern in the distance. *Damn it, Urien! It will be a bloodbath if this doesn't end now.*

Ed grappled with the second lupine as its fangs tore into his neck. More lupines appeared, darting toward the rest of the pack.

Ann raised her hand and blasted the lupine attacking Ed. It did nothing to deter him.

Damn it, think. I overpowered the lykaes when the elves came here, can I do it again?

Stop! she thought.

Nothing happened.

Wait, Lucien said something about a moon curse, and how the archdruid forced them to shift. Ann closed her eyes and reached out with her mind. If there was indeed a curse, she should be able to find it wrapped around the lykaes.

She slammed to the ground as one of the lupines snapped its fangs at her.

Ann gasped as her breath left her in rush.

"Ceangal," she muttered. Light burst from her fingers as she gripped his arm.

The lupine howled as energy binds wrapped around his body.

She shoved him away from her and paused. If lupines were lykaes, it stood to reason that they might still be bound by the curse. It wouldn't matter if they had no souls.

Ann grabbed hold of the lupine again and scanned his body. He snarled, and the binding burst free.

"Ceangail é go daingean agus go tapa."

The lupine yelped as he fell to his knees.

Come on, where is that curse? she wondered.

"Taispeáin dom mallacht na gealaí."

Orbs of light flashed around the lupines and lykaes. Tendrils of blue and red glistened over their bodies as the curse flared to life, etched into their very skin. This was a spell designed by her

217

grandfather, Fergus. He'd reigned for almost five centuries, so it didn't surprise her he'd been the one to cast the spell. It would be hard to break, but that would wait until much later.

Ann raised her hand, and the tendrils blazed with power. "*Stad.*"

The lupine grappling with Ed let go of him and rolled away. Every lykae around them doubled over as Ann's power roamed free. More power rose from deep inside her. Her eyes blazed with light, and her glamour fell away.

Ann, stop! Ed scrambled up. *Pull your power back in before they realise who you are.*

Not yet.

She turned to the lupine. "Tell me how you got here," she ordered.

The lupine growled. "I'll kill you."

"No, you won't. You're bound," she hissed. "I know my brother sent you. What does he have planned in Lulrien?"

Ed clutched his injured neck. "I'd answer her if I were you."

All the lupines struggled under the force of the binding. The other lykaes remained immobilised.

Ann glanced up, saw the wyvern still circling. Why hadn't it attacked?

"I —" the lupine began. Runes flared to life over his skin, blooming with red light.

No, Urien's magic! Ann gasped and let go of the binding, but it was too late. Urien's magic pulsed over the lupines, and all of them fell to the ground, dead.

Lucien flew at Ann. "You did use magic on my people," he snarled, grasping her throat so tight her eyes bulged.

"Lucien, stop!" Lia rushed over. "You can't hurt her."

"She's the archdruid. I should have known," Lucien snapped. "You almost killed me and my people."

"No, I…" Ann gasped. "I had to stop the lupines…"

"Lucien, if you hurt her, I will stop you," Ed warned, eyes blazing emerald. "Let. Her. Go."

Lucien's eyes turned bright amber. "You dare challenge me over her? After what she did?"

Ed, don't, Ann told him.

"Yes, I do. She's my k'ia. Look." Ed pulled off his shirt. The marks she'd seen on herself the other night appeared on his chest.

Lucien shoved Ann away so hard she hit the ground. She coughed, her throat still ached.

Lucien caught hold of Ed and stared at the marks. "Impossible. Lykaes—"

"It's a trick," Jessa spoke up. "No doubt caused by her magic. You should kill her."

Ed moved to Ann's side as Lucien reached out for her again. Blue lightning sparked between his fingers. "Don't touch her," he warned.

Lucien hissed out a breath. "This bond isn't natural."

Jessa gasped. "Rohn has magic."

"Yes, something your alpha refuses to believe is possible," Ed snapped, helping Ann to her feet. "I'm an overseer, sent to guide her. That's why I was sent away."

"Get out of here," Lucien said through gritted teeth. "I won't have the archdruid among my people. You're banished from village under pain of death."

"Fine, we'll both leave." Ed wrapped an arm around Ann.

Lucien gaped at him in disbelief. "What?"

"I have magic too. I can't stay," Ed said.

Ann touched his arm. "Don't. I'll leave." She transported out before anyone could say another word.

Ann reappeared back inside the hut. She rubbed her throat. Damn it, she'd wanted to help. Instead, she'd got herself banished.

Ed blurred in behind her. "He's unbelievable!" he fumed.

"You shouldn't have told him you're an overseer," Ann replied.

Ed gaped at her. "He would have killed you."

She shook her head. "He can't." She grabbed hold of her pack. "It doesn't matter. We both know I couldn't stay here forever. Urien sent them to remind me he can get to me no matter where I am."

Ed ran a hand through his hair, then sighed. "Let's go. I can't—"

"No. I'm leaving, you're not."

Ed's mouth fell open. "What? I can't stay here after what just happened."

"Talk to your father, I'm sure he'd let you stay. Blame it on me if you have to." She swung her pack over her shoulder.

"Ann, you can't be serious. I won't stay with them. Not after—"

"Ed, you came here for a reason that's more important than me."

"Not to me, it's not," Ed snapped.

"Maybe that's the problem. You're letting your feelings for me get in the way."

She touched his cheek. *Play along.*

What? What are you talking about? Ed's eyes narrowed.

I think Urien has a spy here. I sensed something earlier when I cast the binding, she said. *Play along. Make it look like we're having an argument. Knowing Urien, he probably wants to split us up, so let's make it look believable.*

"My feelings for you aren't an issue," Ed insisted.

You think Urien knew what we'd do?

She nodded. *That's why those lupines died. He doesn't want me here, which is why you have to stay and watch over the lykaes.*

"Aren't they?" Ann retorted. "You were sent here. You're an overseer, that's your calling. I don't need you to protect or guide me anymore." Her last words stung.

"Ann, I —"

"Just stay. I have to go." She wrapped her arms around him and kissed him hard, pouring all of her emotion into the kiss.

He held onto her. *I don't know if I can let you go.*

You have to. Besides, it's not forever. We've been apart before. Ann sighed and pulled away. *We'll see each other again soon.* She transported out before Ed could say anything else, so he wouldn't see her tears.

CHAPTER 19

Urien stumbled into Ranelle's chamber. Since the wyvern had attacked him a few days earlier, the wound had festered. Nothing he tried would heal it. Blood magic gave him little energy now. Killing numerous slaves did no good, and nor would any spell or potion.

Ranelle looked up from where she sat at a table covered in papers. "You can't be here," she hissed. "Your sister is here, along with Ceara and Jax."

Urien growled at the mention of Ann. Had she caused him to become like this? Something must have weakened the spell Darius had cast to bind Urien and his siblings together. It should have healed him.

."Ann won't sense me," he replied. He'd cast a spell to shield himself. At least some spells worked on him. "How did you get her away from Edward?"

"Ceara has been ill."

Despite his aching chest and throbbing head, Urien smiled. "Good, my magic worked well then. You haven't healed her, have you?"

Ranelle bit her lip. "Of course I have. I couldn't let the poor woman die."

Urien scowled. "She almost caught me, thanks to your interference," he snapped, pulling off his shirt. The wound had been leaking pus. "I can't heal. If this body dies, your people die too." He lifted the Arcus stone. "I've already given the command. The magic will still work."

All colour drained from Ranelle's face as she rose. "I've already apologised for—"

"Find a way to fix this. You're a council leader, you must know something!"

Ranelle hesitated. "I'm a leader, but I'm not an elder. This is beyond my skill to heal." She touched his shoulder. "This body is dying."

"I can't find my own body—Edward and my sister took it and hid it the night Ann banished me," he growled. "I don't feel any connection to it either. Why is my father's spell failing?" He caught her hesitation and gripped the stone. "You know something. Tell me."

"I don't…" Ranelle clutched her stomach. "Please don't force me to change again."

"Then talk." He'd force her to talk if he had to, he didn't have time to waste. He had no idea what would happen to his soul if he didn't have a body. Would it move on? Could he possess another body? Neither appealed to him—they ran the risk of Ann trapping him in limbo again.

"I don't know for certain." Ranelle gritted her teeth as the stone's power clutched at her. "I think the bond between her and Rohn might be weakening Darius' spell."

Urien's eyes narrowed. "How? What bond?"

She shook her head. "I don't know. It's the connection they have to each other."

He rubbed his chin. "Must be a soul bond then."

"You can't break that."

"Death could." He grinned. "But there must be a way to find my body. You'll cast a spell." He pointed at her. "I need an outside force."

"But my magic—" Ranelle protested.

"You'll do it, or I'll force you to." He clutched the stone to his chest. Its power hummed against his skin.

"Your sister is here," Ranelle snapped. "She'll know. You will expose yourself—something I doubt you want."

"Ann isn't here. I'd sense her if she were. Let's cast a spell," Urien ordered. "Then we'll go below ground. We're getting close to the door—I can feel it."

"Not here." Ranelle moved to the secret door and pressed the knot on the wall. The door slid open.

Urien followed her down the winding tunnel. His chest tightened as he gasped for breath. Gods below, how much longer would this body last? The flickering torches blurred, and his head resumed its usual pounding. *Not again.*

"Hurry," Ranelle called after him. "I don't want to risk your sister sensing you."

Urien didn't want to risk that either. This damned body felt so weak. He knew he couldn't fight Ann off until he got his true body back.

The elders wouldn't help—not until he gave them what they wanted: Ann.

Urien stumbled on, forcing Xander's stiff limbs to move. This tunnel seemed much shorter than the one that led to the underground caverns where the lupines and wyverns were being housed.

He followed Ranelle into a larger chamber. Gnarled roots covered the earthen walls, glistening a deep blue and humming with energy. A spell circle etched with sigils lined the floor. This woman was full of surprises.

"Stand in the circle." Ranelle motioned to it.

Urien hesitated. He hadn't had anyone use magic for him like this in a long time. What if she used it against him? His body wouldn't be able to withstand any sort of attack. Urien slipped the Arcus stone around his neck. Attaching it to a chain had been the easiest way to ensure its safety. "Don't do anything stupid," he warned her. "The command on the stone will still work." The Arcus stone glittered with power.

"Just stand still. I can't guarantee this will work." Ranelle's jaw tightened. "Your sister will have hidden your body well."

"Just do it." Once he found his body, Urien would plan his next move. Whatever that may be.

Ranelle threw salt around the circle for purification.

Urien bit back a laugh. It'd take a lot more than that to cleanse him.

Ranelle's eyes flared with bright green light as she chanted strange words of power. Blood pounded in his ears so hard he couldn't make out her words. The circle hummed as the sigils flared to life.

A burst of light shot through Urien's chest. His eyes snapped shut.

"Follow the magic with your mind," Ranelle instructed, repeating the words louder so he could hear her.

Urien hated the feel of her magic. So pure, like it came from nature itself. The pounding in his head eased a little, but his brow creased. "I don't see anything," he growled.

"Concentrate. Let it guide you."

His head exploded with pain, forcing him to his knees. His mind had hit a wall of impenetrable energy. "I can't get through," he hissed. "Do something. Try harder." He wrapped his fingers around the Arcus stone.

"I told you it'd be difficult—perhaps impossible—to break through their magic."

Urien crawled out of the circle. The humming from the tree roots beat in time to the pain in his aching skull.

Healing energy. He'd heard Ranelle say something about that before. "Use the tree to heal me," he rasped.

Her mouth fell open. "What? No."

"Do it, or I'll make it a command."

"It won't work. The tree heals people only when it chooses to. I can't force it to do anything," Ranelle insisted. "I'm telling the truth."

"Do it anyway. I need some strength."

Ranelle shook her head. "I can't. Compel me if you have to, but I still can't do it."

Urien's mind raced. Darius had insisted he be taught the druid ways and magics, but Urien had hated it. He had no connection to nature like the druids did, but could he convince it to help?

As he drew closer, the tree roots curled around him in response.

"Heal me," he ordered. He didn't bother using the druid tongue, just using magic to send out the command.

"No, don't. Please," Ranelle begged. "You might drain too much power. My people need the energy to survive."

Urien ignored her. He didn't give a fuck about a worthless tree. Energy flowed through him, cool and soothing. The wound on his chest closed and scabbed over but didn't fully heal.

Ranelle slumped to the floor, pale with dark circles suddenly ringing her eyes. "The tree's energy won't sustain you for long. That body is still dying."

"It's enough for now." Urien smiled. He hadn't felt this good in days. He moved away from the circle and yanked Ranelle to her feet. "Come, time to go below and see what progress you've made."

Underground, they passed by a cage of red-eyed lupines who thrashed and growled when they saw Urien. He'd put the worthless beasts down soon, they were much harder to control than the wyverns, but he wouldn't kill them just yet, in case he had need of them again. They had proved useful in keeping Ann and the other rogues distracted.

There it stood, a glowing circle etched with ancient runes—one of the door's outer locks. According to the scroll, there were three locks. Each had to be opened individually.

"You don't have to do this. Those things were locked away for good reason." She touched his shoulder. "You can—"

He shrugged her off. "Quiet, woman."

Urien examined the glittering runes. They weren't just druidic, but elder. The first lock called for blood. He snapped his fingers, and Ryn appeared in a flash of light.

"My lord?" She sounded uncertain.

Urien slashed his blade across her throat and smeared drops of blood over the seal. The runes bloomed with power. The first phase of unlocking the door had begun, now he had to wait and see what came out of the door first.

CHAPTER 20

Ann roamed through the garden that surrounded hometree, glancing around. No buzz of thoughts came to her as she moved.

She felt relieved to get away from hometree, having left Jax to watch over Ceara.

At first, they'd thought the elves had done something to Ceara. Ranelle had explained it was mist sickness. There hadn't been a mention of a cure in Darius' journal entry on it.

Ann and Jax hadn't displayed any symptoms so far. Ann knew her father's spell would protect her from such things, and Jax was convinced he was immune. Ed hadn't shown any symptoms either, but Ann suspected he had immunity too, since he'd come from Lulrien.

Ranelle had given Ceara a potion that had helped with the sickness. Ceara had of course complained about being laid up in bed for the past few days, but at least she seemed to be getting better.

Ann moved beyond the garden into the forest. Blue wood trees loomed overhead, almost black in the dim light. She'd walked around hometree too and found it a fascinating place—though guards blocked her at every turn. She breathed a sigh of relief, leaning back against the tree. She hadn't seen Ed in over a week. Just thinking of him made an ache form in her chest.

By the spirits, I miss you.

She hadn't been back to the village since Ceara fell ill. She and Jax had taken it in turns to watch over Ceara. She hadn't wanted to leave Ceara alone, even though the elves hadn't done anything threatening so far. It still felt odd not having him around. Ed had wanted to see Ceara too, but the elves stopped him whenever he got near the tree.

Movement caught her eye, and she turned to see Ed standing beside her. "What are you doing here?" She gasped.

"You needed me, so here I am."

"I never said—"

"You didn't have to, I felt it."

Ann threw herself into his arms and hugged him. "I missed you."

"I missed you too." He bent to kiss her, but she put a finger to his lips.

"Not here." She took his hand and led him away as the door to the vault flashed into existence.

They hurried through. Ed grabbed her and kissed her hard. She eagerly returned his kiss with just as much passion.

"Why didn't you call more often? I've been going out of my mind worrying about all of you," Ed said. "It's taken everything in me not to come and see you."

Ann shook her head. "I called as much as I could. Jax doesn't seem to be affected, thankfully. Probably due to his stone magic."

"Were you sick?" He stroked her cheek.

"No, I'm fine. Papa's spell must protect me from it." She sighed. "I still haven't met the council yet—and I still think we should talk to them. Ranelle seems to be stalling. She's hiding something. Jax and I have been watching her and the other elves." She paused. "I'm still not sure they *are* elves, but at least they don't seem to mind me using magic."

"Things have been tense in the village. What else have you found out staying at hometree?"

"Not much. The elves stay away from me for the most part. Jax and I tried to look around, but guards block our way no matter where we go." She tucked a lock of hair behind her ear. "Something feels strange underground, but I can't figure out what."

"I found something strange too. Marcus, Jessa, and I hunted down some of Ranelle's people who were torturing another lupine prisoner. They had shock rods with them—the kind used by Gliss. I never had a chance to tell you before you went to stay with Ranelle."

Her eyes widened. "That doesn't make any sense. I know Urien has probably already approached Ranelle's people—and I suspect they're working together." She ran a hand through her hair. "But why would they use Gliss weapons?"

"I don't know. I tried talking to my father, but he won't listen." Ed scowled. "I don't understand it. He despises them, yet he seems reluctant to make a move against them." He wrapped an arm around her as they moved down the hall. "What's Ranelle like?"

She shook her head. "Hard to say. She seems helpful—well, seems to *want* to help. I don't trust her motives. She and her people are up to something."

Despite Ranelle helping Ceara with the sickness caused by the mist, Ann had her suspicions. "She asked me things about you too, which seemed odd."

"Why would she be interested in me?" Ed's frown deepened. "I'm a lykae, someone she should despise." He rubbed his chin. "Do you think she had something to do with me being chased away from Lulrien? I still think someone forced me to leave that day. Someone *wanted* me gone."

"I don't know. I guess anything is possible." Ann slumped down onto a divan. "I need to talk with the council. If Urien manages to sway them to his side—well, I'm no match for all of them. They're made up of the strongest Magickind leaders." She sighed. "Maybe Sage was right, I do need allies." Before they'd left Trewa, the old druid had advised Ann to start making allies among the other races. That would be easier said than done—most races despised the archdruid, or believed Ann had killed her parents.

"You do have allies." He sat beside her and ran his fingers through her hair. "You have me. One way or another, I'll get the lykaes on our side."

Ann laughed. "That won't be easy, more like impossible. Lucien hates me."

"He doesn't know you like I do."

She smiled and rested her head against his shoulder. "I've missed this. Us. Being together like this."

"I love it when you say us." He brushed his lips over her neck.

"How are you getting on with the other…" She moaned as his lips trailed lower. "Ed, we're supposed to be…planning. Problem-solving…" She closed her eyes, loving the feel of his lips on her skin.

We are, Ed said. *Every second we're apart I'm craving you, so I'm fixing that.*

She giggled, cupped his face, and captured his mouth in another kiss. Their tongues mated together. Reluctantly, Ann pulled away when his eyes started glowing hot emerald.

"Fuck, not again." He rubbed his eyes and growled.

She touched his cheek. "I don't care about that. Your beast side has never bothered me," she said. "Well, I might not kiss you when you're in your full beast form. You should go. I have something I need to do."

Days of being bored and stuck at hometree had given her a chance to practise the spell more and research using her father's books from the vault. Jax had been helping too, reading kept them both occupied.

"What?" His eyes narrowed.

"Nothing. Just a spell. Then I have to go back to—"

"You're hiding something."

She sighed, hating how well he knew her. "I'm not. I'm going to test out my unlinking spell." She tucked a lock of hair behind her ear. "I haven't seen Xander anymore. I have to save him."

"How can you test it without Urien being here?" Ed frowned at her.

"I can in the spirit realm—or the Grey, as that strange entity called it," she admitted. "I can't afford to be distracted during the spell." Ann didn't want to risk Ed being there and getting dragged over to the other side like the last time she'd crossed over. She feared what might happen to him if she did.

"You won't be. I'll be there with you."

Ed followed her inside the work room. The candles flared to life as Ann focused her power on them. She kicked off her boots, wishing she could feel the earth underneath her feet rather than hard, wooden floor. She set a pillow down to lie on. "Remember, don't interfere, no matter what happens. I won't risk your life. You got dragged over to the other side when I crossed over looking for Xander before."

"I'm your anchor," he insisted as he sat beside her. "If something goes wrong, I'll—"

"No, I need to stay under longer. It's the only way I can free Xander. Promise you won't do anything, and don't touch me when the spell is in progress."

"I can't. If the spell goes wrong, I'll pull you out," he said. "One day your father's spell might not bring you back."

"Fine, but only do it as a last resort."

Ed sighed. "Okay."

Ann opened her mouth to drink the potion that would hold her in death, but hesitated. This would be the most dangerous magic she'd ever performed. If the spell that revived her from death did fail, her death would be permanent.

Grabbing the back of his neck, she kissed Ed hard, pouring every ounce of desire and emotion she had into the kiss.

Ed pulled her onto his lap, returning her kiss with just as much emotion.

"I have to go," she said after a few moments.

"I know." He pressed his forehead against hers. "Just come back to me. No matter what. I won't lose you." His fingers tangled in her hair. "I wouldn't be—"

"I know." She cut him off with a kiss.

She pulled away and gulped down the potion, then let blackness drag her under. The gloom of the other side surrounded her like a heavy cloak. The greyness seemed cold and empty as usual.

"Xander?" Ann called. "Xander?" She waited. No sign of her brother appeared.

Come on, Xander. I know you can hear me.

She needed him here.

"Hello, sister," said a cold voice.

"Urien." His true form stood there, with the same raven hair and coal-black eyes as she remembered. In spirit form, he couldn't hide behind Xander's image.

"Trying to call our little brother again, I see," Urien sneered. "He won't give you any secrets this time."

"What have you done?" Something felt wrong. She couldn't feel Xander's presence as her mind reached out for him.

"I knew you'd try something eventually. No doubt you thought to trap me here." Urien smirked.

Ann raised her hand, sending a ball of glowing fire at him.

Urien dodged it and blasted her with lightning.

She ducked out of the way and began her spell, invoking the words of power. *"Díbirt agus ceangail a spiorad."*

Urien stumbled and laughed. "You won't force me to remain in the void this time, sister."

"No?" She muttered more words of power. *"Ní dhéanfaidh na ceangail a cheanglaíonn anois dínn."*

She felt something inside her snap, and the vines of her father's spell flashed over her wrist. Even in her astral form, pain burned through her. Ann yelped, but grinned. It had worked! The spell Darius had cast on them five years ago had lifted—for now at least.

Urien gasped as she blasted him with another fireball.

She recited the familiar words she'd spoken all those years ago to remove his soul from his body and banish it. Power flowed between her fingers as she reached for his soul, ready to trap it here for eternity. This time, she'd make sure the spell remained permanent.

The mark on her wrist burned with light as it returned.

Urien yelped, staring at his own wrist. He laughed. "Even you can't undo Papa's magic, it seems." He hurled another lightning bolt at her.

Ann cried out as her spirit reconnected with her body. Pain tore through her chest where he'd struck her. She looked down, feeling her flesh scalding, but saw no mark.

"What happened?" Ed brushed her hair off her face. "You started choking, but I couldn't wake you."

Her limbs felt heavy, and her stomach recoiled. All her energy had been spent.

"It didn't work." She buried her face against the cushion beneath her. "My father's spell came back after I lifted it, so I couldn't bind him. He got away."

If the spell remained, she may never be able to rip Urien's soul from Xander's body. Urien had found a way to use it to protect himself—no doubt with the help of the elders.

Ann closed her eyes and let sleep drag her under.

When she woke again, she found herself in bed with Ed's body wrapped around her. His arms were tight around her as he held her close. She sighed, enjoying the feel of him there. She missed waking up next to him.

Her head pounded, and her limbs still felt heavy. Facing Urien had cost her more energy than she'd realised and she made a move to get up. With a groan, she tried to wriggle free of his embrace. She'd need time, meditation, and a connection to the earth to restore her strength.

Or did she? She'd taken energy from Ed before. His primal power felt better than anything even the elements could give her. She'd channelled it the last time she'd been stuck in the Grey. Even though druid law forbade such practice.

Ann sighed. She'd broken druid law long before now, just as her father had. He had told her once their power went beyond that of nature. Ed's grip tightened as if he didn't want to let her go.

"Ed, we need to get up," she murmured. "It must be late." Normally, she could easily sense the time of day. Her magic felt too weak to tell her anything.

"Why?" he mumbled.

"Because you have to get back to the village. People will notice you're gone."

Ed buried his face against her neck. "It won't matter if I'm gone a little longer."

Ann gave him a shove. "We still have work to do. I want to look around more of Mirkwood away from any prying eyes." She turned and kissed him, slowly at first, and then deeper.

Energy jolted between them as Ed returned her kiss, and strength slowly flowed back into her as she channelled it.

"Come on, we can't stay here all day." Ann pulled away from him.

Ed rolled his eyes. "One day soon, I will have you in this bed all day."

She flashed him a smile before getting up.

Ann and Ed reappeared on the edge of Mirkwood, walking further away from Ranelle's tree as the door to the vault disappeared behind them.

"What are we looking for?" Ed asked.

"Ranelle's people are hiding something, but neither Jax nor I have been able to travel very far inside her tree palace, or get near the underground entrances." Ann scanned the area with her mind to make sure there were none of Ranelle's people around watching them. "It's early enough to have a look around. Maybe we can get a better look at things without anyone seeing us."

"We'll have to be careful. If they find me here, it'll lead to more problems." Ed took her hand and Ann felt their powers join as she cast her senses out. That wyvern and those two lupines had to have come from somewhere close by, and one way or another, she'd figure out what Ranelle was hiding here.

They pushed through the trees and enormous leaves that formed a canopy down from the blue woods. The air smelt of fresh dew and a sweet aroma like honeysuckle.

As they moved into a clearing, something zipped past them.

CHAPTER 21

Ed's eyes burned emerald as his claws and fangs came out. The beast felt excited, eager to take control. Something whizzed past them again, blurring so fast he couldn't tell what it was. *Now what?*

"What the—?" Ann muttered as something knocked her to the ground. She jumped up, a fireball forming in her hand.

Ed blurred, grabbing one of the creatures by the throat. It looked to be about three feet tall, with a pointed snout, whiskers, and beady eyes. It resembled a rat. "Fir deargs." He snapped its neck and tossed the body aside. "That's odd. I haven't heard of them inhabiting Lulrien in centuries."

Ann muttered something, and the rest of the creatures froze around them. "What are they?"

"They're pests."

She raised her hand, making each creature burst into flame, then explode.

Ed winced as his claws and fangs retracted. The beast growled. It had wanted to fight, to hunt. *Not today, my friend.*

"How did you know what they were?" Ann asked.

He shrugged. "Must be overseer knowledge. They're not that dangerous, but they can play gruesome pranks on people."

"Where did they come from?" She glanced around, as if expecting to find an answer in the clearing.

"That's a good question," Ed replied.

Ann's hand went to her throat. "My crest is gone," she gasped. "One of them must've taken it."

More of the fir deargs ran around them, laughing as they went.

"Oh, you'd better run while you can, you little rodents. I've got to get that crest back. It's the only way to access the vault." She ran off in the opposite direction.

Ed stumbled as one of the pests blurred around his legs. He growled, letting the beast take control again. He threw one of them against the tree, hearing the crunch of bone as he did.

He blurred again as two more came at him. His eyes burned hot emerald. "Do you want to die?"

Ed, I think I've found a patch of the mist, Ann called. *Hurry. See if you can lure the other little buggers this way.*

Ed blurred, trees rushing past him as he appeared where he'd sensed Ann's presence, yet he saw no sign of her. The beast snarled when it didn't feel her either.

The fir deargs whizzed after him, and a shimmering white light danced over the landscape. The mist.

Ann, where are you? He grabbed two of the creatures and shoved them through the light.

No answer came.

He snarled, fangs bared as more creatures came at him. They cowered, then vanished back through the mist. Ed sniffed, his heart pounding. Ann had been here, but her presence vanished.

Ann?

Laughter echoed around him, and he thought he caught a blur of movement.

"The mist between the worlds weakens," a voice goaded. "Will you stay, or run home with your tail between your legs?"

Oh not that thing again, he thought. *I don't have a tail!*

Why did this strange entity keep following them around? Ed had hoped it might stay gone for good this time.

"Where is she?" Ed snarled. "If you harm her, no power on Erthea will protect you."

More laughter followed. "Fool, I'm far beyond your powers."

He blurred again, leaping at the light and hitting the ground hard. "Where is she? What do you want with me?"

"Who says I want you?" the voice replied. "I enjoy watching lesser beings. It's so amusing."

Ed growled, then flew at it again. "Where is Ann?"

"Strange how obsessed you are with her. She's not a lykae, she can never be yours."

"She's already mine." This time the beast spoke, low and guttural. "I'll tear you apart and drain every drop of your blood. I'm immune to magic."

More laughter rang out. "Fool, you are nothing."

Ed doubled over in agony as his bones twisted and fur sprouted over his skin. His hands replaced by long, gnarled paws.

Ed felt his self-control slipping away as the beast took full hold of his body. It wanted blood. He couldn't fight something intangible, but he'd damn well try. This thing had dared to take what was his—Ann.

The laughter grew.

He rose on wobbly legs—legs more muscular than his own. He felt stronger than before, no longer encumbered by his human form.

Ed clenched his fists, trying to regain control. *Stop this,* he thought.

The laughter rang louder, and the voice hissed in his ear, "She'll never accept you like this. Beast. Demon."

He ignored the goading, sniffing the air as he dove headlong into the mist.

Light burned his eyes, and smells assaulted his senses as he tried to pass through. The beast only had one goal: finding Ann.

"You will give her back to me," he hissed, moving free of the mist. "Ann!" he bellowed, his voice echoing around him.

The laughter and the presence belonging to it had faded.

"Ed?"

At the sound of her call, he blurred, appearing in front of her a second later.

Her eyes widened as she took a step back. "What happened?" Although her voice sounded calm, he heard her heart pounding. "Did that stupid voice trick you into going to the mist too?"

Laughter echoed in the distance.

Ann threw a fireball at the mist. It bounced off, exploding a nearby tree. She glanced at the beast, and then took off, muttering, "I will find that thing and blow it apart."

The beast gritted his teeth and blurred, picking her up and throwing her over his shoulder.

Ann gave a cry of alarm. "Put me down!"

If his k'ia wanted the strange being, he'd get it for her, but he'd keep her safe regardless. Trees blurred as he followed the laughter, moving faster than ever before. He stopped when he reached the outskirts of some ruins. Buildings rose into the trees that loomed around them.

He set her down. "Stay close."

Ann let out a breath and slumped back against the wall. "Don't do that again." She scrambled up. "The mist is torn here. I can feel it." She smiled and slipped her crest back over her neck. "Let's try a tracking spell. See if we can find out where all these creatures keep coming from."

She turned, raised her hand. *"Taispeáin dúinn cad atá á lorg againn."*

Ed clenched his fists, trying to regain control, but could he? The beast had appeared in his true form now—a true lykae. It wanted to remain in control. Magic charged the air as fire flared over the glowing mist. So strong he could taste it.

Ann had magic that went far beyond a druid's abilities. Power whirled deep inside her. It came from something beyond nature, yet she seemed unaware of it.

He watched in awe as light encompassed the mist. Lykaes were supposed to hate magic, yet his beast revelled in the feel of it.

She chanted more words of power, her magic burning brighter.

Ed gritted his teeth, his fangs digging into his lips as he fought to regain control of his body. He hadn't changed, and Ann had asked him to more than once.

Ann stumbled. He blurred and took her hand. Something jolted between them.

Ed gasped as his claws, fangs, and fur retracted.

Ann glanced at him in shock. She felt it too, her power and his strength combined, merging as if they were one. "What are you doing?" she asked.

"We can find them. Do it, keep going." He gripped her hand tighter.

Together they watched as the mist stretched, shimmering a fluorescent white.

He moved to wrap his arms around Ann from behind, letting his strength flow to her. The mist finally parted with a flash of light.

Ann sagged against him as their power and energy faded. "That felt incredible." She looked up. "You're you again." She wrapped her arms around him in a tight embrace.

He smiled and held her close. His heart twisted with a familiar feeling he'd spent years trying to ignore. Love.

A clearing had appeared through the surrounding mist, Ed let go of her, relieved to be back in human form. He felt stronger and more powerful than he felt before.

Hand-in-hand, they moved along the trail until they came to a lake.

"I think the cold feeling in this area can't be traced to its source." Ann glanced around. "Maybe we should head back to the vault in case that entity shows up again."

"You wanted to search."

"That was before that thing forced you to change. What if it does something worse?"

"I'll be fine. I feel more in control now than I've ever felt before."

"Maybe Lia's techniques are working."

"Or maybe it's because I have you. Our bond helps." Ed inhaled again. He smelt trees, earth, and something foul deep below ground. "You're right, something is wrong here."

"Can you trace it?" Ann pushed through the trees. A branch snapped back and almost knocked her off her feet.

Ed blurred and picked her up.

"Great, more carrying," she grumbled. "I can walk."

He blurred past the dense foliage until they reached the lake. "The stench is stronger here. Like fire and sulphur," he said as he set her down again.

The lake looked unusually calm and still, like a mirror reflecting their images back at them.

"The coldness is stronger here," Ann muttered words of power, and the lake shimmered. "Maybe we need to go in."

"How do you know there aren't any creatures in there?" Ed crossed his arms. "If this is where they're coming through, it might not be a good idea to go in there."

"I forgot how scared you are of water. How can we find out where all these creatures are coming from if we don't go in there and explore?"

"I am not afraid of water." He scowled.

"I don't blame you, you did almost drown. You would have, too, if I hadn't sensed you." Ann walked over to the water's edge.

"Yes, but it brought me to you. I can't believe I'm doing this."

Ann jumped in, sighing as the cool water enveloped her. "I sometimes think you've lost your sense of adventure. You used to be more fun."

"My sense of adventure got replaced by a sense of caution." He glanced around, wary.

"There's no one here but us." She splashed him.

Ed hesitated. Something didn't feel right about this place. Where was the ward he'd seen during the hunt? "Ann, maybe—"

The lake shimmered with bright blue light, then whirled around Ann and swallowed her up.

CHAPTER 22

Ann landed on a hard stone floor. *What the heck just happened?*

Her head spun from where the portal had sucked her under before she'd had a chance to transport herself out. She remembered seeing Ed's panicked face.

"Ed?" she called.

The room around her appeared small and empty, with grey stone walls, but no door and no windows. *Wonderful.*

She hated being closed in and took a deep breath to calm her racing heart. *Ed?* She reached out with her mind and felt…nothing. *What the…no! This can't be happening! We're bound.*

Ed, answer me. Are you alright? She screwed up her face and reached for her magic. Nothing there either.

Ann reached out. The walls felt cold, hard and real. "Damn it, where am I?" she yelled. "Urien, get in here! I know you're the one who did this."

Laughter followed as a gorgeous blond-haired man appeared.

"Who are you?" Ann demanded. "Where is Urien? Are you one of his minions?"

The man cackled. "Oh, good grief, no. I'm no one's minion."

Ann took in his rich clothing. A nobleman, no doubt. She'd met enough of those growing up. His appearance didn't indicate his race, though. His blonde hair fell past his shoulders, and his electric blue eyes seemed to see her very soul. Power rolled off him like waves crashing against rock.

Like Domnu's power, only harsher.

"You're an elder," she realised, and her heart sank.

"One of many." He smirked, showing too much teeth.

Ann had always suspected the elders had helped Orla and Urien to kill her parents and take Caselhelm, but she had never proved it. Going after the elders had never seemed possible. They were higher beings, and most didn't even live on Erthea.

"Why am I here?" She raised her chin, she wouldn't show fear. The archdruid never showed their true emotions. She forced her expression to become impassive.

The elder gave another snigger and raised his hand.

An invisible blast slammed her against the wall. The air in her lungs left her in a rush. She gasped and slumped to the ground. Her shoulder ached from where it taken the brunt of the blow. Ann used her other hand to summon fire. Still nothing.

"You didn't really think we'd let you go, did you?" he asked.

"It's been five years. Why now?" Ann backed away from him, retreating to the furthest corner of the room. Not that it offered her any kind of protection.

"The spell Darius cast on you not only protected you from death, but it shielded you from us." He raised his hand, and an invisible noose tightened around her neck. "Your father betrayed us, the very people he was sworn to serve. Someone has to pay the price for what he did."

Ann's lungs burned as she fought for breath. "I haven't done anything to you," she rasped when he finally loosened his grip.

He laughed. "Of course you have, you've turned against us. Darius may have kept you from us when he was alive, but you know the role of archdruid and what it entails. Instead of turning to us, you chose to become a rogue," he hissed. "You've turned so many against us. At least your brother has the sense to work with and worship us."

Ann laughed, although it came out as more of a cough. "You're not gods, you're just powerful beings who control our world and like to keep it in chaos. My father saw you for what you are, that's why you killed him."

"Darius stole things from us, and we want those items back. The fool thought he was stronger than us, and he paid the price."

Ann braced herself for more choking and reached for her magic again. Nothing. She guessed this might be a void—a rare place where no magic flowed and anyone with power became powerless. She should still have some power—she knew magic didn't dissipate right away in a void. Maybe she had enough to call Ed or the others.

Ed? she called again. *I'm in a void, trapped by an elder.*

"You really think Urien will make a good archdruid?" she said aloud. Maybe if she could keep the elder talking, it would hold off the torture for a little longer. Then what? If she and Ed couldn't sense each other, how would he find her?

Guess I'll have to find my own way out of here.

"Of course not. He is little more than a petulant child, but we can control him. He's so desperate for power, he'll do anything to please us."

Ann checked her body over. Her knives were gone. No surprise there, but had they found all her weapons? "He won't serve you for long. Urien has always been hungry for power." Ann reached into her left boot to find there was still a knife there—they'd only taken her visible weapons and hadn't checked over her very well.

They probably think I'm no threat without my magic. She'd have to wait for the right moment to use it.

"Oh, he'll behave himself."

Ann slid the knife out whilst the elder paced the length of the room and hid it down her sleeve. "How can you make him archdruid?" An archdruid was born with their power, not chosen as people were led to believe. At least Ann had been. Darius had told her that made her special.

252

He turned around. "We'll take the power from you, rip it out. Unless you choose to join us."

Ann shook her head. "You know I'd never do that. You stand for everything I'm fighting against."

He made a tutting sound. "Stubborn, just like your father. I'm offering you a chance at freedom here, Rhiannon," he said. "You must tire of running, of always looking over your shoulder. We control Erthea. If you joined us, you could take your rightful place in Caselhelm as the true archdruid. You'd be free to lead the life you should have always led."

"And be controlled? That's not freedom. I saw what you did to my father. You gave him the illusion of power, freedom, and authority, but he was a puppet, forced to serve the will of fake gods," she spat. "People who sought to control and destroy life rather than nurture it. No, I'd never agree to that. My ancestors may have served you, I won't. I might be a rogue, but I'm free to make a difference. To make my own choices." She shot to her feet and jabbed the knife through his jugular.

His eyes widened in shock, but no blood came gurgling out. He yanked the blade out and backhanded her so hard she hit the wall. Stars flashed before her eyes from the force of the blow, and Ann slid to the floor, her vision blurred.

"You blasted girl! How dare you attack me!" He rubbed his neck. "Fool, your weapons can't hurt a god." He caught hold of her hair and yanked her head up to force her to look into his searing eyes. "I gave you a chance at redemption. You failed."

Ann spat in his face. "You'll have to kill me before I ever agree to join you."

He laughed again. "Oh, we'll do much worse than that. You had your chance to avoid this. Now we'll have to rip your power from you." He pulled her hair so tight strands of it broke away.

Ann gritted her teeth to avoid crying out in pain. "You can't. The power is mine. It never came from you."

"We'll see."

Light flashed around them as they reappeared in a much larger, brighter room. Ann hit the floor with a thud as her captor let go of her, landing inside a metal spell circle that glittered with sigils she didn't recognise. Around her stood glowing figures, at least twenty men and women whose bodies glittered like diamonds. Ann guessed they were projections, yet their energy crackled in the air. They were all elders, a select group of them. Each wore a pendant bearing a triangle with a circle of thorns in the centre.

The Crimson Alliance. The name came into her mind like a forgotten dream. Where did she know that name from?

"Behold, Rhiannon Valeran. The rogue archdruid herself," her captor said.

Her heart thudded in her ears. Could they really take the archdruid gift away from her? Just because she never wanted the rank or power didn't mean she would relinquish it. Over recent months, she'd come to accept it. The power had always been part of her, whether she acknowledged it or not. She couldn't let Urien have it, he'd use it for destruction and murder. That wasn't what being the archdruid meant, nor was serving the gods.

"Tell us, archdruid," another male voice spoke up. "Will you—?"

"Who are you people?" she demanded, deciding to feign ignorance. "You can't punish me for something my father did. I never took vows to serve you. I'm not bound by you, or your laws."

"We are the Crimson Alliance. We control and govern Erthea from the shadows," said the male voice. "We are the true gods."

"No, you're the bastards who almost destroyed Erthea during the dark times," Ann snapped. "You're always squabbling over territory and power. Trading people like they are cattle. And you dare to call yourselves gods." She gave a harsh laugh.

An angry murmur ran through the group.

Watch your tongue, Rhiannon, a voice whispered in her mind. *These people are not to be trifled with.*

Who are you? she asked. *Domnu?*

No, I am—

"She'll never join us," her captor spoke up. "We must strip her of her power and kill her. Darius' spell has weakened thanks to her bond with the overseer."

"She should suffer eternal torment for her crimes," a woman spoke up. "Who is she to challenge us?"

Ann's heart raced faster. She called her magic, but it still wouldn't come. *Ed, please, I need your help!*

"Kill her!" the crowd chorused.

Another man stepped forward, this one with long white hair and a long white beard that shimmered like moonlight. He raised his hand and chanted unfamiliar words of power, words that sounded so strange she couldn't make them out. The circle around her flared to life.

Ann clutched her chest as icy cold fingers reached inside her. The fingers turned to claws, scratching and ripping through the shields inside her. Her tunic burned away from her arms as the invisible marks she'd earned during her druid training flared with heat—the crescent moon, the oak tree, the lines of power. Each symbol that protected her and represented her power one by one faded away.

Ann screamed as the claws dug deeper, trying to find what they wanted.

The elders' chants continued, increasing to a staccato.

The circle whirled around her, a tornado of light and sound that clawed at the power that made her the archdruid.

Ann reached for her magic, but it refused to respond.

The elders' power held her down as they continued to search for her gift.

"Where's the power?" one of them demanded.

Every inch of her body hurt as their unnatural power seared and crackled through her skin.

One of the hands reached for the source of her gift. Ann squeezed her eyes shut and saw a glowing ball of white light. The hands tugged and pulled at it, but the light refused to budge. Pain ripped through every nerve ending as they yanked at her power.

Glowing vines appeared, black and twisted. They curved up around her legs, and over her thighs and chest. The hands retreated, and the elders let out screams of frustration.

"What is that?"

"It's a spell Darius weaved into her flesh," her captor cried. "We can't take the power from her."

"You have dark magic in you," that strange shadow entity had told her. *"Power that doesn't come from nature."*

Ann reached deep into that part of herself, tapping into power she wasn't supposed to possess. It felt raw and dark. Nothing like the constant flowing power of her druid magic, which came from nature itself. This was something else.

She wanted these people gone. Why should she have to pay for her father's mistakes? She wasn't him. She'd never be the archdruid he had been. These people had no power over her, Ann would never take the vows that would bind her and her powers to them. She was the rogue archdruid, not bound by anyone or anything.

She called this new power to her, and lightning crackled at her fingertips. She screamed, channelling all her pain, anger, and energy into this new power. Light exploded around her, and screams echoed as one by one each of the figures faded. The light continued expanding outwards, sweeping away everything in its wake like an oncoming tidal wave.

She collapsed. Were they dead? She doubted even she had the power to kill an elder, let alone an entire group of them, but they were gone, that's all that mattered.

Ann let the blackness swallow her, grateful she no longer had to endure the agony.

CHAPTER 23

Ed jumped into the lake. The cool water hit him like a thousand knives. He swam around then dove under but found nothing but blackness. Both Ann and the portal were gone. *Spirits be damned!*

He used his speed and shot out of the lake. Water flew from his body as he blurred toward the great tree. Blood pounded in his ears. He moved so fast he reappeared inside Ceara's room within seconds. The large room had been built out of the tree itself. Wood rings were etched on the walls, and vines hung from the ceiling.

Ceara and Jax sat on a low-level bed surrounded by books. They both jumped when they saw him.

"Wolfy, you can't be here." Ceara scrambled up. "Are you mad?"

"Ann is missing. Someone took her," he growled. His eyes flashed bright emerald. "Where is Ranelle?"

"Not here." Jax rose too. "What happened?"

Ed shook his head. "Doesn't matter. I have to find her. Ranelle is behind this, I know it." His fists clenched. "She's been working with Urien all along."

"Won't her people attack you if they find you here?" Jax glanced behind Ed, uneasy.

"Let them. I'll rip them apart," Ed growled.

"Ed, we found something." Jax gripped his shoulder. "A text that talks about why Lulrien got cut off from the other lands."

Ed waved a hand in dismissal. "As if that matters."

"We think we've found out what Urien's planning," Ceara said.

Ed's jaw tightened. Everything in him screamed at him to go find Ranelle and demand to know where Ann was, but he knew this was important. "What is it?"

Ceara picked up a book. "Here. Darius' father came here a couple of centuries ago. He opened the door to the underworld, and a load of nasty buggers came out."

"Including the Fomorians," Jax added. "That's where they came from."

"But the archdruid lost control over them," Ceara continued. "So the elders ordered him to seal the door shut. Too many people died, and the elders didn't like the fact they couldn't control the demons."

"The archdruid sealed it shut and used a spell to make sure no one in Lulrien ever found it," Jax said. "Urien wants to open the door.

Think of how powerful he'd be if he had legions of demons at his disposal."

"What does this have to do with Ann?" Ed demanded. His mind reached out for her again. The feeling of emptiness that greeted him made a hollow form in his chest.

"He needs the power of the archdruid to open it," Ceara replied. "If he hasn't already. I felt something dark last night."

"I've gone to look around, but haven't found any signs of demons," Jax remarked.

Ed thought back to the fir deargs he and Ann had encountered earlier. He groaned. "I think you're right. Ann and I were attacked by some low-level pests earlier."

Ed blurred out of the room and through the halls until he found the person he sought.

Ranelle's eyes widened when she saw him. "Rohn, what are you doing here?"

Ed grabbed her by the throat. "Tell me where Ann is right now, or I swear I'll kill you," he growled as Jax and Ceara appeared in a puff of smoke. *Where did Ceara get a transportation potion from?*

"Ed, don't!" Ceara grabbed his arm. "She's your mother. You can't kill her."

"Rohn, please don't do this," Ranelle said. "I can explain."

Ed shoved her away. "How can she be my mother?" He turned to look at his siblings.

"Think about it. You have magic, and Lucien bonded with a non-lykae," Ceara said.

"Her eyes are green—just like yours glow," Jax remarked. "And you can commune with wyverns—which is what her people are."

Ed frowned. "Is that true?" he asked Ranelle. He'd known her people were more than what they seemed, but hadn't been able to prove it.

"You're not so good at hiding things," Ceara said.

"That's what I said," Jax added. "We did some digging while we stayed here—Ann helped."

"Where is Ann?" Ed demanded. He didn't want to think about the revelation about Ranelle. It didn't matter.

Ranelle shook her head. "The elders have her now." She touched his face. "I'm so sorry, I didn't have a choice."

Ed slapped her hand away. "Don't touch me. I knew I couldn't trust you." The beast clawed at the edge of his mind, demanding to be let out. "Why do the elders have her?"

Lucien shot into the room. "Because she is considered a traitor to the gods."

"Why are you here?" Ed demanded.

"Because I felt her pain. Woman, what have you got yourself into now?" Lucien touched her cheek.

She shoved him away. "At least I kept our son safe." Her jaw clenched. "Even if the elders tried to stop it from happening."

"But you brought me back, didn't you? You sent me that dream telling me to come here." Ed ran a hand through his hair. "Never mind your petty disputes, I only care about finding Ann. Where's Urien?"

"Wait, why would Ann be a traitor?" Ceara spoke up.

"Because Darius dared to turn against the elders. He broke away and stole from them," Lucien replied. "The gods won't let that go unpunished."

"How do you know so much?" Jax frowned.

"He's an overseer too. My power had to come from somewhere." Ed crossed his arms.

Lucien nodded. "I was overseer to Darius, but that's a long story."

Ed glanced between his parents. "You're both unbelievable."

"Let's put all the hard feelings aside and focus on finding Ann," Ceara suggested. "Ranelle, you need to tell us everything you know."

Ranelle shook her head. "I can't. Urien—" She flinched, as if saying his name caused her pain.

Lucien gripped her shoulder. "It's the Arcus stone, isn't it?"

She nodded. "I don't have a choice. I can't risk my people by turning against him."

"Arcus stone?" Jax asked.

"It's the manifestation of a spell the old archdruid used." Ceara held up the book. "Darius wrote about it in here. Lykaes were bound by the moon curse, and wyverns were bound into human form."

"I don't care about Urien. I need to find Ann." Ed turned to leave.

Ranelle moved over to him. "Wait. The spell Darius used on her is weakening. She's not shielded from the elders. Did you seal your bond?"

He shook his head. "No. Instead, I wasted time trying to figure out what you were hiding," he hissed. "How can Darius' spell weaken? Ann hasn't unbound it."

"You and Ann have always been linked. That's why Darius and I bound you to each other," Ranelle explained. "And why I sent you to her."

Lucien's eyes flashed. "You sent my son away on purpose?"

"I had to. You wanted to raise him as a lykae. What kind of life would he have had growing up here with us fighting all the time?"

"Enough, both of you," Ed snapped. "How does the bond weaken Darius' spell?"

"Darius would have bound Ann's life to her brothers', but her bond with you would break that," Ranelle said. "Once your lykae side awoke, the spell would have weakened as you grew closer."

"Can you call Urien here?" Ceara asked. "We could take him down."

"I'll rip him apart." Ed gritted his teeth and fought for control.

"I doubt Ann would appreciate you hurting Xander," Jax remarked.

"Maybe we can trade him something Urien wants and get Ann back...I have to get Urien's body back."

Ed, Jax and Ceara used a potion to transport out to the beach adjoining Trin. Ed was glad to get away from his parents. He couldn't deal with either of them now.

"We can't give Urien his body," Jax remarked.

"I can, and I will if there's a chance to get Ann back with it." Ed glanced up as the water shimmered above them, held back by the island's power.

"I agree with bird boy on this one." Ceara crossed her arms. "We don't want Urien getting stronger or hurting Xander in the process."

Ann had submerged Trin to stop Urien from getting it. The island was sacred, the final resting place to all the former archdruids. Their power was part of the island too.

"You really think Urien will give Ann up for his body?" Jax asked.

"I'll force him to. If Darius' spell is weakening, Urien's body won't be protected. If he doesn't give Ann over, I'll destroy it."

"Wait a minute, brother. Even if you can do that, there's no telling what Urien would do. He had our mum killed, remember?"

Ceara shuddered. "Please don't remind me of that." She sniffed. "I still miss her. Thanks to Urien, I'll never get the chance to talk to her again."

Jax wrapped an arm around her. "Don't worry, we'll see her again one day. Even if she's in spirit form."

Ed nodded. "He's right."

He moved across the beach until they reached the bottom of the tor. The great stone tower loomed on top of the grassy mound of earth like a silent, watchful guardian. A long gravel path circled the tor itself.

Ed moved to the base of the tor. "I'm not going to let him hurt Ann. If he does, he dies too." Ed sighed. "I shouldn't have taken her to Lulrien in the first place."

"She would have come anyway. Nothing has ever separated you two for long." Jax patted his shoulder. "We'll get her back."

Ed nodded, scanning the grass for signs of the secret door that led below the tor. It took a few seconds before he spotted the almost invisible orange lines that marked the way. *"Oscailte." Open.* He waited.

Nothing happened.

"That's odd." Ed ran his hands over the doorway. The runes that he, Ann, and other druids of the past had used to lock and conceal the entrance glittered to life. "I never had any trouble getting through when I brought the body here."

"Maybe we need Ann here, since she's the archdruid," Ceara remarked.

Ed's hand flared with light and he said, *"Oscailte agus dighlasáil."* *Open and unlock.*

This time the door swung open.

Ed headed into the tunnel. He conjured an orb, and the torches flared to life.

"What is this place?" Jax asked. "I don't remember seeing this when we lived here with Mama and Sage."

Ceara shivered. "I sense dead people here. Why didn't you tell us we were walking around a bunch of tombs?"

The walls were of carved stone and shone with different runes that glittered like gems. Some were protection spells, and some were tales of former archdruids and their conquests.

"All archdruids are brought here after they die, except for Darius. We buried him somewhere else on his orders." Ed moved through the tunnel. He hadn't set foot here since he'd brought Urien's body here a few months earlier. It had been the only place powerful enough to conceal it. Urien's body hadn't always been here. He'd kept it concealed in Darius' hidden tomb, which lay elsewhere, and had only moved it here after Ann had submerged the island.

Ed moved past countless doorways that glittered with runes.

Energy vibrated against his skin as he headed to the one marked with Darius' name. The door swung open as he pressed his palms to the stone, which creaked and groaned as it slid aside. Ed went inside to where a stone sarcophagus stood. It too bloomed with symbols he, Ann, and Sage had all drawn onto it to conceal Urien's body.

"Are you sure we should be doing this?" Jax rubbed the back of his neck. "This is the only leverage we have against Urien."

"I'm not going to leave Ann alone to suffer at the elders' hands."

Ceara appeared behind them. "Hey, we need to hurry. Things are stirring below ground." She froze. "That him?"

Ed nodded and shoved the top of the sarcophagus off. The runes covering the lid turned black as the spell broke. Inside lay Urien's true body, with the same mop of curly black hair, pale skin, and coldly handsome face.

"He looks like he might wake up any minute." Jax raised his staff, as if expecting a sudden attack.

"Ranelle said Xander's body is dying," Ceara told them. "If we kill this body, maybe we'll free Xander."

Ed shook his head. "Urien's soul is still bound inside Xander's body. Killing this body wouldn't do any good." He caught hold of Urien's shoulder. "We'll take the body back and—"

Ed froze as pain ripped through his very soul. He doubled over, and clutched his chest, feeling something inside him snap. His bond with Ann was broken, torn like an invisible cord that had linked them together. She was gone. His heart ached, then filled with an emptiness he'd never felt before.

"Ed, what's wrong?" Jax touched his shoulder, his face etched with concern.

"Oh no," Ceara muttered. "Something has happened to Ann."

Bone and muscle cracked as Ed shifted into his true beast form. Fur covered his body, and his claws and fangs came out. Rage, hot and furious, burned through his blood. His eyes turned a deep shade of red that reflected back at him in Ceara and Jax's gazes.

"This is not good," Ceara remarked, grabbing hold of his arm. Light flared between her brows as her magic flared to life. "Ed, listen to me. I know you're hurting right now, but—"

Ed shoved her aside and shot away before either of them could say or do anything else.

CHAPTER 24

After a while, the pain faded, and then only blackness remained. Empty darkness, void of anything. No time. No place. Nothing. Ann floated around in the emptiness. It didn't matter where she was as long as she avoided pain, but it threatened to call her back.

Damn it, I've got to get away from here. Ann didn't want to go back. Didn't want to feel the ripping at her soul again. Only death would be a release—and probably a temporary one at that. Darius' spell still clung to her, although it was weaker than before. The spell protected her from the elders, but how long would it last?

Damn it, why did you do this to me, Papa? Why did you leave me to clean up your mess?

Something inside her snapped, like an invisible cord breaking. Her body couldn't take any more of the elders' power and had failed. Ann knew she should have felt relieved. Instead, an intense sadness swept over her. She'd never get to see Ed again.

What would happen to her now? Would the spell revive her? Maybe she would remain here in the void. Lost and alone.

I need answers. She wasn't about to leave the others. *Where are you, Papa?*

Light blinded her as the blackness whirled like a tornado.

Ann blinked and found herself in a place she hadn't seen in years, her father's study. It still smelt of wood smoke and cedar with a hint of leather and evergreen—just like him.

"Papa?" she gasped.

Darius sat behind his desk, his long blonde hair and pale blue eyes so like her own. "Rhiannon." He rose and held his arms out to her.

Ann didn't go to him as she once would have. "Am I dead now?"

Darius shook his head. "Not yet. This is a safeguard I put in place in case my spell ever failed."

"You mean if the elders ever got hold of me." She crossed her arms. "Papa, there's so much about your life I never knew. So many secrets."

"And I wanted to spare you all of it." Darius touched her cheek. "I thought the spell would be enough to shield you from them." He gave her a sad smile. "You wouldn't hide away, would you?"

"How could I? There's so much chaos in the five lands that I can't pretend it's not happening." Ann shook her head. "The elders told me they killed you because you turned against them."

"That's true. I couldn't serve false gods any longer. I lost so much because of them, including your mother."

Ann flinched. "You mean the woman who gave birth to me?" She'd always known Deanna hadn't been her true mother. There had never been a bond there. Deanna had been jealous of Ann's close relationship with her father.

Darius always told people Deanna was her mother, though. Ann never wanted to know otherwise. She'd had her father and hadn't needed anyone else.

She'd changed so much from the naive girl who'd worshipped her father.

"Urien has to be stopped. He's inside Xander's body. Xander is dying too—I can feel it," Ann said. "You have to tell me how to end the spell for good."

"The spell was meant to protect you from the elders. I bound you to your brothers so even they couldn't hurt you. You can't—" Darius protested.

"Some things are more important than my life. What about Xander? He's your son too." Ann stared at him, incredulous.

"He was always Deanna's, not mine." Darius sighed.

"The spell is already weakening thanks to my bond with Ed." She missed the feel of their connection. "Why did you bind us together? Was that to keep me safe too?"

"No. I sensed the connection you had with him. I linked you both because I knew he would help balance out the power inside you," he said. "In return you'd help him to control his beast sides. I would never have bound you to him unless I knew he was made for you."

"I have other magic inside me. Dark and unnatural power that doesn't come from nature."

Darius didn't look surprised by that revelation. "I know. I hoped binding you to Edward would keep that part of you hidden."

"Where does it come from? What is it?"

"It doesn't matter. You need to keep that power locked away."

Ann's fists clenched. Even now, in a vision that might only be a figment of her imagination, he still wouldn't give her the answers she needed.

"You bound me to Ed because it served a purpose. Did you ever think about how it would affect us?" she demanded. "I have feelings for him—feelings I don't even know are real." Fire crackled and spurted from the empty hearth.

"I tried to keep you away from all of this," Darius said. "I gave Edward information on where to take you after I—"

"After you died and left me all alone!" She felt tears spring to her eyes. Ann wiped them away, horrified. He'd never liked her to cry. He always said tears were a sign of weakness unbecoming of the archdruid. She had to be strong.

"I can't change the past, Rhiannon. But I can fix this." Darius waved his hand. Black vines appeared over her arms like she'd seen on her chest when Ed had cast the revealing spell. "I'll reinforce the spell—on you alone. That way you can stop Urien and save Xander."

Ann shook her head. "No, I'm tired of having this…unnatural magic wrapped around me. I want it gone."

Strands of light fluttered around her like ribbons, each a different colour, red, blue, black, purple, and everything in between. A multi-layered spell binding her to her brothers and sealing her soul and body off from death.

"Rhiannon, you can't do this." Darius gripped her shoulders. "Please. The elders will make you suffer a fate worse than death for what I did. I stole from them and made people question their belief in them."

Ann tugged at one of the threads and caught a flash of Urien. "I'm tired of running, Papa. If ending this spell will save Xander, so be it. If it weren't for you, I would never have been dragged into this mess."

"Rhiannon, please—"

The study faded as she appeared back in her cell, the threads still wrapped around her. She closed her eyes and gripped one thread. A new image of Xander flashed in front of her as she did. His body was weak, pale, and worn out. Bound by the spell that Urien had used to his advantage.

Another thread revealed Urien, protected by the spell, and a glowing red thread represented her link to Ed. She saw him, Ceara and Jax standing around Urien's sarcophagus.

"Are you sure we can transfer Urien's soul into his body from here?" Jax asked. "He's protected Xander's body with spirits-only-know-what kind of magic."

Ann tugged Urien's thread, narrowing her eyes. The black thread burned away. One link broken, but she knew she'd have to be with Urien in person to fully break the spell. She couldn't do it from here. "You're not protected from death now, brother."

She smiled and hugged Xander's thread.

"Rhiannon, don't do this," Darius's voice echoed around her. Was it really him, or another trick? It didn't matter. She didn't care what happened to her, Xander had suffered enough.

"You've no idea what you're doing," Darius implored her. *"Without the spell, the elders—"*

"I don't care what they do to me. We're done paying for your mistakes," Ann said. "This spell's done more harm than good."

She untangled more threads, destroying them one by one to release her brothers from the spell that bound them together. Ann closed her eyes and saw Urien in Xander's body standing in front of a sealed door that led to evil. Demons clawed and growled on the other side.

That's why he came here.

One by one, she burned more threads away.

Urien's eyes widened.

"You've been in that body too long, brother. Time to get out," Ann hissed. She raised her hand and chanted, *"Bain a anam…"*

Urien stumbled, laughed, and stared right at her. "You don't have the strength to stop me, sister. You're dying. I can feel it."

"I'm not dying until I know Xander is safe."

The thread between her fingers flickered. She didn't have much time left, but she had to stop Urien first. She picked up another thread.

Ed, she thought. An ache formed in her chest. If she could reach him, maybe she could help him and the others to remove Urien's soul from Xander's body.

One by one, the glowing threads fell away. She knew time had run out for her.

Ann gasped as her soul reconnected with her body. She still lay on the floor of her cell. Her body ached where the elders had tried to rip her power from her, and blood dripped from her nose. Drops of red fell onto the dirty stone floor.

Ed? She reached out with her mind, but she couldn't sense him. Was her magic still gone? Why couldn't she feel him?

"Ed?" she called aloud.

No response. He had to hear her, he was her overseer. More than that, he was her partner, the other half of her. One way or another, she would see him one more time before her body gave out.

"Ed, answer me. Please." Ann resumed her crawl. She attempted to get out, but her limbs refused to comply.

Her magic felt weak and lifeless from warding off the elders' attack. She shivered as she remembered the icy fingers reaching inside of her. Clawing at her power, at her very soul. Like it or not, she was the archdruid, and she'd be damned if she let the elders or Urien take it from her.

"Ed?" she called again. Why wouldn't he answer her? Had removing Darius' spell somehow unbound them as well? If so, how? They had a true bond, nothing could break that.

When this is over, I'll tell him how sorry I am for doubting that.

Ann stopped and rested her cheek against the cold, hard stone. She couldn't move. When she reached for Ed, emptiness greeted her. What if Urien had killed him?

Jax? Ceara? she called.

No response came.

She moaned in pain. The elders might be gone for now, but she knew they'd come back sooner or later. Why wouldn't the others answer her either? Were they gone too?

Her heart twisted. Had she led her friends to their deaths?

No, she'd know if Ed was gone. She'd feel it in her heart, her soul.

Everything in her ached from where the elders had almost taken her power.

Something hit the outer door. She looked toward it—it hurt to even open her eyes. The door remained out of reach.

"Get up, Rhiannon," she heard her father's voice say. *"An archdruid doesn't cower on the ground. Get up. You're stronger than this."*

"You didn't fight, did you, Papa?" she murmured. "You left me and Xander alone."

Her stomach clenched at the thought of Xander. Was he alive, or had Urien disposed of him too?

Another thump.

Ann squeezed her eyes shut, too weak to look at what it might be.

Whack!

Ann peered up to see glowing amber eyes blazing down at her.

"Rhiannon?" the voice sounded like Lucien.

Now I must be dreaming.

Strong arms yanked her up. "Good spirits, what happened?" Lucien's face changed beast to man once more.

"Lucien?"

"Yes, druid. I'm here."

Her head lolled against his shoulder as blackness threatened to embrace her once again.

"Stay awake," Lucien ordered. "Tell me what they did to you." His footsteps made no sound as he carried her out.

Her vision wavered, and warmth radiated over her body, seeping into every fibre of her being.

Ann blinked. Her body still ached, but her mind felt clear. "You're an overseer."

"That was a long time ago." Lucien descended the steps. "I served your father. He was my appointed charge."

Ann frowned. "You? How's that possible?" She shook her head. "Where's Edward? I need to see him."

He ignored her last question. "Before my brother died, I led a very different life. Darius and I were like brothers," Lucien explained. "We fought in the realm wars together."

"You hate magic."

"I didn't always, but magic killed my brother when he stumbled on that accursed doorway," Lucien said. "I gave up my calling to protect my pack."

"What about Ranelle? I know she's your k'ia."

Lucien gave a harsh laugh. "You're definitely his daughter."

"Why did you come to save me? You hate me."

"I don't hate you, I hated what you were capable of. I outlawed all magic because it cost me so much. My brother, my love and my son." He sighed. "I realise now what a fool I've been."

"Where's Ed?" she asked again. "Are my friends alright?"

"They're dealing with Rohn." Lucien's expression turned grim. "He is in the primal rage. That's why you can't sense him."

"What?" Ann gasped. "How?"

"I think he sensed what the elders did to you. Losing one's k'ia to death can trigger the rage."

"Hurry up and take me to him then." She glanced down the spiral staircase. "Why aren't you using your speed?"

Lucien winced. "It took a lot of strength to get in here. I need time to recover."

"We don't have time, Ed needs me." Her face scrunched up, but no magic came to her. "I'm too weak to transport out."

Lucien halted. "All overseers are connected to the person they're meant to protect. Perhaps you can use that to take us to Rohn."

"How? I can't feel him anymore."

Lucien gripped her hand. "I have some power. Use it. Focus on Rohn."

White light flared against her palm, and she closed her eyes and thought of Ed. Nothing.

"Stop searching with your mind," Lucien said. "You must use your heart. You and Rohn are connected on a soul level, not just as charge and overseer."

"How do I do that?" She opened her eyes and frowned at him.

"You love him, don't you?" he said. "Use that. Your father always used his head over his heart too."

Ann gulped and closed her eyes. Orbs of blue light sparkled around them.

A moment later, the pair of them reappeared outside Lucien's hut. A huge man-shaped hole had appeared on the side of it.

"Lia?" Lucien called.

Anger radiated on the air like an ill wind, hot and fiery.

"Take me to Ed," Ann said.

Lucien ran through the village, heading in the direction of the anger. Ann's heart thudded in her ears. "You're the only one who can reach Rohn now," Lucien said as they passed several ruined houses.

"How? You said lykaes lose their souls when they lose their k'ia. I died...for a while."

"You and Rohn have an incredible bond. I can sense it," he said. "What you have is powerful. I should never have questioned that. You can reach him, I know it."

Up ahead, Ann spotted Jax stumble back as a blur of light shot toward him. Jax's skin hardened, easily taking the brunt of even Ed's blow.

"Jax?" Ann called.

"Thank the spirits," Jax muttered.

Lucien set Ann on her feet and grabbed hold of Ed. The two lykaes blurred in a rush.

"You okay?" Ann put her hand on Jax's shoulder.

"I've been better. Ann, I think he's gone. He's not Ed anymore, I can see it in his eyes."

"Where's Ceara?"

"At hometree with Marcus."

Ed slammed Lucien into the ground so hard the earth vibrated.

"Ed, stop! He's your father," Ann said loudly.

He didn't look like Ed anymore. This was the beast in its true form. Fur covered his body, his face had a long snout with fangs. He had bowed legs and glowing red eyes.

"Ed, please stop." Ann stumbled over to him. "You don't want to hurt him."

The beast growled.

"Listen to her, Rohn," Lucien rasped. "I was wrong, she is your k'ia. I never should have doubted that."

Ed gripped Lucien's throat so hard the alpha's eyes bulged.

"Ed, please." Ann touched his arm. "Don't. He's your father. He saved me from the elders."

Ed backhanded her so hard she hit the ground. She saw stars for a moment.

Jax swung his staff. Ed dodged the blow and Lucien blurred out of reach.

Talk to him, Lucien told her as he gasped for breath.

Ed knocked Jax away as if he was nothing more than a pest, then turned his attention to Ann and snarled.

Ann pushed her hair off her face. "Are you going to kill me, Ed?" she hissed. "Go ahead. Try." She was willing to bet he wouldn't hurt her if it came down to it. She only hoped she was right.

The beast hesitated.

Ann scrambled up and took hold of his clawed hands. "I know you're still in there somewhere." The beast hissed and made a grab for her, Ann backed away. "Think of everything we've been through together, whether by fate, blood, or fire." She caught hold of his face. "We've always been part of each other, not only when I saved you from drowning, but always." She touched his cheek. "You made me want to live again after my parents died. Without you, I would have given up. You're my strength, my heart. I can't live without you. Losing you to Orla for three months was torture. It made me realise how much you mean to me."

The beast snarled and backed away from her as if her words hurt him.

"You said I guided you back when you lost yourself to the darkness," she continued. "I need you to come back to me now. I need you with me. I need you to be by my side." Tears dripped down her cheeks as her hands flared with golden might. "Always and forever, remember? You promised me that. We've survived elders, demons and even death. Please come back."

The beast roared as the light enveloped his body.

Ed sank to his knees as the fur and fangs vanished. He took a shuddering breath. The redness blurred until his eyes returned to their normal hazel shade. "Ann?" he rasped.

She smiled and wrapped her arms around him, then laughed through her tears. "Don't ever do that to me again."

CHAPTER 25

Ed held onto Ann tight as he wrapped his arms around her. He breathed a sigh of relief. Moments before, he'd been consumed by the rage. All he'd been able to feel was the hot anger of it, the fury and the need for death and blood. His soul had been slipping away, at least until Ann had brought him back. It hadn't just been her power that had saved him, it had been the connection they shared with each other.

Ed buried his face against her shoulder. "I thought I lost you. What happened?"

"The elders tried to rip my archdruid power from me, but I fought them back." Ann gave him a quick kiss. "Your father got me out."

They both turned to look at Lucien. "Thank you, Father," Ed nodded.

A large wyvern circled overhead, followed by several others.

Jax frowned. "What are they doing here?"

"I have a bad feeling about this," Lucien remarked.

"Please tell me you broke Darius' spell," Ed said to Ann.

She shook her head. "I only weakened it. I think I need to be close to my brothers—both of them—to fully break it."

"We have Urien's body. Let's go."

Ann waved her hand, and they returned to Trin, hurrying back to the tomb where Ceara had been standing guard over the body.

Ed stopped dead when he saw Urien with his arm wrapped around Ceara's neck in a headlock.

"About time you got here," Ceara muttered.

"You are too late, sister," Urien sneered. "I control the wyverns." The Arcus stone glittered around his neck. "We'll break the final seals on the door to the underworld, and I'll finally have the power that is my birthright."

Ann shook her head. "Not this time, brother."

She turned to Ed. "I'm sorry, love. This is the only way."

She muttered words of power that Ed recognised as a death spell. All light drained from her face as she slumped to the ground, dead.

Urien hit the ground too, gasping for breath. Tendrils of power flowed around them, then erupted in a violent explosion as Darius's spell finally broke, taking the Arcus stone with it. Without the power of the archdruid present, it would no longer bind the lykaes or the wyverns.

Ed knelt beside Ann. "Come on, I'm not going to lose you now." He placed a hand on her chest. "Life to life and mind to mind, now spirits intertwine. In life and death, I make you mine." He recited the words of the joining vows, and tendrils of light wrapped around their wrists.

Ann gasped and opened her eyes in shock. "What did you do?"

"I sealed our bond. I've already lost you once today, I won't do it again." He wrapped his arms around her and held her close. "I love you, Ann."

Ann clung to him for a moment, then muttered a curse, shoving Ed out of the way as a blast of lightning came at them.

Urien leapt to his feet, still very much alive. "You've broken our father's spell, but don't you dare think you can stop me." Light flashed around him as he disappeared.

Around them chaos reigned. They had appeared outside Mirkwood mine, where lykaes and wyverns were fighting hideous demons. Some had hulking apelike bodies and several limbs.

Light flashed as the demons jumped into the creatures' bodies.

A demon came at them, its iron-tipped claws flashing. Ed raised his hand and blue lightning shot from his fingers. It sent the demon staggering backward in a smouldering heap. He glanced at his hand. "That's new."

"I've got to find Urien." Ann took off in the opposite direction.

Ed blurred after her, blasting demons as they went. He spotted Marcus wrestling with a demon, and hurried over to his cousin. He yanked the demon off Marcus and blasted it.

"Rohn," Marcus gasped.

"You alright?" He held out a hand.

Marcus grabbed it, and Ed pulled him up. "I am now. Lucien and Ranelle are inside."

He shot away. Inside the mine, Ranelle and Lucien cast spells to conjure fire and bolts of lightning as demons came swarming out of a black hole in the earth. A hulking demon came at them, and Ed blurred and blasted it away, then hurried over to Lucien.

"Son," Lucien grinned. "You're not hurt."

"Not yet." He ducked as a massive demon threw a boulder at his head.

Ranelle screamed as another demon knocked her to the ground, its iron-tipped claws flashing at her throat.

Ed blurred and punched his fist through the demon's chest, yanking out its heart. The demon turned to sludge as he crushed the heart.

"Rohn," Ranelle gasped. "You're here."

She reached up to touch him, but he brushed her off. He didn't have time for family reunions.

Lightning and fire flashed around them as Urien and Ann continued to hurl magic at each other ahead of them.

"We've got to get the doorway shut," Ed said. He caught hold of the massive boulder that had been blocking the doorway and tried to push it, but it barely moved. "Lucien, Marcus, help me."

Lucien and Marcus blurred to his side, and they tried heaving the boulder together, but still it refused to budge.

Ranelle scrambled up. "Rohn, Lucien, help me. Together we should have enough power to move it." Lucien and Ed both blurred to her.

"What do we have to do?" Ed asked.

Ranelle grasped his hand, then Lucien's. "Give me your strength. Together we should have enough power."

Lucien's eyes turned white with power, and Ed felt his own eyes burning. The boulder rose into the air, hovered for a moment, then slammed into the gaping hole.

"We did it." Ed felt a stab of pain. No, not his pain—Ann's.

He turned to see her stumble back and hit the ground hard.

"You two get above ground. There are still a lot of demons up there, as well as people who need help. Hurry, the mine could come down any minute," Ed told them.

"We're not leaving you," Lucien protested.

"I'll be fine. Go."

He blurred toward Ann.

Jax swung his staff, knocking Urien to the ground, and Ceara jabbed her rod against Urien's neck, making him cry out in agony.

"Get off me!" Urien screamed.

Ed blurred, punching through Urien's chest and grabbing hold of Xander's heart.

Ann grabbed Urien by the throat, her eyes turning black as she said the same words she'd spoken five years earlier.

Urien screamed as light pulsed through his body. Ann placed her hand on his chest, capturing a glowing ball of blue light. His eyes rolled back, and Xander's body collapsed.

The light flickered between Ann's fingers as Ed let go of Xander's heart and pulled away.

"Is that Urien's?" Ceara frowned, pulling her shock rod away.

"This is his soul." Ann nodded.

"I'm surprised he even had one." Ceara sneered. "Send him to the underworld then. Make sure he suffers."

Ed moved to her side and took her free hand. Lightning crackled between their joined hands.

"How do we know anywhere is strong enough to hold him?" Jax asked.

"Limbo will hold him," Ann said, then began the chant.

A blast of energy sent all four of them crashing to the ground.

"What the fuck was that?" Ceara demanded.

Ann's eyes flared with power, and light shimmered between her fingers as Urien's soul reappeared. "Blood might bind you here, demon, but it no longer binds you and Xander together."

Ed yanked over the coffin holding Urien's body, removing Urien's own heart, and she sent his soul floating back inside it before shoving his heart back in his chest.

Urien gasped, his eyes widening as he awoke, but he remained still.

"You got what you wanted, brother. You're back in your own body." Ann raised her hand again, and light enveloped him, holding his spirit in place once and for all.

She crawled over to Xander's body. "Xander? Xander, wake up." She touched his face.

Ed moved to her side. He heard no signs of life coming from Xander's body. "Ann, love…"

"No, don't tell me he's gone. He can't be gone." Tears streaked down her face.

Ed wrapped an arm around her, and light flashed between them as she muttered words of power.

Xander still lay there, lifeless.

"Why isn't it working?" She clutched her brother's hand. "Come on, little brother. Wake up, breathe. Please, Xander."

Ceara looked away, and Ed thought he saw tears in her eyes.

"What did I do wrong?" Ann muttered. Black vines shimmered over her skin as Darius' spell flashed back into existence. Lightning flashed between Ann and her two fallen brothers, striking her in the chest.

"Shit, what just happened?" Ceara asked.

"Darius' spell must still have been active." Ed touched Ann's forehead. He didn't hear her heartbeat.

"What does that mean? Will she and Xander wake up?"

"I don't know," Ed admitted.

EPILOGUE

Ann blinked, surprised to find herself standing in front of the archdruid's throne back in the great hall at Larenth Palace. The very throne she had destroyed a few weeks earlier.

"Xander?" She didn't see any sign of her brother. Strange, she'd never expected death to be like this, to lead her back here, of all places.

"All paths seem to lead back here, don't they?" said a familiar voice.

Ann turned to see Urien beside her and took a step back.

"There's no need to be afraid, little sister. I can't hurt you. Not here." Urien flashed her a smile. It looked almost genuine, making him resemble the Urien he'd been before the revolution.

"Why am I here? If this is an attempt to defeat me in death, then—"

"No, you've defeated me. I was destined to die anyway. Blood magic comes with a heavy price—my soul." Urien shook his head. "I had to die; I see that now."

"I didn't want that." Ann sighed. "Despite everything you've done, you're my brother. What happened to you? You used to bring me gifts when I was little. You made me feel special when my mother ignored me."

"Perhaps I was always meant to turn out this way."

"I never wanted things to end like this. Not even after everything you did." She moved over to the dais. "I guess they had to. You would never have stopped."

"I inherited our father's lust for power."

"Everything does lead back here," she agreed. "I never wanted the throne, or anything that comes with it, but I couldn't escape either."

"Father wasn't surprised that night. He must have known what I'd do, and he let it happen anyway," Urien remarked. "I never knew why."

"He knew." She sat down on the steps of the dais. It was strange, but she didn't feel threatened by Urien here. What could he do to her here in death? Perhaps this wasn't real either. "He never did anything without it serving a purpose. Spirits only know what his purpose for letting himself be killed was."

Urien sat down beside her. "The elders were going to kill him anyway for betraying them. They used me and my need for power to do it."

"I met the Crimson Alliance. They tried to steal my archdruid gift." She shuddered at the memory.

"They are the true power here on Erthea. They like to think of themselves as gods, and perhaps in a way they are. They're more powerful than anything I've ever seen."

"Papa betrayed them, but we will have to deal with the consequences." She shook her head and glanced back at the throne. "That thing never did any real good. I'm glad I destroyed it."

"It won't change anything. The elders—the Crimson Alliance— won't stop trying to get back whatever our father took from them. Nor will they allow anyone to challenge their rule."

"You mean me? I'm surprised they would view me as a threat."

"You're the archdruid. You still have power, but you're not under their control as our ancestors were. That makes you a danger to them. The Crimson don't abide threats against them," Urien told her. "They won't stop coming after you or using the people you care about against you."

"I know that."

"Do you? You're not protected by Father's spell anymore."

"Yeah, no thanks to you," she muttered.

Urien flinched. "I can't change what I've done, Rhiannon. I wanted to warn you about the elders before you leave."

"Now I know this isn't real." Ann stood up and backed away from him. "You'd never want to save me, you did your best to kill me."

"Well, let's call it the last desperate attempts of a dying man." Urien rose too. "The seer Domnu told me something I need to tell you before you leave here and return to your body."

She gritted her teeth. *And here I thought Domnu might be on my side.* Maybe she *had* had to come here for a reason.

"Who helped you kill our father? Which elder?" Ann knew this might be the last chance she had to ask Urien for the truth, but would he admit it to her?

"Does it matter?" Urien scoffed.

She crossed her arms. "It does to me."

Urien shook his head. "I don't know her name. They call her The Morrigan. She is an assassin, and she hated Father. It seemed personal for her. The elder I've had most dealings with is called Arwan. They will never stop coming after you. Xander and I are already victims of the Valeran legacy. Don't let yourself become one too."

Ann thought of Xander, remembering her fallen brother was not dead, but not alive either. One way or another, she would get him back.

If you enjoyed this book please leave a review on Amazon or book site of your choice.

For updates on more books and news releases sign up for my newsletter on tiffanyshand.com/newsletter

ALSO BY TIFFANY SHAND

ANDOVIA CHRONICLES

Dark Deeds Prequel

The Calling

Hidden Darkness

Morrigan's Heirs

ROGUES OF MAGIC SERIES

Bound By Blood

Archdruid

Bound By Fire

Old Magic

Dark Deception

Sins Of The Past

Reign Of Darkness

Rogues Of Magic Complete Box Set Books 1-7

ROGUES OF MAGIC NOVELLAS

Wyvern's Curse

Forsaken

On Dangerous Tides

EVERLIGHT ACADEMY TRILOGY

Everlight Academy, Book 1: Faeling

Everlight Academy, Book 2: Fae Born

Hunted Guardian – An Everlight Academy Story

EXCALIBAR INVESTIGATIONS SERIES

Touched By Darkness

Bound To Darkness

Rising Darkness

Excalibar Investigations Complete Box Set

SHADOW WALKER SERIES

Shadow Walker

Shadow Spy

Shadow Guardian

Shadow Walker Complete Box Set

THE AMARANTHINE CHRONICLES BOOK 1

Betrayed By Blood

Dark Revenge

The Final Battle

SHIFTER CLANS SERIES

The Alpha's Daughter

Alpha Ascending

The Alpha's Curse

The Shifter Clans Complete Box Set

TALES OF THE ITHEREAL

Fey Spy

Outcast Fey

Rogue Fey

Hunted Fey

Tales of the Ithereal Complete Box Set

THE FEY GUARDIAN SERIES

Memories Lost

Memories Awakened

Memories Found

The Fey Guardian Complete Series

THE ARKADIA SAGA

Chosen Avatar

Captive Avatar

Fallen Avatar

The Arkadia Saga Complete Series

ABOUT THE AUTHOR

Tiffany Shand is a writing mentor, professionally trained copy editor and copy writer who has been writing stories for as long as she can remember. Born in East Anglia, Tiffany still lives in the area, constantly guarding her workspace from the two cats which she shares her home with.

She began using her pets as a writing inspiration when she was a child, before moving on to write her first novel after successful completion of a creative writing course. Nowadays, Tiffany writes urban fantasy and paranormal romance, as well as nonfiction books for other writers, all available through eBook stores and on her own website.

Tiffany's favourite quote is *'writing is an exploration. You start from nothing and learn as you go'* and it is armed with this that she hopes to be able to help, inspire and mentor many more aspiring authors.

When she has time to unwind, Tiffany enjoys photography, reading, and watching endless box sets. She also loves to get out and visit the vast number of castles and historic houses that England has to offer.

You can contact Tiffany Shand, or just see what she is writing about at:

Author website: tiffanyshand.com

Business site: Write Now Creative

Twitter: @tiffanyshand

Facebook page: Tiffany Shand Author Page

Printed in Poland
by Amazon Fulfillment
Poland Sp. z o.o., Wrocław
19 July 2022

a64d9cb1-e375-49d1-aa73-b293ee15b441R01